No Grater Danger

No Grater Danger

Victoria Hamilton

BEYOND THE PAGE
PUBLISHING

Beyond the Page Books
are published by
Beyond the Page Publishing
www.beyondthepagepub.com

ISBN: 978-1-946069-76-4

✐ One ✐

JAYMIE LEIGHTON MÜLLER hugged her stepdaughter, Jocie, closely to her knees as the ferry from Heartbreak Island to Queensville chugged up to the dock. Jocie, a *little* little person, as she called herself, held the leash of Jaymie's dog, her three-legged Yorkie-Poo Hoppy, and talked to him. Jocie had been nervous about the ferry ride — their summer trip out to the Leighton cottage after Jaymie and Jakob Müller's wedding in June had been scary for her when a storm came up — so Jaymie reasoned that having Hoppy to look after this time would focus her attention. It had worked.

"No, Hoppy, you can't go to the edge of the boat," Jocie said, in her calmest tone, with the slightest charming lisp. Today, her blonde hair up in a ponytail, she was wearing her favorite outfit: pink jeans with a pale blue T-shirt and a pink jean jacket altered by her Oma to fit her tiny, stocky frame and short arms. Hoppy had a matching collar and leash, in pink vinyl! "We're going to stay right here, nice and safe, by the benches with Mama Jaymie."

Jaymie felt the little thrill of happiness she always got when Jocie called her by the name she had settled on . . . for now. She had announced it in solemn tones the first day of their family portion of the honeymoon; she'd call her Mama Jaymie, with the provision that she might shorten it at some point. Whether that meant she'd take to calling her *Jaymie* or *Mama* had been left unsaid. They had been out to the cottage to clean it preparatory to closing it up for the season, after having rented it out all summer except for the couple of weeks reserved for Jaymie's parents, Alan and Joy, to use it.

It was mid-October; a week ago she, Jakob and Jocie had been in Canada to visit her Grandma Leighton and celebrate Canadian Thanksgiving with her, along with her parents. Becca and her new-ish husband, Kevin, were on their much-delayed honeymoon in the UK, but had Skyped in, and together they made plans to gather in Queensville for Christmas. Grandma Leighton had enjoyed her visit there in December the year before, when she had stayed at the Queensville Inn and visited with old friends from her youth, so they were going to repeat that adventure over Christmas this year.

So far the warm weather had held, but that could change any day. In Michigan in autumn you could go from having the air

1

conditioner on to snow on the ground in twenty-four hours. The ferry slowed and the captain expertly brought it alongside the dock beyond the marina, where a few last die-hard sailors still had their boats in slips, even though it was fall.

"Do you see now, Jocie? The ferry is nothing to be afraid of. The captain is very experienced; even on that stormy crossing he kept us safe, right?"

Jocie nodded, but she was too intent on keeping Hoppy calm— not that the little dog needed any such help, since he had been over to the island and back on the ferry dozens of times—and talking to him in soothing tones. They waited until the captain gave the all clear to disembark. Jaymie picked up Hoppy to carry off the boat and had Jocie hold on to the railing as they walked along the passenger gangplank.

Jaymie and Jocie held the leash between their clasped hands as they walked down the wharf toward the shops that lined the marina, a collection of old and tired stores constructed of weathered gray wood that leaned against each other for support. There was a bait and tackle shop alongside a feed and tack store and a couple of other boarded-up shops that had been empty as long as Jaymie could remember.

Some folks were clustered outside the bait and tackle shop and voices were raised, signs of a squabble. Jaymie tried to steer Jocie and Hoppy around the cluster, but a group broke away to chatter among themselves, blocking their passage. In the center of the main group one man, a tall silver-haired fellow dressed in robin's egg blue pants, white loafers, a pastel plaid shirt, and with a sunshine yellow knit sweater draped over his shoulders, berated an elderly woman. She faced him with a fierce expression on her deeply lined face.

"You don't give a damn about this town anymore, do you, Lois?" he shouted, flinging his hands up in the air. "All you care about is your rotting empty buildings and this smelly bait shop. Who would want to eat ice cream sitting next to a place that sells worms?"

"Fergus, that ain't fair!" said Trip Findley, Jaymie's behind-the-house neighbor in Queensville. "Lois Perry is a founding member of the Queensville Heritage Society. She's been looking out for this town longer than you've been alive, for cripes sake!"

"I don't need you to stand up for me, Trip, much as I appreciate it," Miss Perry said. Petite and hunched, with tightly curled gray hair, wearing a wool coat over a dress despite the warm weather, and low-wedge heels, the elderly woman put both hands on the head of her cane and stood firm. She was a frail figure, all the more interesting for being the tiniest among a crowd of taller, younger folk.

"It's gotta be said, Lois," Trip stated to the woman, then turned back to his opponent. "You been gone for years, Fergus. Lois cares about this town, but she has a right to do what she wants with her own property, don't she?"

Jon Hastings, a paunchy fellow in overalls and a red T-shirt bearing an image of a worm on a hook, his hair a shock of greasy gray locks standing straight up from his head, stepped forward. "Now, Trip, Fergus is trying to make things better," he said. "I understand where he's coming from." He turned to the older woman, towering over her. "And Miss Perry, you know we got your back. We've been renting the bait shop for fifteen years, and you've always been fair to us. We can work something out, though, if you want to go along with Fergus here and sell the land. It would rest your mind. Woman your age shouldn't have to fuss over property in her golden years."

"I don't need *your* support, Jon," the tall man said to the overall-clad fellow, who was joined by a plump woman in matching overalls and bait shop T-shirt, her blonde hair teased into a high hair-sprayed pouf.

"Jon's just trying to help, Fergus," she said, hands on her hips.

"I know that, I know. I'm just frustrated. Thanks, Jon, sincerely," the fellow said, thrusting one hand through his silvery hair, then patting it down.

Jaymie tried to move on with Jocie, but the little girl was interested and hung back, watching and listening. Adults' conversations always fascinated her, and something about the elderly woman, so tiny and so fierce, drew her attention.

Still leaning heavily on her cane, the elderly woman squinted in the autumn sunshine and glared up at the tall man, ignoring the couple in overalls. "The bait shop and the feed store have been here for fifty years," she said, her voice crackling with tension but loud and authoritative, with a husky tone Jaymie's Grandma Leighton had always called a whiskey voice. "They employ Queensville folk; they *serve* Queensville folk. You say you want to develop the empty shops, but I've heard that before! Empty shops, empty promises." She banged the cane on the wood plank walkway. "I told you before, I'll *rent* you the empty shops, but I won't sell them, or the land that goes with them!"

Jaymie recognized others in the group as members of the heritage society. She had missed a few meetings and it seemed something was up. Now she was interested, too. She picked up Hoppy in one arm and still held on to Jocie's hand, but sidled over to Haskell Lockland, head of the heritage society. "What's going on, Haskell?"

He leaned toward her to speak in a murmur. "You know Miss Lois Perry, right? She owns these dockside buildings."

"I've heard the name, but I've never met her." Besides owning the dockside shops, Miss Perry was notorious locally for being a recluse *and* for having the most magnificent home on Winding Woods Lane, a street in an exclusive historic enclave north of the village of Queensville, but still officially part of it. Jaymie also knew of her as the cousin of Mrs. Martha Stubbs, born Martha Perry, an elderly friend and coconspirator of Jaymie's from past murder investigations. Jaymie had a habit of finding dead bodies and then discovering who killed the person. Mrs. Stubbs, an avid mystery reader, was sometimes instrumental in figuring out the solution.

"And that fellow is Fergus Baird of Baird Construction," Haskell continued, pointing to the man dressed in Easter egg colors. "He was born and raised here, but went off to university and didn't come back until a few years ago when he settled in Wolverhampton. He owns a construction and development company. They built that new plaza in Wolverhampton with the medical clinic in it. He wants to buy the dockside shops and develop them, but Miss Perry doesn't want to sell."

"That's her right."

"Sure, but there's more to it," Haskell said impatiently. "Baird has promised to develop tourist-friendly shops that will give a better image to those coming off the ferry and coming over on boats than a smelly old bait shop and a feed store, for crying out loud!" Haskell straightened. "Can you imagine a sweet shop, a tea shop, and a boutique? That could be folks' first impression of Queensville instead of the odor from the bait shop."

"Haskell, I've passed by here hundreds of times and I've never smelled the bait shop. What you're *smelling*, if anything, is the St. Clair River on a hot day!"

He shrugged. "I just wish she'd sell. She's holding back progress."

Jocie tugged on Jaymie's hand. "Look at her cane!" she whispered.

Jaymie noticed the cane that Miss Perry was leaning on. It was unusual, dark twisted wood with an enormous silver head shaped like some kind of nut. "It's amazing!" Jocie had shown great interest in historical items lately, inspired by Jaymie's love of vintage kitchenalia. They had shared picnics over the summer using some of the vintage picnic baskets Jaymie had collected and no longer used for business, and had tea using the Fire King snack set Jaymie had received as a wedding shower gift. "We should get going, though, honey," Jaymie whispered.

Just then an old green pickup truck screeched to a stop in the parking lot by the shops, kicking up a wave of gravel, and Dani Brougham, who owned a riding stable with her new wife, Emma Spangler, flung herself out of the cab. She paused when she saw the crowd, then strode over, greeting Jocie first, crouching down to talk to her as Jaymie let go of her hand so the two could hug. Jocie had been out to the stable last June for a first riding lesson and had enjoyed it somewhat—mostly because of her admiration for Emma's talents as a rider—but not enough to go back. Dani straightened and asked what was going on; Jaymie answered briefly.

While Jaymie was distracted it appeared that the discussion had gotten heated. The developer, red-faced, shouted, "You're so pigheaded, Lois! If you gave a damn about this community you'd sell to me!"

Trip Findley was about to step forward but Miss Perry swung her cane at Baird and missed. Dani dashed forward and caught the elderly woman as she was about to take a tumble. She steadied the woman, murmuring to her gently, but Miss Perry looked shaken.

"You're crazy, old woman," Baird shouted, backing away. "Best thing that could happen for this town is if you would croak and Morgan inherited. She'd sell these shacks to me in a heartbeat. I could tear them down, build something nice and help this town get back on its feet!"

Hoppy was barking and squirming, sensing the tension, and Jocie threw her arms around Jaymie's legs. Did the developer *really* think that badgering an elderly woman was the way to get Queensville on his side? And that the town needed him to survive? They were doing fine . . . better than fine!

"Fergus, you'd best get out of here," Trip said loudly. "Lois don't need this trouble right now!"

The developer stormed off past Jaymie and Jocie, heading up the hill in a swirl of fallen autumn leaves. Dani left Miss Perry in the care of the bait shop owners and returned to Jaymie and Jocie.

"*That* was uncomfortable," Jaymie said. "Is Miss Perry going to be okay?"

"Jon and Bev will take care of her," Dani replied.

"Jon and Bev Hastings, right?" Jaymie said. "I've seen them around, but we're just nodding acquaintances."

"They've owned the bait shop for years. I don't fish, but I know Jon pretty well. He steps in when Hank, from the feed store, needs a hand. Or a day off."

"So they own the business?" Jocie was beginning to get antsy, so Jaymie gave her Hoppy's leash, and the little girl let him sniff along the hillside where a group of saplings attracted the dog's attention. Hoppy was a boy dog, but being three-legged—he had lost one of his front legs as a baby by getting it caught in the puppy-mill cage where he was born—meant lifting a leg to pee was not an option. He did the wobbly best he could, but still managed to leave his mark at the base of one of the newly planted saplings.

"The business, yeah, but they rent the actual physical shop from Miss Perry, as does Hank. She owns the buildings and land from the marina shops and north a ways."

"All that undeveloped land along the riverbank?"

Dani nodded, pushing her straight blonde bangs off her high forehead. "At least three, four hundred feet of waterfront."

"I always wondered why homes had never been built along there; I guess that's my answer."

"Anyway, Hank would be fine if Miss Perry sells the shops, even if he had to move; his feed shop would be better situated in

Wolverhampton anyway. But the bait shop . . . it pretty much has to be by the river, right? If she sells to Baird the Hastings would be out of business."

"Odd that they were so conciliatory toward the developer."

Dani shrugged. "Jon doesn't like a fuss," she said, watching as the crowd broke up. Smaller groups formed, the townsfolk chattering and gossiping, as Jon Hastings and his wife helped the landowner along the marina to a bench so she could rest. "Miss Perry has been good to them. She only takes a fraction in rent compared to what she *could* take. I know Hank pays a lot more than they do."

"I guess it is kind of a tourist industry in a way, isn't it?" She felt a twinge of worry for the lady; as intrepid as she seemed, she was also elderly and not completely steady on her feet. But it looked like she had people who cared looking out for her; the bait shop owners were solicitous.

"Yeah, I suppose." Dani watched with a frown. "I kinda think Miss Perry is being taken advantage of by the Hastings, though. I know she doesn't want to, but it probably would be best for her to sell the marina property. She's not getting any younger."

"I suppose. We'd better get going. Jocie, come back now!" she called to her daughter. She turned back to her friend. "Say hi to Emma for us, Dani."

"Come out and see the horses sometime," she said, giving her a farewell hug, then crouching down to hug Jocie and pat Hoppy on the head. "Even if you don't want to ride. I'm starting up a hayride business on the side with a team I saved from the slaughterhouse. They're sweet old dudes, a matched set of roan geldings that have been friends for over ten years. Would you like a hayride?"

Jocie nodded. "Can my friends come?"

"As many as you want." She kissed Jocie's plump pink cheek, a loud smack that made her giggle, then stood and met Jaymie's gaze. "They used to be carriage horses, but they're semi-retired now; the hayride business is only for the fall. Hey, Emma is into goats now! I thought she was crazy, but they are the cutest things! Goats in pajamas running around the paddock and leaping over hay bales are the funniest thing I've ever seen. She films them for her video channel online, so . . . I have to get some goat chow for them." She rolled her eyes but smiled, her broad face pink-cheeked with happiness at the mention of Emma.

Jaymie smiled; that was *so* Dani, who couldn't bear to think of any horse being mistreated, and *so* Emma, who loved anything four-legged. "We'll make a point of coming out near Halloween." The stable owner waved and set off back to the feed shop to get the goat chow.

"Let's get home, honey," Jaymie said, taking Jocie's hand and ascending the hill up to the walkway above with a weary Hoppy lagging behind.

• • •

WHEN JAYMIE AND JAKOB GOT MARRIED they decided they'd spend time in Jaymie's family's yellow brick Queen Anne home in Queensville, but also in Jakob's hand-built from-a-kit log home in a corner of his Christmas tree farm outside of town. The schedule had proved to be complicated at times, but they were working on it. This week, while Becca and Kevin were on the last week of their honeymoon, Jaymie, Jakob and Jocie were staying in the Queensville home. Jakob drove Jocie to school each morning and Jaymie picked her up.

Sunday night was a normal evening of homework check, bath and bed for Jocie, snuggled in her tiny room with Lilibet, the name she had now settled on for her tiger-striped kitten that was quickly growing beyond any kittenhood. Jaymie and Jakob were lying together in the bed she had had since her childhood years, a lovely old iron double bed with a butter yellow quilt. After a little marital fun, Jaymie had let Hoppy back into the room — he had not, so far, taken in stride being banned from the bedroom at certain times, but he'd have to get used to it — and he was now curled up in the crook of Jaymie's knees.

She yawned, snuggled under Jakob's arm around her and told him about her and Jocie's trip out to the island that morning while he attended an auction out of town. She described what had happened on shore, and all about what she knew about the shops lining the dock.

"How do you feel about it?" he asked.

That was a typical evolved-male Jakob question. She gazed up into his slumberous brown eyes in the faint moonlight coming in the window. Sighing, she kissed him full on the mouth and snuggled closer.

"Mmm, what was that for?" he asked.

"Just for you being you. I've never had a man who always asked my opinion. It's nice."

"Jeez, and here I thought it was because I was somehow sexy when I'm sleepy." He yawned widely.

"You are," she said with a soft chuckle, cupping his bearded cheek in her palm. She had always thought beards were scratchy, but his wasn't; it was soft and luxuriant thanks to beard oil and beard balm, masculine hair products he used religiously. She joked that he had more "product" than *she* did for hair! "Now, about the docks—"

"Whoa, wait a minute, young woman," he growled. "I want to hear more about how sexy I am."

She giggled. They spent a few more minutes kissing. "Mmmm . . . you know, I think a lot about kissing now," she whispered.

"Is that so?"

"I do. Jocie was in a silly mood one day and asked why we kiss with our mouths and not our ears."

He chuckled, a rumble of warm, rich sound. "What did you tell her?"

"What could I say? I gave her an ear kiss." She paused, then murmured, "But I think we kiss with our mouths because that's where the sweetest words come from. That's where we say 'I love you' from. And that's where promises come from, promises to love forever." They kissed. Jaymie sighed, and he held her close against his body. "You don't mind staying in Queensville, do you?" she asked after a few minutes.

"Of course not. I love this room; it's a part of your life. And I know how much you care about this town. It's good for you to be so close to all your friends."

"I do love Queensville." Her mind returned to the problem of the marina. "You know, as nice as it would be to have a tearoom and sweet shop down there by the river, it *is* Miss Perry's property," Jaymie murmured. "It's not fair to try to bully her into selling, like

Fergus Baird is doing. Or *guilt* her into selling, like Haskell was trying to do."

"I agree." He yawned and stretched. "Good night, Mrs. Müller."

She made herself more comfortable in his arms, and checked that Hoppy was settled. "Good night, Mr. Müller."

✄ Two ✄

MONDAY WAS BUSY, as usual, getting Jocie ready for school and Jakob hustling her along, since he had an appointment and needed to drop her off first, but it was noisy, too, which was *not* completely usual. Grant and Mimi Watson, who had owned the house next door to the Leighton home for many years, were having their place fixed up; they had decided to sell and live permanently in their condo in Boca Raton.

It was the end of an era . . . an *earsplitting* end of an era. A worker was using a noisy paint gun plugged into an even noisier generator to paint the trimwork on the house. Jakob kissed her goodbye, as did Jocie, and the pair left. Jaymie tried to tune out the noise while washing the dishes and putting dinner ingredients in the slow cooker. The sale was concerning. After so many years it would be strange to have new Queensville neighbors, ones who lived there all the time.

Would they play loud music? Have a barky dog? Or rent the house out on some vacation rental website? The houses on their street were close together, since they didn't have driveways and garages to separate them. Instead a parking lane ran along the back separating them from their backyard neighbors, whose houses faced the parallel street. That meant that one could, if so moved, reach out a window and shake hands with their next-door neighbor. It would be a stretch, but technically it was possible. She hoped whoever bought the house would be congenial neighbors, the kind you'd *want* to shake hands with.

It was one of her mornings to work at the Queensville Emporium. Lunch afterward with Valetta Nibley, her lifelong best friend— literally lifelong, since Valetta was fifteen years older than her and had babysat her many times—would be a definite benefit of the morning shift. Valetta had recently been instrumental in solving a problem concerning Jaymie's crabby tabby, Denver. He was set in his ways, and barely tolerated Hoppy, let alone Jocie's young cat, Lilibet. He would not have taken to moving back and forth between the Queensville home and the log cabin on the farm.

Valetta had solved that by offering to pet sit him, but that had swiftly changed to a more practical solution: she wanted to adopt him. Jaymie had been uncertain. Was it fair to rehome an adult cat who was perfectly happy with his routine? As Valetta had pointed out, his routine would have changed anyway, and this change was more to his benefit. So they decided to give it a try. In July Denver had moved to her friend's Queensville cottage home and instantly loved it, adapting more quickly than anyone thought possible. He was king of the castle, almost literally. Valetta had ordered him a pet bed with *King of the Castle* and his photo on it, and had Bill Waterman, their local handyman, build a catio — an enclosed cat patio — on her back porch with kitty door access so he'd have outside time with no danger to himself. He had his own room, with a super-deluxe cat tree by the window, where he could look out into the bushes and get excited about the birds, or more likely sleep the day away.

It was the perfect solution all around. Jaymie was a touch miffed; she had a feeling she missed the little dude a lot more than he missed her.

Jaymie had a great morning working in the Emporium, dashed over to Valetta's cottage for lunch and to visit Denver, who she missed more than she cared to admit, then returned home and wrote her food column, "Vintage Eats," sending it off to Nan in Wolver-hampton. She took Hoppy for a long walk, played with Lilibet for a while, and by then it was time to pick Jocie up at school.

October in Michigan is gorgeous much of the time. When it isn't rainy, or windy, or — heaven forbid — snowing, there is, some days, a beautiful balance. This Monday was one of those days, sunny but not unseasonably warm, with the scent of falling oak and poplar leaves on the breeze. She pulled on a long cardigan over her flowered rayon tunic top and peach leggings, locked the kitchen door, then exited through the summer porch, locking that door too. She hoisted her purse over her shoulder and headed down the flagstone path to the parking lane behind the house.

Trip Findley, thin and wiry, the senior beau to every older lady in the village and a favorite at card parties and Rotary Club dances, was hammering a board onto his back fence. He waved with his hammer, his mouth spiky with nails gripped between his lips ready to use. He spat them out into his palm. "Say, Jaymie, you don't have that awful noisy white van no more," he called out.

"I finally replaced it." She pulled out her keys and hit the unlock button. Her newer—not brand-new; she preferred pre-owned—SUV, a nondescript white Explorer, beeped cheerily. "Mom and Dad insisted on giving me a wedding present, enough money to buy a better vehicle. They made the point that if I was going to be ferrying around precious cargo like Jocie it was time for me to get something a little safer. I spent the summer looking around. We couldn't use my van and definitely not Jakob's truck to drive to Florida, so we rented an Explorer. I liked it a lot, so when we got back I bought this." She patted the door frame, then slung her heavy purse into the vehicle over onto the passenger seat.

"Good going. Time you had something better to drive! What did you do with the van?"

"They're using it on the farm to move stuff around." She strolled over to Trip, shoving her hands down into the cardigan pockets. "What did you make of all that fuss down by the docks yesterday?"

"I kinda wish Lois would sell and be done with it, but that woman never met a fight she didn't intend to win."

"She seemed . . . doughty, I guess I'd call it."

"I call it feisty. That's Lois! Spoilin' fer a quarrel," Trip said and chuckled. "Y'know, she got used to running society in this town many years back. But things have changed, and she don't like it." He nodded, stuck the nails back between his pale lips, and returned to nailing.

Jaymie got in her SUV and headed out to Jocie's school. She pulled into the parking lot of the long, low, sixties-era school just as the school principal, Sybil Thorndike, did.

"Jaymie, my favorite parent! Don't tell the others," she said with a laugh as she locked her sedan. "I'm coming back from a meeting at the county school board."

Sybil was a woman about Becca's age, stalwart, sturdy, and no-nonsense, much like Becca, too, in those traits. She was a dedicated educator who loved kids, and Jaymie had found her excellent to deal with in the short time she had known her. At Sybil's urging Jaymie had joined the parents' council along with Jakob, and they met to work on enhanced educational opportunities for the students using local community resources.

Sybil leaned into Jaymie's car window. "You've got a creative mind; I have a question for you."

"Join me in my office," Jaymie said, grabbing her purse from the passenger seat and tossing it in the back.

Sybil slid into the passenger seat and turned to face Jaymie. "Have you ever heard of a teaching technique called learning through objects?" Jaymie shook her head. "Well, it's exactly what it sounds like. Many kids are visual learners. Tactile objects help to cement things in their brains."

"I think we're all like that," Jaymie responded. "I learned to cook when I was young because my grandmother had me stir batter and measure ingredients. It became second nature to me, whereas my sister never had that growing up, since Mom isn't much of a cook and Grandma didn't move in until Becca was sixteen."

"Exactly. That's the theory behind experiments in science class, to develop hands-on skills. But it hasn't been applied to reading and history, not yet, anyway. I'd like to develop a program section in history using objects from the heritage house—and, if it works, in other subjects—and I was wondering if you could help."

"I'd love to. I've got some ideas on how to show history through kitchen tools!"

Sybil nodded enthusiastically. "Excellent. Could I make a suggestion? I'd like to start with a section on the history of trade routes, especially the spice trade."

Jaymie's mind started working—spices? Spices were good in cookies: cinnamon, ginger, cardamom, nutmeg, even allspice! "So you mean for the spice route, maybe, like, nutmeg graters? Pepper grinders? That kind of thing?"

"Exactly! Do you have anything in your collection at the house?"

"Hmm . . . a few, but let me look into it and get back to you," Jaymie said, as she saw Jocie exit the school, hauling a book bag that looked overfull.

"You got it. We'll touch base another day." Sybil got out of the SUV and greeted Jocie somberly, asking about her progress in her new grade.

"C'mon, kiddo," Jaymie said. Jocie got into the backseat, which had a specialized seat meant to protect her small yet sturdy frame in case of an accident. She caught her daughter's eye in the rearview mirror. "Buckle up! And tell me about your day."

• • •

THE NEXT MORNING was typical of Jaymie's new normal. While Jakob made breakfast, familiar now with the Queensville kitchen, Jaymie fed Hoppy and Lilibet, then helped Jocie finish her homework at the trestle table. Together they all ate French toast, and Jocie tried out some jokes on them. "Why are ghosts such bad liars?" she asked.

"Why?" Jaymie and Jakob said together.

"Because you can see right through them!"

They laughed and finished breakfast. She then kissed them both goodbye, making sure Jocie had her lunch and her homework. Jakob was taking Jocie to school then heading out of town. He was going to be late coming home since he had to deliver items from his store, The Junk Stops Here, to customers in Wolverhampton, Marine City, Algonac and Port Huron. He had taken on more work at the store since his partner, Gus, was dealing with some family crises, but he was looking to hire more help. Jaymie was pitching in whenever she could, as was Helmut's partner, Sonya. Helmut, Jakob's older brother, was his closest sibling in every way.

Also, it was the countdown to the Christmas tree season and Jakob had to plan this year's cut with Helmut, who was also his partner in the Christmas tree farm. This time of year, in early autumn, they marked the trees available for self-cutting, as well as the ones they would cut themselves for sale at local spots.

His parents were scaling back their farming activity as they moved toward full retirement. Always ambitious, Jakob was going to be partnering with his brother Helmut in a new branch—he made that joke himself!—of his business, growing trees for local landscaping businesses. Jaymie and Jakob were alike in so many ways, not the least of which was a boundless enthusiasm for self-employment and a quick imagination for new ideas.

But today she wasn't working at any one of her jobs and had the day to herself. She did laundry, finished up the dishes, then opened her laptop and checked the weather. The internet informed her it was going to be cooler than the day before, so she dressed in a pair of cute, colorful leggings and a tunic top, over which she put on a cool jacket Jakob had given her, with sturdy walking boots.

Singing a happy tune, she leashed Hoppy and began a long walk through her village, pausing to say hello to friends and take in the fall scents and sights. After he was good and tired and begging to be carried — poor little tripod pup needed that sometimes — she headed to the Queensville Inn to visit her friend Mrs. Stubbs, who lived in a suite of rooms modified for her by her son Lyle, who owned the inn.

As Jaymie approached the inn she saw that Mrs. Stubbs was not in her room but out on the flagstone terrace, sitting in her motorized wheelchair in the early fall sunshine with a book, which she set aside as she saw her friend approach. Jaymie bent over to hug her, and Hoppy promptly begged to be set on her lap, then curled up and went to sleep while Mrs. Stubbs stroked him, massaging the scarred area where he had lost his leg.

"What are you up to today, missy?" Mrs. Stubbs asked, her voice crackly and her tone good-humored, for once. She was known locally as a rather cranky woman, but being ninety-something was, as she often said, not for sissies. Some days were bad, with crippling pain in her arthritic joints. Today was a good day; sun on her hands made them better, she had once told Jaymie, flexing the knotted joints.

Jaymie told her friend all she had been doing and caught her up on everything to do with her new family. Jakob was good, working hard as always, and with more ideas for businesses than he could keep up with. Jocie was doing better. She had already told her friend about their trip in the summer, when they had gone to a hospital in Delaware for Jocie's annual checkup to keep an eye on her skeletal dysplasia, a part of her achondroplasia dwarfism. They had also, at the same time, consulted with the geneticist who was keeping an eye on her progress, something always done for children with genetic conditions. She was on track, progressing normally, hitting all her growth markers. Jaymie had been pleased to learn what she suspected, that Jocie was in the highest percentile of intellectual development for her age group, despite occasional setbacks physically that made her miss school sometimes.

"She's had a rough go, lately. We drove from Delaware down to Boca Raton to visit Mom and Dad," Jaymie said. "Jocie adored the beach, but we think the ocean water got into her ears. She had a nasty ear infection in August that kept her from starting school immediately after Labor Day." Jocie and other little people were prone to ear infections, but antibiotics had helped and she was almost all better, rapidly catching up in school. Only time would tell if she'd need tubes inserted in her ears to keep her from suffering hearing loss.

"Poor little duckie," Mrs. Stubbs said softly. "I miss having little ones around. I have two great-grands, but they live so far away. If Dee's boys get started having kids I'll enjoy it. Will you bring Jocie to see me soon?"

"I sure will. She'd like that. Let's do a proper tea party in your room sometime soon!" She paused, then continued, "Actually, Ms. Thorndike, Jocie's principal, stopped me to talk yesterday. She's initiating a learning through objects program at the school." Jaymie explained what learning through objects was. "She suggested using items from the heritage house in the lessons. I jumped on it and said okay, but then started thinking . . . Haskell is so fussy about the house. Do you think he'll be on board with having a bunch of kids there for a couple of hours, rather than just touring through?"

"I'll make sure he is," Mrs. Stubbs said, her tone starchy. "I had plenty of trouble keeping him in line when he was young. He and Lyle were friends and he was always a nuisance." She had volunteered for many years at Wolverhampton High through the seventies and eighties, while her boys were growing up. "I'll remind him what a pain he was and how important learning opportunities are for the children."

Jaymie spoke about where she was going to start, with things related to the spice trade to explain global exploration and the spice route. "I'm going to have to beef up my collection of spice storage, graters, cookbooks and the like, though."

Mrs. Stubbs stroked Hoppy and he sighed a contented doggy sigh and curled into a tighter ball on her lap. "You should start with my cousin, Lois Perry."

"Huh. It's funny how you see someone or hear of someone and all of a sudden you hear about them again and again!" Jaymie related that she had seen Miss Perry down by the dock in an argument with the developer.

"That sounds like Lois. She's spirited when it comes to our family history and legacy."

"What does she have to do with spices, though?"

Mrs. Stubbs stared at her in dismay, her eyes crinkling at the corners. "You really don't know? Haven't you ever heard of Captain Perry and the Nutmeg Palace?"

"Well, I know about the Perry family a little; Perry Street, Perry Park and Perry Place are named for them . . . for your family." The Perry name was ubiquitous in Queensville, and she knew they were among the founders of the town, and had something to do with shipping.

"I'm disappointed. Thought you knew local history better than that." Mrs. Stubbs loved to tell a good story, so this was a good excuse to relate some family history. "I'm a Perry by birth, as you know. Lois is a little younger than I; as a very little girl she was as much a stubborn pain in the bee-hind as she is now. Anyway, about the Perry family: back in the mid eighteen hundreds my some number of great-grandfathers, Captain Jonas Perry, who started working as a spice trader from the east, settled here in Queensville. Built a wood house first, but he liked to be better and higher up than everybody else, so he bought a big chunk of land on the prominence north of town and built himself what folks around here thought was a gaudy and unnecessarily large house for his family — just himself, his wife and three boys.

"And the servants, of course. In those days everyone had servants, even if it was just a maid-of-all-work. The house is on the headland that looks north and south along the river, on what's known as Winding Woods Lane now. Because of how big it was, and how many finials and gewgaws he put on it, folks around here started calling it the Palace. He liked to have the last laugh, did Jonas, so he went even more extravagant, added more gingerbread, and called it the Nutmeg Palace, built on his spice fortune. That's what it's been called ever since."

"I did *not* know all of that. It fits in perfect with the section on spice trade routes! Gives it a local spin."

"Lois is the official family guardian of the palace. There's a book on the spice trade in America that mentions the Perry family; I'm sure she has a copy. She also has maps, rare botanical prints, and every kind of spice grinder, grater and the rest you could ever imagine."

"That would be so awesome for the students!" Jaymie paused, watching her friend, starting to get sleepy in the warm autumnal sunshine. "You don't think . . . would she — "

"I'll call her and set up a meeting for you," Mrs. Stubbs said, her eyes closed, hand on Hoppy, cradling him. She opened one eye. "I can't promise what she'll agree to, but if you go with my blessing she's more likely to loan you bits and bobs from the collection than if you go in cold."

"Thank you, *thank* you! My daughter thanks you. Her school thanks you!" She paused a beat. "Can you call her soon and maybe I can go out there this afternoon?"

Mrs. Stubbs chuckled. "Never one to let moss grow under your feet, are you? Let's go in, have a cup of tea, and I'll call her."

Jaymie came away with a two p.m. meeting with Miss Lois Perry, and a bit of a headache. Life seemed to move so quickly at times. She had met and married Jakob much more quickly than she had ever thought possible, but they both knew it was right. She had always been flexible and adaptable: working at several different jobs, becoming a food columnist, aspiring to write a cookbook, marrying a man with his own range of businesses, becoming the mom of a soon-to-be nine-year-old . . . all required flexibility and adaptability at heightened levels.

But she was adept at making every visit or trip serve many purposes; she might triple up with this new venture, helping Sybil with her learning through objects idea. Hopefully she could borrow items for the heritage house displays, use them to teach the kids in Jocie's school about spice trade routes, and perhaps in doing so find a vintage recipe using spices for her "Vintage Eats" column.

She returned to the house and deposited a sleepy Hoppy in his basket by the stove, where Lilibet was snoozing. Then she headed right back out again, walking over to her sister and brother-in-law's new store, Queensville Fine Antiques. It was a lovely day to walk and reflect, the autumn sun warm on her face, neighbors out walking their dogs and doing yard work, chrysanthemums blooming in shades of gold and burgundy as red and yellow leaves drifted.

The last year and a half had been a thrill ride in some ways. She could have done without the presence of murder in her life, though there was great satisfaction in helping the police solve them. But she could *not* have done without meeting and marrying Jakob and his little daughter, Jocie, and her closer relationship with her sister, and her sister's new husband, Kevin. It was a good time to be alive, she often felt.

She climbed the front steps and entered the antique shop, on time for her lesson in antiques from Kevin's older sister, Georgina. "I'm here and ready to learn!"

The woman looked up at Jaymie, checked her watch and frowned. She was two minutes late. Jaymie sighed but didn't comment as she stowed her purse under the desk and took her place beside her teacher. Georgina was even more English than Kevin. Petite, dyed blonde and slim—she called herself well-preserved, and she was that—she managed the antique store for her brother and Becca, and lived in an apartment in back, which she complained about constantly. Becca took the complaints in stride and was trying to alter it to please her new sister-in-law.

Becca wanted Jaymie schooled in fine antiques in case anything else happened like the event that had put Kevin and Becca's honeymoon off until now, Georgina's emergency gallbladder surgery and recovery, which had taken most of the summer. Though Georgina was better now, Becca wanted to be able to fall back on Jaymie to take care of things if need be. Unfortunately, neither Georgina nor Kevin thought her antique knowledge was deep enough. Becca had been offended—not an unusual state for her, but this time it was on her younger sister's behalf—but Jaymie, the more she learned, agreed with them.

At first she couldn't have told the difference between an étagère and an epergne, but she was beginning to get a grasp on that and much more: historical periods in antiques, from Georgian, Victorian, and Edwardian on through the more esoteric differences between art nouveau and art deco. She was learning how to recognize a silver hallmark and how to identify silver plate. Today's lesson was in antique china: how to recognize quality; the different makers; and what to look at when appraising pieces.

"Of course, you won't be buying or appraising any yourself, but it doesn't hurt for you to have an understanding of it," Georgina said.

"Of course," Jaymie murmured, examining a mark on the back of a piece of Sèvres with a loupe, a jeweler's tool that magnified them.

The front showroom of Queensville Fine Antiques had been designed by Becca to make everything look much more valuable than it was. Glass cases holding hallmarked silver antique pieces lined one end of the showroom; Minton and Wedgwood china, and fragile prewar crystal, lined the other, sparkling under halogen lighting, bright but cool. Good pieces of furniture like a burled walnut étagère and a mahogany Duncan Phyfe dining set with lyre-back chairs took up the front space by the big picture window. Place settings of Royal Crown Derby Old Imari china and Acanthus patterned sterling silver flatware atop a vintage damask tablecloth dressed the table, while lovely ruby-colored crystal vases sparkled on an intricate Victorian étagère. The sales desk was a reclaimed, repurposed kitchen island made out of pickled-finish maple with a marble top. Georgina spent much of her time behind it answering questions on the phone, updating the store's website and social media, and polishing silver. She had been involved in antiques her whole life, she had told Jaymie, and was as passionate still as she had been as a girl.

She was deeply knowledgeable and Jaymie was enjoying her lessons, though Georgina was prickly at times and ill-tempered toward children, aloof and frosty any time Jocie was around. So far they had covered how to tell the difference between hand-painted design and transfer print on china, and even how to recognize a combination of techniques. Hand-painted was worth a lot more, and the primary rule of thumb Georgina offered was to look for tiny errors or dissimilarities in pieces, which indicated hand-painting. Jaymie correctly identified a piece of transfer-printed china by noting, under the loupe, the stippling, raised dots rather than brush strokes.

Jaymie looked at her watch. "Oops, I'm going to have to get going, Georgina," she said, handing her back the china plate. "I have to be out to Miss Lois Perry's place by two. I don't think she'd like it if I was late."

"Miss Perry? I've *met* the lady."

Her frosty tone stopped Jaymie in the act of grabbing her purse.

She examined the woman's face, her look meaningful, her blue eyes glacial behind large plastic-rimmed glasses. "Is there something I should know?"

"Ask her why she came barging in here one day saying we had some of her family's silver that had been stolen from her home." Georgina's tone was crisp and offended.

↫ Three ↫

"AS IF WE WOULD BUY from anyone suspect!" Georgina said with a sniff of contempt. "We are *not* a pawnshop."

"I didn't hear about this!" Jaymie said.

"It happened while you were on vacation." She turned her computer monitor to face Jaymie. "She claimed this, a hallmarked set of Savoy by Buccellati that we bought, was hers."

Jaymie knew that Buccellati was an Italian maker of fine sterling silver flatware, among other things. On the Queensville Fine Antiques website they had listed the service for twelve plus serving pieces of flatware for eighteen thousand dollars. Jaymie gasped. Eighteen *thousand* dollars. She'd been told antiques had plummeted in value in the last fifteen years; apparently that was not true of sterling silver! "What happened?"

"She called the police. They shut our establishment down for an afternoon. I was appalled and *dread*fully embarrassed!" She was at her snippiest, mounted on the highest of high horses. "It was humiliating."

"Why didn't anyone tell me?"

"Why would they?" Georgina asked. "Nothing came of it. We had provenance. It's not like we're some flea market . . . or junk store." She swiftly cut a glance at Jaymie as she turned the computer monitor back into place.

That was a shot at The Junk Stops Here, Jakob's store. With a big smile, Jaymie said, "I'll stick to my junk shop Pyrex and melamine, thank you very much."

"Anyway . . . watch that woman," Georgina said. "She's not entirely balanced."

"I'll keep that in mind."

Jaymie retrieved her Explorer from home and drove back through town, past the Queensville Inn to River Road, which gently ascended from the village to a wooded prominence that overlooked the river. River Road moved away from the waterway briefly, circling around an enclave of historic, wealthy homes, most concealed from each other by bends, turns and trees. The neighborhood as a whole, made up of a loop—Winding Woods Lane—and two streets, was called Winding Woods. After curving around Winding Woods, River Road resumed its track along the St. Clair and descended to just above river level once more.

When the Queensville Heritage Society had first started looking for a house to buy and convert to a historic home attraction, they had considered one in Winding Woods, but the homes, most over a hundred and thirty years old, were out of the society's price range, every single one elegantly outfitted and perfectly preserved, like wealthy dowagers with precise surgical facelifts every half century or so. Instead the heritage society had been fortunate to purchase Dumpe House, now the Queensville Historic Manor, away from the river and slightly out of town. They got it for a song and had renovated it to a high standard, including fire safety upgrades, new wiring and other modern amenities. It was a good purchase since it was on a large parcel of land with room to add parking and build a historic interpretation center. That wouldn't have been possible in Winding Woods.

The best view of the river was commanded by the star home of Winding Woods, stately in its regal splendor and isolation, the residence known as the Nutmeg Palace. It was a large, intricately painted Queen Anne–style home, the first, Mrs. Stubbs had told her, and therefore the oldest. Though it sat on the highest prominence overlooking the St. Clair River, because of the heavy woods surrounding it only the widow's walk and turret rooms were visible until one rounded the bend of Winding Woods Lane, the great loop off of River Road that was the highest, furthest point of Winding Woods, with Laurel and Linden streets the only others in the enclave.

When she pulled up and turned off the engine, Jaymie sat staring at the house for a few minutes, trying to take it all in. It was magnificent. Bewildering. It was, in fact, a tumult to the senses, an explosion of gingerbread, gabling, scrollwork, coffered panels, paneled friezes, porches sticking out hither and thither, all adorned with an intricate color scheme of mauves and lavender accented with charcoal. Turrets! A widow's walk! Every detail screamed Victorian, and in 1850 was likely a marvel for the locals. Back then, it would have been clearly visible from almost anywhere, since the trees had all been chopped down so construction could proceed.

Since then, of course, every effort had been made to restore the wooded splendor to Winding Woods Lane, and so trees were abundant. Even across from the homes was a circular glade of laurel and linden trees, along with thick undergrowth and pleasant, shaded walks. Each home along the lane felt secluded and private, even from the others.

To the right of the Nutmeg Palace was a sidewalk leading around to the back of the house, lined with an overgrown hedge of japonica that straggled over the walk, already shadowed by a bow window overhang. It would be like walking through a tunnel of branches and architecture. The backyard was concealed by a wooden gate that had seen better days, the wood bleached to a gray pitted appearance. The grass was overgrown, and there was a spirea bush that crowded the walk. Jaymie remembered that on the other side of the hedge was Haskell Lockland's home, which she had passed driving up.

She climbed the creaky front steps slowly, passed through a semicircular wooden arch, crossed the board porch and lifted the knocker on the double oak door. Before she could release it, the door was pulled open and Miss Lois Perry stood in the doorway leaning heavily on her cane, a plain, serviceable aluminum one today.

"You're Jaymie Leighton," she said, her voice scratchy and curt.

"I am. Mrs. Stubbs called and you said I could come by at two to talk to you."

"Something about school, or your daughter or . . . something." She turned away and hobbled down the hall toward the back of the house.

Jaymie stood for a moment on the threshold, but deciding that was all the invitation she would receive, she followed, closing the big door behind her. She paused and looked around her. The entryway was spacious enough but felt smaller because of the overpowering décor and lack of lighting. The walls were papered in a busy pattern of vines in browns and golds, and there were all manner of furnishings, including an enormous Victorian mirrored hall tree laden with coats and hats and a holder full of canes and umbrellas. Across from that was a carved mahogany table holding a china dish on a stand and an oil lantern.

The hall felt even more crowded because of the elaborate wood gingerbread details that topped the arches and the oak staircase that turned ninety degrees on a landing and ascended out of sight. On the right, beyond the staircase, overlooking the porch, was the turret area, which simply held a semicircular bench with fussy patterned cushions, and draped windows, the gloom preventing her from seeing much but that.

On the left, through a doorway arched in dark-stained spindled gingerbread, there was a parlor with glass and oak cases filled with silver along one wall, as well as documents and botanical prints framed in rich dark wood clustered on the painted walls above them. There was an intricately carved fireplace along the far wall, and settees and chairs filling the space by the draped window. The furnishing in the parlor was antique, but not heavy Victorian. It looked, to Jaymie's newly tutored gaze, to be art nouveau opulence, with leaf and vine motifs. As her eyes became accustomed to the clutter she began to discern intricate details in the home, like the carved nut shapes in the gingerbread, showing how the home was designed to be unique.

"Are you coming?" Miss Perry said, having returned to the hallway and glaring down it at Jaymie. "Don't stand there gawping; come!"

Obediently she followed the woman down the long hall, past a dining room, through a worn and scuffed kitchen that looked like it had last been renovated in the fifties to a popular style and never touched since, to a small dim room off of it, what appeared to be Miss Perry's lair. There was a recliner oriented toward a newer flat-screen television, another chair for a guest, and shelves with books along two other walls. There was a small TV table beside her chair that held an assortment of vitamin bottles and a weekly dosette, which held her prescription medications; it was divided into days of the week and times of day, as different drugs needed to be taken with meals and at bedtime.

This is where, for the most part, she probably lived. The woman put on a brave face but age was taking its toll, as it was with Jaymie's beloved Grandma Leighton and good friend Mrs. Stubbs. Did she live here all alone? Jaymie considered what Georgina had told her about the theft the woman had endured and wondered if she was ever frightened.

As Miss Perry lowered herself into her chair with an *oof* of weariness, Jaymie moved the other chair to face hers and sat down too. She was about to open her mouth to ask about the home when the phone on the side table rang; it was a landline, one of those phones with the huge number buttons and a cordless handset.

"Hello? Who? *Who?* Speak up!" Miss Perry listened. "Oh, hello, Estelle . . . no, I *told* you, I'm still thinking about it and I don't care if you're on a schedule!" She hit the Off button and set the handset in the cradle on the TV table. "Used to be you could slam the phone down in someone's ear and it had an impact," she grumbled.

"Was that Estelle Arden?"

"You know her?"

"She's on the heritage board," Jaymie said. "I'm a member of the heritage society."

"Which I cofounded umpteen years ago. Estelle is a pain in the bum, is what she is. She and that boyfriend of hers, Conrad what's-his-name—"

"Conrad Reese?"

"That's him."

"I don't think they're a couple."

"Hmph. They want to not only talk to me at length for their little project, but they want me to let people wander all over my property!" She sat up taller in her recliner, a glint of anger in her eyes. She glared at Jaymie and continued, "They're writing some fool walking-tour pamphlet—"

"'Walk Historic Queensville,'" Jaymie supplied. "It's going to be a booklet to give folks self-guided walking tours of the town and area. The sale of it is to help the heritage society."

"I don't care if it's to support bonobos in the Congo, I am *not* going to let those two into my house to case the joint, and I'm *never* going to let strangers wander all over my property pretending they're tourists! I should have told her that, but I don't like doing that on the phone. I'll tell her in person." White foam flecked her lips and a vein throbbed in her forehead. She plucked at the floral sleeve of her silky shirtwaist dress and pulled a handkerchief from it, like a geriatric magician, using it to dab at her mouth. "The only reason I let *you* in is because Martha said you were okay!"

"I'm glad you feel that way. Mrs. Stubbs is an old friend of my grandmother, Mrs. Lucy Leighton."

"Lucille! I remember her. She's older than I. So is Martha, by the way. They're *all* older than I am," she said with satisfaction. "But none of 'em have the responsibility of living in this museum. Sometimes I think I should sell it, but it's our family heritage. It's a legacy." She was getting worked up, sitting forward in the chair, her tiny frame trembling with ire. "So are the land along the river and the marina shops, but everybody, including my niece, wants to tell me what to do with *my* property!"

"Miss Perry, may I make you a cup of tea?"

Startled and disarmed, she nodded and sat back in her chair. "Kettle's on the stove, tea is over the sink. I don't know where the teapot is; Morgan never bothers with one. She makes my tea in a mug, like a damned heathen!"

Jaymie knew old ladies — and young ladies — and tea was almost always the answer to anything upsetting. When Jocie found out she had to go to a doctor again for another round of medication she cried, but a tea party made her feel a little better. Jaymie took one wrong turn looking for where a teapot might be stored and found herself facing a back staircase, chilly and dusty, with dark paint on the stair that was worn in the center. It rose from an alcove — almost as big as a mudroom, but not as self-contained — that overlooked the back lawn through a window in the door. She then discovered a butler's pantry, with looming shelves of serving ware. There she found a pretty rose-flowered teapot — an inexpensive Sadler, stained from years of use, but that was the best kind — and returned to the kitchen. She made a pot of tea, found mugs, sugar, spoons and milk and plopped it all on a dollar store tray that was on top of the elderly humming fridge. She carried the tray into the television room and set it down on a low table that was pushed against one set of bookcases.

Miss Perry had her eyes closed, but she opened them and said, "Two sugars and no milk."

Jaymie fixed up their cups, set Miss Perry's on her table, and sat down with her own. Where to start the conversation, she wondered. The lady seemed to have a lot on her mind, so she'd start there. "So Estelle and Conrad want you to allow people to come on your property during the walking tour."

"My idiot neighbors have already allowed it, and they expect me to give them right-of-way across my property to go from Haskell's house south of me to the Zanes on the north side."

"I know Haskell well from the heritage society, of course. He's also some kind of cousin to my friend Heidi Lockland."

"Hmph. Pain in the bum."

"I saw you all on the dock on Sunday, Haskell included. I was coming back from Heartbreak Island on the ferry with my daughter and saw you speaking with that developer, Fergus Baird."

"*Another* pain in the bum. He wants to buy that land and tear down the buildings, build all new. I told him I'd *rent* him the two empty buildings, but he said no. Not my fault if he won't compromise. Those places were built in the twenties by my folks. If they want to tear them down they'll have to drive bulldozers over my cold, dead body."

Jaymie felt a chill down her back. "Please don't say that, Miss Perry." She searched for something to change the subject from Baird's evil plans. "Um . . . I understand that a few months ago you had a break-in and some silver was stolen. What happened?"

Between sips of tea, Miss Perry told her that one night while she slept upstairs, someone broke a window in the utility room, managed to unlock it and get through, and took a few items of great value. "They knew enough to pick and choose: an entire set of flatware; an epergne; a silver tray and fruit bowl. All sterling. Worth a fortune."

"That would be pretty heavy," Jaymie remarked. "What did the police say?"

"That I was lucky they didn't kill me where I lay, and that I should get an alarm system or a big dog."

"But you didn't get either?"

She twisted and glared at Jaymie. "I am *not* going to be a prisoner in my own home, and those alarms are impossible . . . all number keypads and codes. One fellow came out and explained it to me, but you'd need a science degree to work it. And I *hate* dogs: big, dirty, expensive beasts. If the robbers kill me for my silver next time, so be it." She sighed. "Besides, Morgan is terrified of dogs; if I got one she'd never come, and I depend on her."

"So, the utility room is in the back of the house?"

"Exactly! Under the back stairs. One of my reasons for not

wanting every yahoo in the world trotting across my land. How am I supposed to know who's friend and who's foe if every Tom, Dick and Harriet can claim they're doing a walking tour? I've heard those awful ATVs out there too, even at night; those noisy vehicles tear up the waterfront and scare my cats."

"You have cats?"

"I don't have them, they have me," she grumbled. "I feed 'em, anyway. Just a few strays. They're not hurting anyone and they keep the mice away."

Jaymie thought of asking about her visit to the antique store but decided against it. She had a mission and a reason to be there, and she needed to get on with it. "Miss Perry, the principal of my daughter's elementary school, Sybil Thorndike, is trying to start a section on exploring history through objects, and I want to help her. My area is the kitchen, and we're going to do a section on the spice trade and exploration. I would love to see your spice-related memorabilia and, if you decide it's a good idea, borrow some for the heritage home displays so we can take the kids there for demonstrations."

Miss Perry gazed at her for a long minute. "I'm thinking about it. How would you protect the items?"

"The heritage home does have an alarm system and so far we've never had a theft." Just a murder, but she wasn't about to say that. "I was thinking of having our handyman build lockable cases like the one I had him make for the antique cleaver display I have mounted in the kitchen."

She chuckled. "Didn't want anyone to get the wrong idea, right?" She drank down the rest of her tea.

"Yes, and yours would be securely mounted on the wall, too, kind of double security."

"Auntie Lois!" a voice rang out from the front. "Auntie Lois, I'm here!"

"Here, Morgan," Miss Perry called out. "My great-niece checking in on me," she said to Jaymie. "Don't know what I'd do without her. She's married to that Saunders Wallace, the car salesman fellow who advertises on TV so much, and she works in the dealership office."

A young woman, thirtyish, with long straight blonde hair and wearing a sweater over a summery dress that clung to her plump, curvy figure, poked her head in the TV room door. "Oh! You have company. Sorry."

Jaymie stood and held her hand out. "Jaymie Leighton. I came to talk to your aunt about her spice grater collection."

"We haven't gotten down to brass tacks yet," Miss Perry said. "But I might be lending out some of the collection to the heritage house. That ought to shut Haskell up for a while."

"Mr. Lockland just wants to let folks walk across the property along the riverfront, Auntie," Morgan said. "You should let them do it. Be civic-minded!"

"Civic-minded . . . pfft!" Miss Perry said, waving one hand.

"You're such a grumblepuss!" She flashed a bright smile at Jaymie, then grabbed the tray and exited with it, heading back to the kitchen and running some water.

Jaymie exchanged a look with Miss Perry, who sighed and shook her head. For the next while, as Morgan clanked around in the kitchen, Miss Perry told Jaymie about some of the family history. How Captain Jonas Perry circumnavigated the globe, finding new sources for the spices the family built their wealth on: star anise, cinnamon, allspice, cloves and the all-important nutmeg.

Every Georgian and Regency gentleman carried a nutmeg grater, she said. It was a sign of elegance, like snuff and a walking stick. Silver Georgian nutmeg graters in particular were valuable and highly collectible. Fascinated, since the Regency era was one of her favorite time periods to read about in the romance fiction she loved, Jaymie drank it all in.

After chatting a while Miss Perry shouted, "Morgan, *Morgan!*"

"Yes, Auntie Lois?" she said, poking her head back into the TV room.

"Can you get me the silver Georgian nutmeg grinders from the display case in the parlor?"

The young woman disappeared and came back with three objects, which she handed over to her aunt. "I'm going to throw a load of laundry in, Auntie, and start your dinner."

"Thanks, dear." Miss Perry turned back to Jaymie and handed her one item. "This one is Georgian, pure silver, and dates to the eighteenth century."

Jaymie took it and turned it over and over. It was lovely, almost egg-shaped, made of smooth soft silver, with lines of carved rosettes in alternating bands. It twisted open in the middle to expose a grating surface. "Very neat. I've seen them in photos but never held one."

She handed Jaymie another smaller one that was shaped like a nutmeg, except with a grater surface. Jaymie handed those two back and took the last.

"That one is plainer," Miss Perry said, "but I like it."

If Jaymie hadn't known it was a nutmeg grater she would have assumed it was a small jewelry box or compact. It was oval and flat, with hallmarks on the underside and lovely carved vines on the top, with initials in the center: JMP. "Jonas Perry?"

Miss Perry nodded. "Jonas *Magnus* Perry."

She took the lid off to expose the grater insert inside; the user would grate the nutmeg, then lift the grater insert out and sprinkle the spice over food. "These are lovely!"

"I won't loan you the Perry grater, but some of the others, I will." She heaved herself from her chair and reached for her aluminum cane. "Come see the displays, and bring those with you. We have some botanical prints from the seventeen hundreds and a book or two on the spice trade, as well as the pamphlet I wrote back in the eighties about the Perry family. Also an entire collection of various spice graters."

She led the way very slowly to the front room and for another half hour wandered around it, touching familiar objects and telling Jaymie all about how the Perrys came to settle in Michigan and build the Nutmeg Palace. She showed her the paintings and botanical prints, framed on the wall above the cases, and a few books mentioning the Perrys, as well as the spice trade in America.

As they perused the cases, Jaymie set the nutmeg graters back in place on the deep blue velvet case lining among the others, the empty spaces and cradles indicating where each was missing. There was an amazing array of shapes and sizes, from the ones Jaymie had already seen to ones shaped like acorns, walnuts, cylinders and boxes. There was every material, from carved rosewood and mahogany, brass, silver, aluminum and steel, and a lovely enameled beauty. There were colonial spice graters made of tin, and odd ones with turn handles, like miniature meat grinders.

"This is an *amazing* collection, Miss Perry."

"Every Perry generation has added to it. It's been fun telling you about it," the woman said, leaning heavily on her cane.

"I'm afraid I've worn you out," Jaymie said. "I'll let you think about what we can borrow, and come back another day."

"Give me a few days to consider. Meanwhile, you talk to Haskell. I want a guarantee from him that he'll be responsible for them."

Jaymie quailed at the thought. She and Haskell got along all right, but she hadn't run the idea for the school tie-in past him yet. She exited the parlor toward the front door, turned and said, "Thank you, Miss Perry. You've been so gracious. My daughter's class will benefit greatly."

The woman chuckled, the sound a dry rasp. "It's all in the approach. If those heritage society folks would serve me tea and listen to my stories I'd probably say yes to a lot more of their requests!"

Jaymie laughed with her, opened the door and stepped out to the porch. A very large barking dog charged up the stairs and lunged at her. She stumbled backward.

"Tiberius, *down!*" a man shouted.

Miss Perry erupted from the hallway out onto the porch, almost falling over as she flailed with her cane. "Langlow Zane, you get that destructive mutt off my property before I get out the shotgun!"

"Miss Perry, he got loose, that's all!" the man said as he raced after the large hound, which had bounded down from the porch and now seemed to think the chase was a grand idea. It leaped about, evading capture. "He's a playful pup. He's not hurting anyone."

"Bullfeathers!" Miss Perry shouted, her voice shaking with anger, as Jaymie descended the front steps to the sidewalk. "You walk that mutt off leash all the time and it poops on my property. You don't even *bother* scooping it!"

"That is *not* our Tiberius!" the man said, straightening. He was tall and slim, late fifties, likely, with tidy white hair, one lock falling over his forehead. His clothing was sporty, a polo shirt and tan chinos belted with a woven leather belt, topped by an expensive red Columbia windbreaker jacket, open, the zipper bottom flapping in the breeze. He wore tan leather docker shoes.

Jaymie recognized him; he belonged to the sailing club. He and his wife, Phillipa, had a cottage on Heartbreak Island. The dog took his master's preoccupation as license and bounded down the walk beside Miss Perry's house toward the backyard. He lunged and busted through the gate, which whacked against the house, then the dog disappeared.

"Get that unholy hellhound off my property!" Miss Perry shrieked. She had turned from a lovely, silver-haired laughing elderly lady to a red-faced harridan in seconds. She tottered to the rounded end of the wooden porch and leaned over, peering down the sidewalk that ran to the back of the property. "Get him away from here before he hurts my kitties!"

Jaymie sped into action, sprinting past Lan Zane—the dog owner's face was set in a resentful grimace, and he seemed in no hurry to comply—through the open wooden gate and to the backyard. The pooch was racing around, pausing occasionally to sniff at bushes, but easily evaded her outstretched hand when she dove for him. A cat erupted from under some hydrangea, yowling and rocketing across the yard, the dog in full pursuit, snapping at the cat's flailing tail. "Tiberius!" Jaymie yelled. "Tiberius, *no!*" The yelling made no impact, but the cat had found safety and disappeared from sight into a thick box hedge along the back edge of the yard.

The dog's owner raced into the yard, huffing and puffing, and grasped his dog's collar, but only because Tiberius, deprived of his prey, trotted back to him amiably.

"Old witch," he muttered, leading the dog by the collar across the wide swath of emerald green. "Tiberius was just having some fun."

"She has a right not to have your dog on her property," Jaymie retorted, appalled by his rudeness.

"Yeah, well, notice she didn't mention that those mangy stray cats she feeds on the back porch are a worse nuisance," he said, waving his free hand toward the glowering cat. "They dig and crap in my garden and kill the birds at my feeders! I'm fed up with it."

That was a new wrinkle in their conflict that she had not considered. Jaymie caught sight of a landing by the back door where several empty chipped china dishes sat. She also noticed another cat, more steadfast than the runner, sitting in the middle of the lawn and staring at Tiberius, growling with a low, threatening sound. It was a fat gray cat with a round face and gold eyes; he looked healthy and poised, the feline king of his domain. He turned, tail held high, and strolled over to the hydrangea hedge that separated the Nutmeg Palace from the Zane house north of it, made the motion that indicated he was marking it with his scent, staring with a defiant glare, then disappeared from sight. Lan Zane was still talking over his shoulder as he staggered along, tugging his huge dog toward the front, but his words were lost to Jaymie as she noticed the view of the river from Miss Perry's backyard.

It was magnificent, a portion of it framed by an arbor of roses set to the south edge of the overgrown box hedge that lined the top of the bluff. She moved toward it almost involuntarily, stepping through the arbor and examining the vista. A path followed the cliff edge about twenty feet above the river, but there was also another path that zigzagged back and forth, descending to the water's edge, muddy and rocky below the bluff. Herring gulls wheeled and screeched above, adults with elegant gray and white plumage, and immature birds, clothed in speckled soft brown feathers. She stared down at the silvery blue river gliding past and then looked south, toward Heartbreak Island. A cargo ship majestically churned along in the shipping lane, past the island heading north, toward Lake Huron. There was probably no point along the St. Clair with this view because, for the most part, land along the river was flat and only a few feet above the water's edge. She could see why folks wanted to come up the zigzag path and walk along the bluff trail.

She looked along the bluff to the south; there was another magnificent property there, which she knew was Haskell Lockland's. She could hardly see it, just the second floor above the hedge that divided the properties, but there was a definite path that ascended on his land to the bluff. His second floor at the back of his house was a glassed office with probably the best view of all. It looked newer than the house. She thought she could see a fence through the hedge; if that was there, then his property was better insulated from danger than Miss Perry's.

The Zane property was to the north of Miss Perry's, but Jaymie couldn't see that at all, as it was concealed by Miss Perry's home and the high hedge, and by the fact that Winding Woods Lane curved away past the elderly woman's home. Her wedge-shaped property was the largest of the three, with the wide base of the wedge along the river.

She turned back toward Miss Perry's place, but her attention was caught by some movement below the bluff; she edged forward and peered down the hillside. A flash of red, and whoever it was, was gone. Had someone been coming along the path below but stopped when they saw her? Or was someone watching Miss Perry's house? She glanced back at the house, noting the large window that must be the utility room, given the newish pane that was different than the three other wavy old glass panes. It would give easy access to the house. Once someone had successfully robbed the place and knew what was in it, would they try again?

With an uneasy feeling she turned, headed back to the front of the house, closing the gate carefully behind her, and took her leave of the elderly lady, who leaned heavily on her cane, supported by her great-niece, Morgan. Jaymie promised to get back in touch with Miss Perry as soon as she talked to Haskell Lockland about security measures for the valuable historic items the lady would like to loan the heritage society.

As Jaymie drove away she caught the young woman's expression in the rearview mirror. For some unknown reason that maybe had nothing to do with Jaymie, Morgan Wallace looked perturbed and grim. She supported her aunt into the house and closed the door behind them.

⬡ **Four** ⬡

THE NEXT FEW DAYS were busy with a medical appointment for Jocie (Jaymie and Jakob both took her to her doctor), a vet appointment for Hoppy (his yearly shots and checkup in Wolverhampton), working at the Emporium, helping Cynthia Turbridge move furniture around in the Cottage Shoppe, lessons from Georgina on furniture styles — she learned about the art deco period in antiques — and a hundred other things big and small. She cornered Haskell out at the heritage house and got him to agree to Miss Perry's reasonable requests. Somewhere in there she fit in her weekly column and the recipe book she was still working on. She had a new idea for it, something to make it stand out from the crowd of other cookbooks that were published every season.

Her calendar had gone from busy to jam-packed.

The weekend saw them back at Jakob's log cabin on his property in a corner of his parents' farm. Saturday morning there was a chill in the air, a warning of autumn to come. As she finished drying the dishes and Jocie worked on a project at the trestle table, Jakob wrapped his arms around her from behind, squeezing her.

"Jakob, I can't breathe," she protested with a laugh.

"I love you," he whispered in her ear.

She giggled at the tickle of his beard. She turned in his arms and kissed him full on the mouth. "Ditto, Mr. Müller."

"Come for a walk with me? I need to walk the trees and decide a few things for the coming season."

A Christmas tree farmer thinks about Christmas three hundred and sixty-five days a year, she had discovered. "I would love to, sir. Just let me finish here." He put away the rest of the dishes, speeding up the process.

A few minutes later, with Hoppy keeping up as best he could, they were walking the trees, as Jakob called it, strolling the long rows of pine trees that stretched in a slope up and over some of the Müller land. Many years before, he had begun the project with a friend and a couple of his brothers. He was the brains behind it, though, and the one most committed to making Müller Christmas Trees the success it had become. He now had ten acres of balsam and Fraser fir, Scotch pine and spruce, all at different stages of growth to ensure a continuing supply over the coming years. They walked in step, his arm around her shoulders, his warm body close to hers, a coupled harmony she never thought she would find in her life. She learned more every time she was out in the trees with him, and not all of what she learned was arboriculture.

A small rabbit streaked away, startling a blue jay that flew up to the top of one of the taller Frasers and noisily scolded it and the Müllers. Jaymie inhaled deeply; the heady pine scent, the crunch of dried needles, pinecones and mulch underfoot . . . these were sensations she was learning by heart, and relished. She was a farmer's wife. It still felt new, to her, and unexpectedly exciting in ways she couldn't explain.

Once they got to a prominence, they stopped and turned, surveying the land. The whole Müller farm stretched all the way to the next road, and from the hilltop they could see his parents' farm, a sprawling modern ranch-style farmhouse obscured by a large barn, drive shed, and several outbuildings. Jakob's mother had a huge vegetable garden, and there was a grove of fruit trees.

When they turned they could see Jakob's and her home, the log cabin. She had come to love it, partially for its rustic appearance and the fact that her husband had built it with help from his brothers, but even more for what it represented. It was where she had found a family. The cabin was in a lonely spot, and opposite was nothing but trees, a wood of about seventy acres or so. It was private property, but Jakob and his family knew the owner, and he didn't mind them walking through it. She often took Hoppy for a stroll down a path through the woods, and walked there with Jocie, too, gathering acorns, leaves and twigs for craft projects. They strolled home arm in arm.

Back in front of the log cabin, as she picked dead heads off the purple and yellow chrysanthemums she had planted in pots by the door, Jakob stood, legs spread, fists on his hips, staring at the property on the other side of the Müller farm, his eyes calculating. He was broad and handsome, dressed in a plaid shirt and jeans, his beard luxuriantly growing for its annual winter appearance. From looking at his father Jaymie knew that when he was old his hair would turn white, and she would bet that with those twinkling eyes he would look like a brown-eyed Santa. But that was a ways away yet; for now he looked like a particularly handsome Teutonic lumber-jack. "What are you thinking about?"

He glanced at her and smiled. "Can you guess?"

She looked at him, her head tilted to one side, feeling a tingle in her stomach. "You've got an idea to expand the business," she said. "Tell me."

"How well you know me already!" He approached her and slung his left arm over her shoulder. He turned her to look toward the land that stretched out beyond the log cabin. "That land is up for sale."

Jaymie knew that; she had seen the sign that listed it as fifty acres of farmland, zoned for agriculture or development. "That went up a few days ago. Do you know the owners?"

"I do. They're newish, just owned it for ten years. They're keep-ing the house, which is on the next road, and dividing the farmland off of it. I'm thinking of expanding. And . . ." He looked down at her. "You're going to think I'm crazy."

With a laugh, she said, "Tell me, before I imagine the worst."

"There's a hill in the middle of the fifty acres."

She put her hand up to shade her eyes and looked at the rows of corn stubble that rose in long lines in the distance. A red-tailed hawk soared above, making big, swooping circles as it hunted mice and voles. "I can see the hill."

"Imagine Müller Family Christmas Acres!" he said, his voice sparking with energy and enthusiasm. He stretched his free hand out, waving it as he painted word pictures. "A sledding hill in the middle, more Christmas trees — that way I can convert some of the Christmas tree acreage on my parents' land to nursery stock trees — and there, along the road, a year-round Christmas store!" His words tumbled over each other in his excitement.

"Like Bronner's in Frankenmuth?" Bronner's, a Michigan institution for over seventy years, was one of the biggest Christmas stores in the world, with a building covering seven acres.

He chuckled, a sound that rumbled in his chest. "Not nearly *that* big, Jaymie. But Christmas, all year long. Honey, I can *see* it!" he said, again waving that free hand in front of them like a wand. "Another log building, like the cabin, but bigger, with a wide covered porch, railing like a hitching post, big windows, and white twinkle lights everywhere! A place for families to come and visit, drink cocoa, have a slide down the hill out back, roast marsh-mallows, make s'mores!"

"And in the store sell . . . what?" she asked, practicality forcing her to pump the brakes a little.

"Well . . ." He started, and blinked. "Christmas decorations to go along with the Müller farm Christmas trees, maybe. And locally made Christmas treats."

She felt a tickle of excitement in her stomach. "We could offer Christmas décor year-round," she mused, "but also things for other celebrations, like Easter, and spring and Memorial Day. Bedding plants in spring for gardeners. July Fourth decorations, and Halloween. We could make it a destination, a family event, not just for shopping but for *fun*! Jakob, it sounds wonderful." She turned, looking up into his eyes. "Can we do all that?"

"Of course we can!" He hugged her. "Good thing I married *you*. You're the only woman in the world who would get as excited as me about this."

"Oh! Can we have a pumpkin patch?" she asked with a little hop. "And maybe a road to the sliding hill so that kids with disabilities can get to it too?"

"Honey, you are the *best*. I never even thought about that, but it makes it so much better! If we had a road we could give cart rides to the hill for oldsters, too, so they can watch the kids slide! Wouldn't Mrs. Stubbs love that?"

Jaymie squealed with glee and her eyes prickled with tears. "And maybe . . . oh, Jakob! Dani and Emma have a hayride cart and have rescued a couple of horses. Their stable isn't far from us. We could have them come and give hayrides!"

"That would be amazing!" he said, his voice filled with excitement.

"I'm sold," she said as Hoppy barked in glee and danced at her side. "When can we buy the land?"

"I'll call today to enquire."

"I've got some money saved," she said. "I want to invest!"

"That's my girl," he said, squeezing her to his side.

When they got back to the cabin, Jocie was finishing her homework. She looked up. "Mama, your phone rang!"

Jaymie stopped dead and her eyes teared up. Jocie had called her Mama. Just . . . Mama, not Mama Jaymie. *Mama.* Her breath caught in her throat, though life swirled on around her, Jakob dashing off to write ideas down, Jocie going back to her page of division and math problems. Neither noticed the momentous event, and that was how it *should* be, she decided, not bringing it to anyone's attention. She hugged the moment to herself, relishing it. It was a small thing, maybe, but important to her.

Jocie had called her Mama.

She checked her phone. "It's Miss Perry . . . good. I can tell her what Haskell said." She went out to sit on the bench on the porch, picked up her pup, letting him curl up in her lap, and returned the call. After salutations, she said, "Haskell wants to talk a bit more, but he tentatively agreed that if it's a go, the society would pay for Bill Waterman to make locked cabinets for your spice grinders and have them securely bolted to the wall. He grumbled at the cost, but that's nothing new." He had also tried to enlist Jaymie to intercede on the heritage society's behalf with Miss Perry about right-of-way access across her land, but she told him she wasn't about to do that. Miss Perry had a right to make her own decisions without being badgered by every person with whom she came in contact. "I'm going to meet him at the heritage house to get final approval, but I think we can bet on it."

"Good," the lady said, sounding tired. "I have a hair appointment later today and church tomorrow. Come out on Monday and we can discuss it."

"I'm sorry, Miss Perry, but Monday is bad for me. I have work at The Junk Stops Here, and a bunch of other stuff." Including a school meeting and dinner with Jakob's parents.

"Tuesday, then. But in the afternoon. That damn writer, Estelle, is coming out, and I have another appointment before lunch."

"Okay, Tuesday afternoon, that's perfect. I'm going to meet Haskell at the house in the morning, so I'll have the final answer before I see you."

• • •

SUNDAY WAS FAMILY DAY; Jakob, Jaymie and Jocie were having

dinner at the Queensville Inn with Kevin and Becca. Jocie was excited, since she got to dress up in the frock she wore to Jaymie and Jakob's wedding, a pretty confection that made her look like a lovely doll. After a brief visit to Mrs. Stubbs's room, they found a quiet table for six near the fireplace, a booster seat for Jocie bringing her up to a good height with the table. The Queensville Inn dining room had been completely redecorated over the summer in elegant shades of cream and taupe, with soft silver accents. Even the china dishes used were ivory with a single silver line around the rims. Becca and Kevin arrived. Jaymie jumped up and hugged her older sister. Getting married on the same day, as well as solving a decades-old mystery surrounding Becca's two friends' disappearance, had brought them closer together. Becca finally letting go of some of her desire to control Jaymie's collecting habits had helped even more. They had reached a détente, of sorts, with Jaymie promising that any time she added something to their jointly owned Queensville home, she'd get rid of something.

"You look gorgeous!" Jaymie said, eyeing her up and down. Becca wore her hair shorter, and it curled softly around her round face. She had new glasses, rimless, so her blue eyes were large, and though there were light lines gathered under them, she looked younger, somehow. "It feels like I haven't seen you in forever!" she said, hugging her again.

"We've only been gone three weeks, Jaymie!"

"I beg your pardon, *four* weeks! You spent a week in London with Grandma Leighton too, before you left."

Becca chuckled. "You look radiant, too."

They kissed cheeks while Kevin and Jakob shook hands, and Kevin crouched down to greet Jocie with a big hug, then got to his feet, his knee joints popping. Kevin was some years Becca's senior, but after three brief and unhappy marriages, everyone agreed she'd finally landed a good one.

The dining room had filled with chatting folks, not an empty chair anywhere, but the service was quick and attentive. Dinner was wonderful; Jaymie had scallops in wine sauce and salmon, and happily sampled Jakob's beef burger and Jocie's spaghetti. She finished with a hot cup of tea, then excused herself to go to the washroom. As she threaded her way through the tables, nodding to folks she knew, she spotted someone familiar. She approached the table.

"Morgan, hello!" she said.

Morgan Perry Wallace looked up from her plate of spaghetti carbonara, but her expression was blank. She frowned. Jaymie glanced at her dinner companion, recognizing her husband, Saunders Wallace, immediately from his television advertisements, from his ginger, crisply curling hair to his tartan jacket.

She looked back to Morgan. "It's Jaymie Leighton. I met you at your aunt's, Miss Perry's place, last week. I'm borrowing some of her historic silver nutmeg graters. In fact, I'm going to see her Tuesday afternoon to finalize things." She turned and pointed toward her table. "That's my sister and brother-in-law, and my husband and daughter. I'm borrowing the graters for the heritage house, so we can do a school lesson at my daughter's school on the spice trade."

"Oh, yes," Morgan said, her cheeks pink. "I . . . I'm not good at recognizing folks."

Saunders leaped to his feet and took her hand, smiling. "Since my wife is being so vague, I'll introduce myself: Saunders Wallace at your service, pretty lady. If you ever need a used car, consider me your guy! We've got cars, trucks, ATVs . . . heck, we've even got a tow truck on the lot!"

Jaymie *had* considered going to Wallace Cars for her vehicle purchase, but he had a reputation for cutting corners on service, so she had gone to his competitor. "I'd better move along and let you two finish your dinner," she said.

Morgan stared down at her food and murmured a goodbye. Saunders frowned over at his wife in puzzlement, but nodded.

"What an odd encounter," Jaymie said to her sister when she returned to the table. She told Becca about it and pointed the couple out as they paid and exited the restaurant, silence between them.

"Maybe you caught them in the middle of a marital spat. That does happen from time to time," Becca said. "Not with you two, of course," she added.

"Oh, we've had arguments," Jaymie said softly. No two lives could be joined without them, but they had successfully navigated through some tension and had come out the other side none the worse for wear.

A waiter removed their plates and returned with a coffee urn to refill cups. Once he was done, he brought the dessert menus, leaving them on the table.

"Anyway, presents!" Becca said, her eyes sparkling as she regarded her sister's family.

"You weren't supposed to get gifts. It was your honeymoon!"

"Doesn't matter. We had fun," she said, exchanging a glance with Kevin, who smiled back at her. "You know I like to shop, especially in antique stores." She pulled out gift bags. "One for you," she said, plopping one down in front of Jakob. "And for you, and for you, *especially!*" she said, setting bags down in front of Jaymie and Jocie.

In Scotland they had bought a tartan tie for Jakob, who put it on right away. It was a great color and looked good with his burgundy dress shirt. For Jaymie, Becca had bought, at an antique store in Edinburgh, an art nouveau vintage hair comb for her long hair.

"Oh, Becca, it's so beautiful!" Jaymie said, her eyes misting. It was amber Bakelite shaped like leaves, with pearls for berries.

"Kevin found it. You know how he is with Bakelite. It's mistletoe! I thought you could wear it at Christmas."

Jaymie jumped up and hugged her sister, then turned her attention to Jocie, who was pulling a box out of her gift bag. Jaymie helped her open the box and take out a vintage child's tea set, sized beautifully for little hands. It was pink lusterware with decals of kittens on it, and was in perfect shape.

Jocie's eyes were round and glittering as she picked up each piece, putting the teapot, covered creamer and milk pitcher together and setting the two teacups on their saucers. "Aunt Becca, it's so pretty!" she said, her voice catching.

"I want a picture," Becca said, jumping up and handing her phone to Kevin. She came around the table and crouched between Jaymie and Jocie, with the tea set in front of them, as her husband snapped the photo.

The waiter brought tea, and while Becca, Jaymie and Jocie had a tea party, Kevin and Jakob started talking about Jakob's new ideas, and eventually moved their chairs close to each other. Kevin pulled out a pad of paper and began doing calculations, and by the end of dinner the two men were almost sold on a partnership of sorts.

Jaymie, meanwhile, had filled Becca in on what she had been doing with the school and the heritage house, and the display items she was borrowing from Miss Perry. She also told her an idea she had for the cookbook she had been writing for almost two years.

"You know, it's all vintage recipes, right? Some from Grandma Leighton's handwritten cookbook, and other vintage recipe standards, like meat loaf, that kind of thing. I've been redoing the recipes so far for the 'Vintage Eats' column, mostly with clarification of old cooking terms. But what about if I redid the recipe two ways, like, lightened up for modern eating habits, and then what all the cooking shows call 'elevated' . . . you know, taken to new levels?"

Becca's eyes gleamed. "First, I'm so happy you're talking to me about this! I feel like you and Val are closer than you and I, sometimes, and I've missed so much."

Around Jocie, who giggled, the sisters hugged each other.

"I think it's a great idea! I don't think I've ever seen a cookbook that does that, a recipe done different ways for different needs or wants."

Their dessert order arrived; the sisters and Jocie shared a wonderful slab of brownie with ice cream, while the guys kept talking over hunks of apple pie. Finally there were hugs and kisses all around, and home for both parties.

• • •

MONDAY WAS, AS JAYMIE HAD PREDICTED, A BUSY DAY, so when she and Jakob finally collapsed on the sofa, all she had the energy to do was flick on the TV. It was the news. Normally she didn't tune in, not with Jocie there, but the little girl was almost asleep, Jakob's hand gently stroking her blonde curls.

That summer they had gotten some bad news from Jocie's doctor. Because of her dwarfism, she could not continue to take part in tumbling, an activity she loved and which had given her a lot of confidence. It wasn't safe because of the danger it posed to her spine. Neither should she play contact sports.

Instead, she had signed up for dance class, a doctor-approved activity. She had not even been cleared for that though, until today, because of her recent bout with the ear infection, which had affected her balance. She had celebrated her doctor clearing her to dance by trying out for the school dance team while Jaymie and Jakob attended a teacher-parent meeting. They then went over to Jakob's parents' for dinner.

Dinner at the Müllers' was never a quiet affair, and it ended with Jocie showing her new dance moves to her cousins while the family had a raucous meeting about Jakob and Jaymie's proposal for a Müller Family Christmas Store and Acres of Fun! Part of the fun was that they kept trying different names for the business, with much discussion of the merits of each. Helmut, the detail-oriented financial mastermind who looked after the farm books and also did accounting for other area businesses, promised to start working on a financial plan once a bid had been put in on the acreage.

Finally back home now and chatting quietly, Jaymie and Jakob watched as a Saunders Wallace advertisement came on the TV. With a toothy grin, a tartan suit and red bow tie, he announced that they were having an autumn clearance. *Come in* now! *Get a vehicle* now! *Best prices anywhere* now! It was annoying because he always seemed to shout in his ads. "Do you want any old used car, or do you want a wheely great *Wallace* used car?"

It wasn't the worst of his cheesy commercials. He had another where he pitched shoes and slippers at the camera, yelling, "Tired of walking? Worn out your blue suede shoes? High-heeled sneakers hurtin' your feet? If your boots were made for walkin' then you can walk in, you can limp in, you can wear stilettos or slippers, but don't walk away! Drive away in a wheely great Wallace used car!"

The local news came on. Her eyes were closing, the sound of the TV mesmerizing, when she heard a name she recognized, and then a voice she knew.

"Get offa my property!"

Jaymie sat up and stared at the TV. There was Miss Perry! "Back it up, back it up!" Jaymie said, flapping her hand at the TV. Luckily they had a DVR that allowed Jakob to back up live TV so he did, to the beginning of the piece.

Miss Perry stood in her doorway watching as the news reporter, a young woman with black hair in a smooth bob, interviewed Estelle Arden, the writer, on the street in front of the Nutmeg Palace. Jaymie knew Estelle well for her work with the heritage society. She had stepped in when they had a problem with a previous writer—who had ended up dead—and edited the booklet they now used as a fund-raiser for the Queensville Historic Manor. She recognized the reporter, too, as one who had reported on past problems in Queensville; she was extremely telegenic, and had a nose for trouble, Jaymie often thought.

Estelle Arden was an older woman, thin, with fine dyed blonde hair teased and styled in a flip, framing an aggressively powdered and rouged face, her pale eyes lined with blue eye makeup, mascara spikily emphasizing thin lashes. She was dressed in walking boots, dark green slacks and a quilted patchwork jacket in tones of yellow and orange over a dark green background, leaf appliqués all over it. "Winding Woods is a historic neighborhood," she said, glancing toward the camera and back to the reporter. "The heritage society hopes to do heritage walks along the riverfront. Most of the home owners—including Haskell Lockland, who is the president of the heritage society, you know, and who lives along here, too—have said they will allow walkers to follow the riverbank path. All except Miss Lois Perry, and that's a real shame because—"

That's when Miss Perry, leaning heavily on her cane, stumped out of her house, across the porch, down the stairs, looking like she was going to fall over any minute, and toward the reporter and Estelle, screaming, "Get offa my property! Get! All of you . . . *shoo!*" She waved her cane and hit the cameraman on the shoulder, a glancing blow that didn't appear to do any harm. As the crew, the reporter and Estelle moved away, Miss Perry was still yelling.

The shot cut to the reporter looking into the camera. "Ms. Arden declined to continue with the interview, saying she is too shaken up by the assault. She plans to call the police, she said, since it is evident from our footage that we were not on Miss Perry's property at all and the attack was unprovoked. Miss Lois Perry declined comment. We'll check back with Ms. Arden and the heritage society for updates. This is Heather Drake, reporting from Winding Woods Lane in Queensville."

"Wow, that Miss Perry is quite the spitfire." Jakob yawned and carefully disengaged his arm from around Jocie as he stretched.

"Calling it an assault is a bit much, though. The woman can barely get around." Jaymie sighed. "Miss Perry was nice enough to me, but she does seem to have her troubles. She had that run-in with Fergus Baird, the developer, and her neighbor, Langlow Zane, and now Estelle. I like Estelle! She's very nice, and she and the reporter were *not* on Miss Perry's property."

"Maybe the lady had an upset tummy," Jocie piped up.

"Hey, I thought you were asleep!" Jakob said, kissing her forehead.

"I was. Now I'm not."

"Well, you'll be asleep again very soon," Jaymie said. "Bedtime, kiddo. We're *all* tired tonight."

Jakob winked at Jaymie over Jocie's head. "I'm tired, but not *that* tired," he said.

✠ Five ✠

JAYMIE WAS MEETING HASKELL at the heritage house to finalize plans for the nutmeg graters and the lessons they would be teaching with their aid. The Queensville Historic Manor, on the outskirts of Queensville, though the town was growing, and would someday encompass the property, was a large three-story Queen Anne, freshly painted and with a sign out front touting the heritage property and opening hours. It had been extensively renovated already, but there was more to be done.

The kitchen was Jaymie's province and she had carefully chosen a vintage color scheme — soft green and cream — and found hundreds of vintage items to match. Utensils from the early part of the twentieth century often had painted handles in green or red, and cream. Even the stove was a vintage beauty painted green and cream that had originally come from The Junk Stops Here. It was her happy place; she volunteered as much as she could, acting as a historical interpreter in period costume and using the antique stove to cook and bake. Today, though, she was just meeting Haskell; the house was open, but visitors would pick up a self-guided tour pamphlet at the front door and wander through on their own.

Haskell was meeting with a builder in Wolverhampton who had offered to donate a structure on a property he owned rather than tear it down. The heritage society was studying whether it would work as the office and interpretation center they had always intended to build. As Jaymie found a spot in the newly paved parking lot behind the old garage, Haskell was returning across the open field with the builder.

She got out of her vehicle and waited. Haskell was a tall, nice-looking older man, calm and stately of demeanor. He was also some kind of cousin a few times removed to one of her best friends, Heidi. Thinking of Heidi, Jaymie reminded herself to call her later. Her friend had been struggling a bit over the summer, but Jaymie hadn't kept up with her as much as she should have, given everything that was going on in her own life. However . . . that was no excuse. Heidi had been there for her, and she would be there for Heidi. It was an odd friendship in some ways, given that Heidi had "stolen" Joel, Jaymie's former boyfriend, away from her two years before. Jaymie was grateful; if not for that theft she may have made the grave error of marrying Joel Anderson.

As they approached, Jaymie was startled when she recognized the builder. It was Fergus Baird! He was dressed as she had seen him before in colorful slacks—plaid this time—and a plain mauve shirt, with a pale green sweater over his shoulders.

"Mr. Baird," she said after Haskell had introduced her. "I saw you down at the docks last week. You were a little hard on Miss Perry, weren't you?"

Haskell gazed at her in horror. He was expecting help from Baird, after all. But the developer didn't appear put out in the slightest.

"Someone needs to hold her accountable," he said with a serious but mild expression, far removed from the anger of his confrontation of a week before. "Truly, do you think that rickety bait shop is the best impression for visitors to our village? I *know* you, young lady; I've seen you before. You are one of the most active servers at the annual Tea with the Queen event. As someone interested in the promotion of this lovely town, do you think those gentle ladies who come to sip tea on the lawn of elegant Stowe House are given a good first impression of Queensville as they wander down a decrepit board wharf past a feed store and bait shop?"

He had a point, and she admitted it. A couple of pretty shops would be a much more welcoming first impression from the water.

"Still," she said, chin rising. "You were very rude to her. She's an elderly lady, and frail."

"So, pardon my bluntness, I should just wait until she dies of natural causes before we move this town forward?" He adjusted the sweater over his shoulders. "I'm well acquainted with the family history. Her mother was ninety-seven when she died. Miss Perry has a ways to go to reach that age. It makes better sense to press her to sell now, while I'm willing to do something, not fifteen years from now."

"Jaymie, you are wasting Mr. Baird's precious time," the society president said, his thick brows drawn low over his eyes. He turned to the other gentleman. "Thanks for coming out, Fergus. I think the building will work for us, but I'll need to take it to the expansion committee. We'd love to have it, but could use some financial help getting it here."

"I said I'd underwrite some of the costs, Haskell." The two men shook hands. "You know I'm good for it."

Troubled, Jaymie watched him walk to his car. "I wouldn't think you'd be on board with bullying an old woman, Haskell," she said, turning to the heritage society president. "This is still a free world."

"He wasn't bullying her. Isn't anyone else entitled to a strong opinion? I think you underestimate Miss Perry." Haskell talked about the building Baird was offering to donate. They needed a feasibility study to decide if it was a good fit for the property, he said. It was a thirties relic, a car dealership building from that time, and had a lot of vintage appeal in some ways, with art deco features: long curving windows that could be used as display areas and for good natural lighting.

"Can we go into the house so I can show you where I want to put the cases? I've got to go soon," Jaymie said. They turned together and started walking, a fallish breeze chasing clouds across the blue sky above them. A couple of smaller birds were chasing away a large black crow, squabbling and shrieking in the country quiet. "I'm meeting Miss Perry this afternoon to get the graters so I can take them to Bill to get started on the design for the cases. Hey, did you see the news last night? The part showing Miss Perry chasing Estelle and the reporter away?"

"That woman . . . she's impossible. I don't know what she has against us all, but she's becoming a problem, one we need to talk about and figure out how to deal with."

Jaymie fought back a spurt of anger. She saw it all too often. Once folks reached a certain age they were expected to give up control of things important to them: their property, their homes, even the care they received from doctors and home health care workers. Getting old, as Mrs. Stubbs often said, was not for sissies. "She's not a *problem*, Haskell, she's a woman still in control of all of her faculties. If you truly want to make a deal with her, have you enlisted Mrs. Stubbs's aid? They're cousins, after all."

"Mrs. Stubbs told me to do something physically impossible when I asked her to talk to Miss Perry," he said haughtily.

Jaymie suppressed a snort of laughter. It clearly ran in the Perry family, that streak of irascibility.

"Can *you* talk to her?" he said. "You seem to have some kind of rapport with the old battle-ax."

Her smile died. She didn't appreciate the lady being spoken of so disrespectfully. "I'm not going to bully or cajole her. Jocie asked if she had a tummy ache. Maybe she's got a point; perhaps Miss Perry isn't well. That can make people tetchy."

"Just try!"

"She's *your* neighbor, Haskell. You know her better than I."

"That does not mean I get along with her. We've had our differences, and still do. I don't understand why she won't let us do the cliff walk pamphlet."

Exasperated, Jaymie said, "Maybe because her place was broken into while she was sleeping upstairs and she's edgy about strangers wandering around her property, Haskell!"

"Okay, all right, I get it. Just do your best."

"I'm not promising anything." Jaymie preceded Haskell up the two steps of the side entrance and into the house; this door led directly to the kitchen. She sat down with him at the kitchen table and showed him the sketches Bill Waterman had drawn up of the locking cases for the spice graters—he had used approximate measurements—as well as the learning through objects material she had printed out from the internet. Bill had given a detailed cost projection. Haskell approved it all, while griping about the cost, the notion of the home being used to teach groups of kids, and the added expense it would incur. She reminded him that the whole purpose of the historic house was to be a teaching tool about the past, and that this, more than any program they had so far instituted, furthered that aim.

She would also bring that up at the next heritage meeting, if she had time to attend, to make sure society members were on board with their mission statement, which included a paragraph about teaching the next generation about Queensville's past. With Haskell's approval in hand, she departed to let him brood about money and history.

Two hours later, after doing some other tasks and getting groceries, heading back to the cabin, putting chili in the slow cooker for dinner, walking Hoppy and cleaning up, she was on the road again toward Winding Woods. She had tried calling Heidi while she was home, but there was no answer. She left a message, then tried Bernie Jenkins's number, but Bernie, her and Heidi's mutual best friend, was either working or didn't have her phone on.

The clouds that had earlier appeared so fluffy and white had turned gray and gathered in gloomy groups, closing out the sky. A wind came up, and rain started tapping on the SUV roof. She glanced at her watch. She was already late. Miss Perry's generation did not like lateness. She pulled over to the side and got out her phone.

All she got was the answering machine; that would have to do. "Miss Perry, I'm running a couple of minutes late but I *am* on my way. In fact, I'm almost there! I do apologize. See you in two minutes!"

She turned off River Road and started up Winding Woods Lane. She looked down, trying to adjust the windshield wiper frequency, as it was set too low to clear the increasing rain. When she looked up, a dark pickup was heading straight at her. "Dang, dude! Slow down!" she yelped, pulling as far as she could to the side of the road as he zoomed past.

She drove past Haskell's stately home—he was there, it appeared; his car was in the drive—and pulled up to the Nutmeg Palace. By the time she pulled into the drive her heart rate had slowed to normal and the rain had become a steady, if light, drizzle. She jumped out and ran up the steps to the covered porch, knocked on the door, then waited. She knocked again more loudly after a few minutes. When there was no answer, she began to feel a light tug of unease. She tried the door and it easily opened.

She stepped into the big entry, pausing on the mat inside the door. "Miss Perry!" she called. "Yoo hoo!" She slipped her boots off and hiked her purse over her shoulder, trudging into the house, calling the woman's name, becoming more and more uneasy. She was not in the parlor or dining room, nor was she in the kitchen or her TV room, though the TV was on, tuned to a game show but muted. Maybe she was sick in bed and had left the door unlocked for her niece, Morgan? But her niece had a key, Jaymie already knew that.

Jaymie returned through the kitchen and headed to the back door, but tripped on something . . . or someone! Loud, hoarse breathing alerted her and Jaymie found a light switch. There, at the bottom of the back stairs, was Miss Perry! "Oh, no!" Jaymie cried. She knelt by the woman, who was bloody but alive. "Miss Perry. Miss Perry, can you hear me?" A moan of pain was her only answer.

Jaymie fumbled in her purse and found her phone, plopping down on the floor beside the woman, then jabbed 911, babbling the problem and the Winding Woods Lane address. She answered the operator's questions—*Yes, Miss Perry was breathing; no, she didn't seem to be conscious; yes, her breathing was regular, though labored and hoarse, and no, Jaymie would not attempt to move her*—and left the line open, leaning over her new friend.

"Miss Perry, help is coming." She pulled off her cardigan and laid it over the elderly woman, who only wore a faded housedress, her thin arms pitiably frail and wrinkled, threaded by blue veins and marred by arthritic joints. A *housedress*? She hadn't had time to change before her appointment with Jaymie? That seemed odd. It was two in the afternoon.

Miss Perry and women of her generation and social strata—club ladies, as Mrs. Stubbs called the women she socialized with in the fifties and sixties—would never be caught by company in a faded, worn housedress. Hadn't she an appointment with Estelle that morning? Maybe after that altercation in front of her house it was called off. But she said she had *another* appointment before lunch. Surely she would have been changed out of her housedress for that? Maybe the person had come, but when they got no answer had gone away again. Jaymie would have if she hadn't known Miss Perry well enough.

The woman moaned and tried to move. Her head was bloody, the fluid drying in a crust in her tightly permed hair; Jaymie spotted a dark mark on the staircase newel post where the woman must have hit her head. She looked down to her feet; they were bare, but moccasin-style slippers that looked too large for her were lying near her at the bottom of the stairs, one upside down over the other. It suggested that she had tripped, but had she? The slippers looked brand-new, not like they had been worn.

Now she was imagining things! When Miss Perry recovered she'd tell them all that she slipped coming down the stairs. Jaymie had found too many bodies in her time. Sirens! Jaymie sighed and whispered a prayer of thanks for first responders. They would soon take over, knowing exactly what to do.

The sirens stopped, but she could hear the heavy throb of the motor of a fire truck and a noise in the front entrance. "Back here!" she yelled. "We're at the very back of the house!"

A woman and man in firefighter uniforms came trudging through. Jaymie gladly relinquished her spot as they assessed the situation. They were swiftly replaced by paramedics from the ambulance, and Jaymie was pushed farther away until she was pacing in the front hall, as a police officer came through the door.

"Bernie!" Jaymie said, thankful it was her friend.

"Jaymie. What's going on here?"

Jaymie sat on the second step of the front hall stairs and told her everything.

"So your understanding was that she was expecting two other people this morning?" Bernie checked her watch. "It's two thirty-five. What time did you get here?"

"About half an hour ago now. I was a few minutes late, but not more. She said she had Estelle Arden—she's a writer working on the Queensville walking tour pamphlet—coming this morning, but that may have been called off, given their altercation."

Bernie knew all about that. She pulled a notebook out of a pocket and a pen from another. She flipped the small coil-bound notebook open. "Why was Ms. Arden coming here this morning?"

Jaymie shrugged. "About the pamphlet, maybe? They were trying to talk Miss Perry into letting walkers have access across her property along the river but she was dead set against allowing it. Why are you asking all these questions? Do you think there's something fishy about her accident?"

"Given the woman's trouble lately, I'm not taking chances," Bernie said, her dark eyes riveted on her notebook. "What about the other appointment?"

"She said it was before lunch, but she didn't say with whom."

"What time would lunch be for her, do you think?"

"I don't know."

"We'll be checking with whoever she was supposed to see today, to try to get an idea what time she may have fallen."

"I'll tell you one thing," Jaymie said. "She would not have been greeting *anyone* in that faded housedress."

Bernie cocked an eyebrow. "Why not? My grandma wears hers twenty-four-seven."

"Probably not a faded old one, though. And Miss Perry was starchy, like Mrs. Stubbs. She would have dressed for a meeting or company."

"So you don't know who else she was supposed to see?"

Jaymie shook her head. "She didn't say, but the way she said it—appointment—probably means it wasn't Morgan Wallace. Though I can't say that for sure. Maybe she wrote it down somewhere? People usually mark things like that on a calendar."

"Good point. Morgan Wallace," Bernie said the name aloud as she wrote it down.

"Her niece. I think she visits often, maybe every day, and makes Miss Perry meals." She thought for a minute. "I wonder if she drops in at lunch? Last time I was here she came in the middle of the afternoon. I don't know much about their daily routine."

"But the door was unlocked when you got here."

"I didn't know that at first and knocked for a while. Ten minutes or so at least. Then I tried the door and it opened."

One of the paramedics strode through, out the front door, and came back a few moments later wheeling a gurney that was spattered with raindrops, shedding them on the shiny wood floor as he walked.

"Is she going to be okay?" Jaymie pleaded, tearing up. It had been a horrible shock, finding her like that. It had looked bad . . . very bad.

"I don't know. They'll do everything they can," she replied, her tone no-nonsense but sympathetic. Bernie headed out the front door and to her police car pulled up to the curb; she slipped inside and used the police radio, then returned inside and said to Jaymie, "I've called it in. We're having Mrs. Wallace called so she can come and lock up after her aunt is taken away. What are you doing here today, by the way?"

Jaymie explained, then said, "It's a lucky thing; I don't know when she would have been found otherwise. Not until Morgan came, I suppose."

"Is everything okay? Is Lois all right?" Lan Zane came in the front door, his dog on a leash.

"Outside, please, sir," Bernie said, ushering the man back out.

Jaymie followed, and they all stood on the covered front porch. Jaymie exchanged a glance with Bernie, introduced Lan Zane, Miss Perry's neighbor to the north, then told him simply that Miss Perry had taken a tumble.

"Sir, did you see anyone visiting Miss Perry this morning?" Bernie asked him.

He glanced between Jaymie and Bernie. "What's going on?"

"Please, sir, just answer the question."

"No, I . . . I haven't seen anything."

They went through his full name, address — right next door — and where he was that morning, which, Jaymie overheard, was at work. He was a contract lawyer in Wolverhampton. He had lunch in town at his desk, which he did most days, though he worked alone so no one could verify that, then did a little more work. He had come home to walk Tiberius, which he did at least once a day when his wife was busy. "I didn't see anything, but you can check with my wife, Phillipa; she was late leaving this morning. She volunteers at the hospital in Wolverhampton. And Haskell Lockland lives on the other side of Lois."

"I was with Haskell out at the historic manor this morning," Jaymie said. "He'd been there for a meeting with a local builder. But I think he must be home, because his car is in his drive now."

For once Tiberius was behaving, lying alert and interested on the porch. "What's going on?" Zane asked, his eyes narrowing. "Why all these questions?" Bernie ignored him and simply jotted down what she had learned.

As the front door opened, Jaymie, Lan and Bernie scattered down the steps and out into the rain, which had diminished to spatters coming down. The paramedics wheeled Miss Perry out on the gurney, then carefully down the steps, as Morgan Wallace drove up, screeching to a halt in her silver sedan with *Wallace Motors* emblazoned on the side. She jumped from the car and raced over to them. "Is she all right? What happened?"

One of the paramedics asked who she was, then told her that Miss Perry was unconscious. She was breathing on her own, but her blood pressure was low. Doctors at Wolverhampton General would be able to assess her more thoroughly. Morgan could follow them to the hospital.

She hung over her aunt, murmuring something, then turned and saw Lan Zane. "You! Did *you* do anything? Aunt Lois said you threatened her!"

He put one hand on his chest as his dog, awoken from his passivity by Morgan's shrieking, began to snarl, bark, leap and snap. She jumped back, her face pale, her eyes wide.

"Me? I didn't do anything!" He yanked on the dog's leash, but Tiberius still tugged and growled as Morgan retreated further. "It's your crazy aunt who threatened *me* . . . said she'd shoot my dog if she ever found him on her property again. What kind of person threatens to shoot a dog?"

"The kind who is upset when the dog has attacked her cats!" Morgan retorted.

"*Her* cats? You mean those feral vermin she feeds!" Zane shouted, his face growing red, the glow spreading up from his neck to his cheeks. His dog snarled and pulled at the lead, lunging at Morgan. "How can she blame my dog when those animals prowl all over my property all day and night?"

"Get that thing away from me!" she screamed.

"Sir, keep your animal under control," Bernie said, stepping between Zane and Morgan Wallace.

The ambulance screamed away. Morgan whirled and stalked into the house, but bolted out a few moments later. "Hey, you! Miss Policewoman!" she shouted, snapping her fingers, her plump cheeks suffused with blotchy red. "Didn't any of you morons notice the wire across the staircase? Someone tried to murder my aunt!"

✄ Six ✄

BERNIE STIFFENED AND PUT UP HER HAND in a *stop* gesture, like a traffic cop. "Thank you, Mrs. Wallace. Can you and Ms. Leighton stay out here while I call for backup?"

It swiftly became a crime scene and tape went up. Some of the officers made Jaymie back down the drive to the road. "Can I get my car out of the driveway?" she asked. "I need to go home soon."

The officer said, "I'll check, ma'am. Just wait here."

Jaymie could see the chagrin on Bernie's face as she directed the cordoning off of the home under Morgan's watchful and resentful gaze. Bernie would rather have found the wire herself, but it was clearly not her fault that she hadn't, since she hadn't been able to access that part of the house while Miss Perry was being cared for by the paramedics.

Who would do something like that, try to kill Miss Perry? It didn't make any sense. A murder attempt like that was so obvious. A trip wire across the stairs was something straight out of a mystery novel, a cliché, like arsenic in tea.

More neighbors wandered down the normally deserted road to watch. Haskell came out of his house, frowned, then went back in. Jaymie pulled her cardigan close about herself and glanced over at Morgan. "I'm so sorry. I hope she'll be okay. You seem very fond of her."

"She's the only family I have left."

"Other than your in-laws, I suppose."

"They don't live in the U.S.," she said curtly. "Saunders keeps saying we should go to Scotland and visit them, but there never seems time. I got a letter from his mother when we got married, with a nice picture of them at Loch Ness taken on vacation, but I've never yet met them."

"That's too bad!"

She shrugged.

"Were you here at lunchtime?"

Morgan stared at her. "Why would you ask that?"

"I was just wondering."

"It's none of your business, but no, I come midafternoon most days, to tidy up and make sure auntie has something for dinner."

"Doesn't she have anyone else cleaning for her?"

"No. I do it all. She has a yard guy, but he never comes in the house. She's suspicious of strangers." She sighed. "So I get to do it all."

Another police car arrived, followed by a forensic van, and a new model Cadillac, which pulled into the spot next to Morgan's car. Saunders Wallace, wearing a suit and tie, with a trench coat over the top of it and a jaunty plaid scarf — the red, black and yellow Wallace tartan — looped around his neck, got out and hurried over to Morgan.

"What's going on?" he asked. "I got your message."

"It's Auntie Lois. Someone tried to *kill* her!" Morgan's voice rose with a hysterical note.

In his manic, antic-filled TV ads he always wore a Wallace tartan sports jacket. Morgan often appeared with him, wearing the Wallace tartan as a skirt or dress, quietly at his side while he grinned and sped through the standard car salesman patter. But today he was solemn and appeared perturbed as he glanced from the open door of the house then down at his wife, who sobbed against his chest. He had an odd expression on his face; it looked like uncertainty mingled with distaste. She watched him, wondering what was going on in his head. He patted Morgan's back, then disentangled himself, walking over to speak to one of the male police officers rather than approaching Bernie, who was clearly in charge of the scene. He was *that* type, maybe, a man who sought other men to speak with, preferring male solidarity over feminine emotion. Or was it his wife in particular who caused him unease?

Who inherited the estate if Miss Lois Perry died? Jaymie wondered. She supposed she should be ashamed of herself for wondering, when Morgan had sunk to a crouch and wept into her open hands, but the sobs seemed manufactured.

Bernie approached Morgan, bending over and touching her shoulder. "Mrs. Wallace, could we ask you a few questions, please?"

She looked up, dry-eyed, and nodded, following Bernie toward the house. Who weeps without producing actual tears? Jaymie, unsettled, watched her hop up the steps to the porch and perch on the railing as Bernie got out her notebook.

Lan Zane, back from his dog walking, watched her, then headed toward Jaymie. "You were here the other day, weren't you? You helped wrangle Tiberius. How did you find the old gal, anyway?"

She was not about to answer nosy neighbor questions. "I hope she's going to be okay," Jaymie said, evading the question.

"Poor lady. I don't hate her, you know," he said, not meeting Jaymie's eyes. "But she's not an easy neighbor. Ask anyone. She doesn't want anything to change. I'm all for the status quo, but she complains every time someone on the circle has a party, or gets a second car, or modernizes their home at all. She complained when Haskell put in central air, said the unit was noisy and made her backyard unlivable! She even went to the township about it. They had someone come out to test the noise and had to convince her it was within tolerance. And it's not like she even uses the backyard except as a place to feed those damn stray cats!"

She eyed him with interest, finding him repellent yet fascinating. He claimed not to hate Miss Perry, and yet everything he said about her was negative. If what Morgan said was true and there was a wire across the stairs designed to trip Miss Perry, it had to have been placed there by someone who could sneak into her house *and* who either had a grudge against her or would benefit by her death. There were the obvious suspects, of course: Morgan Wallace or her husband, if they inherited; Haskell, not likely; Fergus Baird, the developer who so desperately wanted to buy the dockside properties; and Estelle Arden, with whom she had such a well-documented feud.

But Lan Zane, too; he had nothing but trouble with her, it appeared, though he wasn't afraid to say it often and loudly. Presumably he wouldn't have access to her home, though. Unless . . . neighbors often held keys to each other's homes, to let in repair people, or water the plants. Were the Zanes and Miss Perry that close as neighbors? Jaymie doubted it.

The young police officer came back and told her she could move her vehicle now or even leave as long as the police knew how to contact her. She assured the fellow that the police did indeed know how to get in touch with her.

It was time for her to go. She was not going to get involved this time.

• • •

THE CHILI WAS AWESOME, Jocie said, accompanied by cheddar biscuits. Homework, bath, bed, and another day was done. Jaymie fell into bed with Jakob, weary in mind and spirit. As she cuddled under his arm, she looked up at him and scruffed his beard, then yawned. "I'm so tired! Such a long day; or maybe it just felt like it."

"My superhero," he teased, gently kissing her forehead. "Poor Miss Perry. You may have saved her life today."

"I hope she'll be okay. She was so pale, and her breathing was so shallow." The blood . . . it was crusted in her hair, so she had been lying there for some time. How long? "She did *not* look good. I have to go into Wolverhampton tomorrow to see Nan about the column, so I may visit Miss Perry, if they'll let me."

"Good idea. It'll make you feel better if you see her bright-eyed and bushy-tailed."

She grinned. "Only my husband would use that old-fashioned term."

• • •

A STEADY RAIN HAD SET IN OVERNIGHT and the gravel roads splashed mud up to the white exterior of the Explorer, but the drizzle stopped as Jaymie drove into Wolverhampton and found a parking space by Nan's little blue sports car in the newspaper parking lot. By the time she got out of the SUV, watery sunshine was peeking through gaps in the clouds, and the fallish scent of wet poplar leaves perfumed the air even in town. *The Wolverhampton Weekly Howler*, for which she wrote her food column, was housed in a long, low red brick building that was once a factory. It held offices fronting the main street; the printing was done in the back. It was one of the very few local print weeklies still left. They did other printing too, like advertising flyers, posters, and pamphlets.

She went around from the parking lot, entered through the front, then was waved and buzzed past by the receptionist, who was on the phone taking an ad. Jaymie threaded through the open space toward her editor, past chattering groups of people and cubicles in which some few sat at computers doing research and writing. It wasn't a large workforce, but it was an enthusiastic young one. Nan's office was little more than another such cubicle surrounded by half walls and frosted glass to the ceiling, with no actual door. In one corner was her desk, more of a corner table, with a desktop computer and two monitors, file cabinets and a printer. Nan was on the phone, a landline, chewing on a pencil while rocking in her swivel desk chair. She motioned Jaymie to join her.

"Yeah . . . yeah . . . I know," she said. "It's a shi . . . *scheisse* show, right now, the whole political landscape. Yeah, I get it . . . of course. Okay. I'll get back to you on that. Gotta go." She hit the Off button and set the phone back in its cradle. "Jaymie! One of our usual crank callers," she said, referring to the call. "I make nice with him because he also spends a lot on advertisements."

"You know I'm learning German, right?" she said with a smile.

Nan threw her head back and guffawed. "Caught me. I know that word in ten languages and I had to choose German. So . . . did we have a meeting scheduled?"

"Yes, we did. A planning meeting for Christmas for 'Vintage Eats.' And you said you had something else to talk to me about."

"Right . . . *right!*" Nan scrubbed her wiry reddish hair and looked wildly around her desk. "I had a piece of paper . . . where was it?" In the flurry of paper on her desk it could have been anything anywhere. "Ah, here it is!" Unerringly finding the one piece she wanted among the mess, she grabbed it, stared at it for a moment, then looked at Jaymie over the top of it. "How would you feel about promoting your column on a radio show about antiques?"

"Radio show? Does anyone do those anymore?"

"Sure, online, of course. You'd be surprised. People listen to them in their cars, on their phones . . . tablets . . . lots of ways. It's nationally syndicated. Sid Farrell, the host, is great. He actually contacted me about you a couple of months ago but I lost track; he called the other day to remind me. He'd like to have you on to talk about vintage food prepared in vintage dishes."

"How do we do that? Where do I go?" Jaymie asked, picturing sitting in a booth somewhere with headphones on across the desk from the host.

"You use your phone and talk to him."

"Like . . . in my own home?"

"Yes! Sid Farrell's an older gentleman who loves everything vintage and antique. Older gentleman," she said, rolling her eyes.

"Listen to me! We're probably the same age. Joe loves listening to him. He says it takes him back to the good old days." Joe was her husband, Joe Goodenough, the owner of the newspaper. In his seventies, he was more the figurehead of the paper now, the one who did corporate events and attended the Little League games of their sponsored team, the Wolverhampton Howling Wolves.

"I don't know," she said hesitantly. "Would people really be interested?"

"Jaymie, have you not been on social media these days? It seems like every other post has an image of *The Beverly Hillbillies*, or *Pretty in Pink*, or Pyrex dishes, and every single one of them says *Click if you saw this and loved it* or *Click if you used this and miss it!* It's annoying. But they get hundreds of clicks and shares! It's like everybody wants to live in the past anymore instead of making the present better."

Jaymie struggled to hide a smile. Nan's inner grump was showing.

"Besides, why don't you let Sid decide what listeners will be interested in? Presumably he knows."

"If you think it will help, I'll do it," she said, before she could think her way out of it. Two years before she would have shied away, but not now. She was working toward her dream of a cookbook deal. The editor she had contacted told her she needed to make a bit of a name for herself if she was going to achieve it.

"Okay, I'll pass your deets on to Sid and he'll contact you. Or you contact him. Or whatever."

After a half hour of planning out the next few months of 'Vintage Eats' and Nan giving her some advice for the radio show, Jaymie wandered downtown, leaving her SUV in the newspaper parking lot. It was now officially a beautiful fall day: blue sky, nip in the air, white puffy clouds slipping by. But she was still haunted by worry about Miss Perry. She headed to the flower shop, where she bought a bouquet in a vase, tucking it into the passenger seat of the Explorer. She then headed to the drugstore, where she picked out a small manicure kit and a mirror on a stand. From the magazine rack she grabbed the new edition of a popular antiques collecting magazine, a crossword puzzle book, and a *Reader's Digest*, then she picked up a package of pens from Stationery.

She was heading down the treats aisle with her basket, wondering if Miss Perry was a sweets fan, when the door opened and a couple entered. It was Fergus Baird; his lanky figure and colorful wardrobe were unmistakable. Today his slacks were pale blue and he wore a sweater that was pastel shades blended in an ombré mix.

Jaymie couldn't tell who the woman was until she turned. Thunderstruck, she recognized Morgan Perry Wallace; she and Baird were engaged in a fierce and very intimate-appearing argument. He pulled her aside, shook his finger in her face, and then kissed her hard, right there in the perfume aisle. Jaymie stumbled and knocked against a chip display. Morgan looked over, saw her, and broke away from Baird, rubbing her mouth with her hand and darting from the store.

None of my business, Jaymie thought, and made her purchases. Baird, oblivious, followed Morgan out, and Jaymie soon followed. When the young woman saw Jaymie, she shrugged off Baird's arm over her shoulder and approached.

"I guess you're wondering what that was about," she said, shifting from foot to foot. She swept her blonde hair aside and pulled her trench coat closer around, shivering at the light wind that had come up.

"It's none of my business," Jaymie replied mildly. "How is your aunt? Is it okay if I go up and see her?"

"Why would you want to do that?" Morgan asked.

Jaymie, taken aback, said, "I've been thinking about her a lot overnight. Hoping she's okay. I did find her, after all. Is she all right?"

She nodded, but her expression was uncertain. "The doctors think she'll be okay, but they have to keep her for a while. She got such a knock on the head and there is some . . . some blood pooled in the brain cavity. Apparently that's not as bad as it sounds because when we get older our brain shrinks, leaving more room in the brain cavity, so there won't be as much pressure as there would be if she was younger. Who knew your brain shrinks when you get old?"

"I didn't."

"Me neither. Anyway, hopefully her body can reabsorb the blood, or something like that, and she'll recover."

"Is she conscious?"

"Not yet. I just left there about an hour ago."

"Can I visit her anyway?"

"I guess," Morgan said uncertainly. She looked over at Baird, and then back at Jaymie, clearly still wondering if she ought to explain.

"I won't stay long. I want to give her some flowers and magazines."

"That's kind of you."

Jaymie smiled. "I'd best get going, then. See you around, Morgan." She walked away, but when she looked back Morgan was *still* watching her leave with that uncertain expression on her round face. It did leave Jaymie wondering . . . what was Morgan Perry Wallace doing kissing Fergus Baird, who was locked in a fierce land battle with her great-aunt?

℘ Seven ℘

"I SWEAR TO YOU, I'm *not* going to get involved!"

Valetta howled with laughter as she sat on the stoop of the Queensville Emporium, mug of thermos tea wrapped in her hands, empty lunch bag beside her. Today's mug, one of a score or more given to her by friends and family that lauded her career, read *Keep Calm & Thank Your Pharmacist*. "Right. I don't believe you, Jaymie." Sunlight glinted off her thick glasses as she pushed back her curly thick dark hair, threaded heavily with silver now. "I'm sorry, but even *I'm* curious about what is going on with that crew. You *know* you're not going to leave this alone."

"I have quite enough on my plate as it is," Jaymie said, then drained the last of her own tea, letting the mug dangle from her finger by its handle. She had shared an early lunch with her friend, half of Valetta's sandwich and a couple of Tansy Tarts butter tarts, which the Emporium now sold. Tansy Tarts, on Heartbreak Island, had been seducing American consumers with the Canadian sweet treat for over ten years now, but Tansy had recently started broadening her base of butter tart addicts.

"When has that ever stopped you?" Val said.

Jaymie rolled her eyes. "I swore to Morgan that I wasn't interested in the *slightest* about why she, a supposedly happily married woman, was kissing the much older and wealthy property developer who is locked in a pitched battle with her supposedly dearly loved great-aunt. In the drugstore. After being up to the hospital to see said aunt, who someone has tried to kill." She frowned and sighed. "I don't get it, and I *am* curious. I can't help that."

"I've never put you down for your curiosity, my friend," Valetta said, bumping her shoulder. "To me it's one of your most endearing traits." Valetta was often Jaymie's sidekick in investigation, her Watson, her Hastings, her Bess and George rolled into one.

But attempted murder on an elderly woman was not entertaining, nor was murder *ever*. Jaymie didn't take it lightly and only tried to help when she thought she could do so without interfering in the official police investigations. "Poor Miss Perry. Val, you should have seen her in that hospital bed! She's so bruised and battered. It broke my heart. She didn't regain consciousness while I was there." Jaymie had needed the comfort of a familiar face after that, and had come rushing back to Queensville and the one person to whom she could openly talk about what she was wondering.

Well, the one of two, she thought. Jakob was also supportive; he never told her to stay out of other folks' business. In fact, he seemed to think she was superwoman, who could do anything she set her mind to. But then, she felt the same away about him. He had his hands full today, though, interviewing potential employees for The Junk Stops Here. He needed a couple of strong, trustworthy guys or gals who could handle money, talk to customers, *and* load and unload heavy furniture, whatever he required.

"I think I'll go see her again tomorrow." She paused a beat and glanced at Valetta. "I did in passing wonder who inherits if Miss Perry dies?"

"I don't know, but I know who *would* know."

"Who?" Jaymie asked, dreading the answer.

"Brock."

It was true; as a real estate agent Brock kept his finger on the economic pulse of their town, and knew who owned what, who *owed* what, and who inherited from whom. Jaymie groaned. "Please please *please* don't ask him!"

"It's the only way to quickly find out. I won't say *you* want to know." Valetta picked up her phone from the board porch, nodding to some locals wandering by, dogs straining on their leashes, and punched in the number. She chatted for a minute then hung up and pushed her glasses up on her nose, looking smug as she met Jaymie's gaze.

"So . . . who?" Jaymie said impatiently.

"Morgan Perry Wallace. The whole shebang: the house, the property, *and* the dockside shops."

• • •

JAYMIE DROVE BACK TO WOLVERHAMPTON for part two of her day. Townships in Michigan perform many functions: regulating fire protection, police services, tax assessment, and election administration. They also control parks and park services, public water and sewers, as well as trash collection. But the function Jaymie was concerned with that day was land zoning and land use policy.

In the mid-nineties the township offices outgrew the old building on the main street in Wolverhampton, moving to a purpose-built structure on a side street on the far end of town. Jaymie was heading there to gather information for the Müllers concerning zoning on the land they proposed buying. Brock Nibley was the property owners' real estate agent and was giving them guidance; she knew he was knowledgeable, but he *was* working for the other side. She preferred to know what she was talking about and so . . . research to be sure the purchase was worth their time and money.

The township office was a low nondescript building, red brick, with tinted windows and a covered entry. Inside was a warren of hallways leading to the various sections, well indicated by signs. She made her way to the zoning department, and with the help of a chatty township clerk — a plump, frizzy-haired older woman she had met before at auctions and yard sales — Jaymie obtained a map of the land around the Müller farm and environs, coded in colors from light green for agricultural use to dark blue for heavy industrial use. The clerk gave her a package with information and copies of the zoning regulations, and also gave her advice on how to access more online.

Jaymie moved to some tables where a few other people were doing research. She laid out the map and could see already that almost without a break the whole area was zoned agricultural, though Jakob's Christmas tree farm was marked as being zoned "Specialty Farm," with allowance for direct-from-the-farm sales. The Müllers had already gone through some rezoning and knew enough to make this work.

It seemed likely that the township would have no qualms about zoning more of the land as Specialty Farm; however, Jaymie didn't think it was safe to make that assumption. If they were going to buy the farmland for the Müller Christmas Acres of Fun, or whatever they ended up calling it, they would need to have some assurance that the township would cooperate with rezoning it to commercial. A permanent store was a far different thing than a seasonal Christmas tree operation.

They'd need plans drawn up to show the zoning officials what square footage they were talking about, what kind of things they'd sell, how much parking space they'd require, what they proposed for sewage, trash and water, and so on. And they'd have to make a million decisions before then. A few family meetings were in their future. There was already a request in to the township by the current landowners to sever a four-acre parcel with frontage on the next road over, where the current owners had their home; sale of the land was provisional until that was finalized.

Once she finished what she came for, out of curiosity she did a little research on the dockside shops in Queensville. They were zoned commercial, which was no surprise, but when the clerk who had helped her wandered past the table and glanced down at the map that Jaymie was examining, she said, "Oh, are you looking up the dock property in Queensville? Fergus Baird was being *such* a pain in the neck about all that."

"I know. He's desperate to buy the shops so he can convert them into tea shops and the like."

The woman stopped and stared, her pale eyes wide with surprise. *"Tea shops?"* If that's the case he sure is asking a whole lot of questions about the township's view on converting the whole property — which is larger than it looks from the map, by the way, several acres in all — to residential zoning for riverfront condo units with marina access and boat slips."

"Is that so?" Jaymie said. Well, how about that. A few things Baird was doing made sense now. Tea shops! Jaymie harrumphed in indignation. She'd have to make sure she let everyone — including Haskell Lockland — know what Fergus Baird was *really* up to.

• • •

JAYMIE STOPPED BY HER SISTER'S ANTIQUE STORE in Queensville, but Georgina told her that Becca had gone home to work on a secret project. That did *not* sound promising. Becca's secret projects usually involved a lot of "purging" — in other words, getting rid of all the vintage clutter Jaymie loved so much. They had compromised lately, but that didn't mean Jaymie was confident Becca wouldn't throw away some of her treasures if left alone. She parked in the back lane beside her sister's luxury sedan and strode up the flagstone walk to the back door. Without thinking she glanced under the holly hedge, expecting to see Denver there, before remembering that he now lived in luxury at his combination cat condo/catio with his maidservant, Valetta.

She entered the kitchen. "Becca? You here?" she called, glancing around at the kitchen. Okay, no damage . . . er . . . cleaning there yet. "Be-cca!"

"Up here!"

Jaymie ran up the stairs and found her sister in the room she had used since childhood and now shared with Kevin. She was sitting on the floor in front of the closet.

"Wow," Jaymie said, looking at the boxes all around her, tissue paper everywhere like drifts of snow. "So *this* is where you keep your clutter."

Becca looked up at Jaymie with a rueful expression, pushing her glasses up on her nose. "Now you know my dirty little secrets. I need to clear some space in this closet for Kevin. Poor guy lives out of a suitcase when we're in Queensville, and that is not right, so some of my past needs to go to make way for my future."

"Good way to put it! I had to do the same thing in my room for Jakob. Now he stores his elegant collection of plaid work shirts in my closet. Lord, wouldn't Dad have had a heart attack if he knew we'd both be sharing our rooms with boys?" She chuckled, and so did Becca.

"Funny girl. You going to hang around and make jokes while I work?"

"How about I help?"

They spent the rest of the afternoon going through stacks and stacks of boxes, a lifetime of collecting. There were family mementos, photos, vintage stuff from Becca's childhood, and much more. She sorted it all into piles: keep, toss, donate, recycle.

"This is hard," Becca said, moving her legs and rubbing her thigh. "And I don't mean physically, though I'm stiff from sitting on the floor. But I keep putting stuff in the donate pile, then putting it back in the keep pile."

"I know. Hey, what's this?" Jaymie, sitting cross-legged beside her, held up a kids' book, the Little Golden Book version of *The Poky*

Little Puppy that she had plucked from a box of old school yearbooks and teen magazines from the eighties.

Becca took it from her and smiled down at it mistily, her eyes shadowed in the dim light. She set her glasses aside, since she was nearsighted and didn't need them for reading. "It's your favorite book, the one I read to you when you were a baby. I kept it in case I ever had kids."

There was a stillness in the air between them, a moment of clarity. "I kind of thought you never wanted kids because you had to look after me so much as a baby and didn't want to be saddled with an infant ever again," Jaymie said softly.

"Oh, honey!" Becca said. She pulled Jaymie into an awkward hug, then released her, rocking back onto her butt. "If anything, taking care of you as a baby made me want kids even more. It was never in the cards for me. I wish it had been, but I'm content as things are, and I'm happy you've got a daughter I can spoil."

"I'm so relieved, Becca, you don't even know."

They continued sorting, as Jaymie told her sister everything that had gone on in the last few days with Miss Perry, how she had seen Morgan Perry Wallace kissing Fergus Baird, and what she had learned at the township zoning office. They finally descended to the kitchen, washed their hands, and Jaymie brewed a pot of tea. They sat opposite each other at the trestle table, mugs in hand, the door to the summer porch open.

"Why would Baird be looking into residential condo zoning for the dockside area?" Jaymie said. "He said he wanted to build new shops . . . a tea shop, a gift shop, that kind of thing."

"Not nearly as lucrative as condos would be, and a lot more trouble."

"True. But Miss Perry is never going to sell it to him, not even for the proposed shops."

Becca smiled over her mug. "I know what you're thinking," she said, and took a long sip, watching her sister and waiting.

Jaymie gave her a guilty glance. Was she that obvious? "I'm thinking that Baird may have found a way around it. If he discovered that Morgan inherits everything from her aunt, and if she divorced Saunders and married Fergus, he'd be able to do what he wants. Eventually."

"That's a lot of ifs."

"But he's started the chain already," Jaymie argued. "That was no light kiss; it was passionate. *And* persuasive." She waited a beat, holding her sister's gaze. "And Miss Perry is in the hospital with a life-threatening injury."

"Whoa, now you've leapt to a murder attempt. Who do you suspect, Morgan or Baird?"

Jaymie shook her head, faintly ashamed and yet defiant. "Neither. Both. *Someone* did it, Becca! *Someone* put that wire across the stairs and tripped poor Miss Perry. It came close to killing her. It still could."

"Don't put all your suspects in one basket," Becca advised. "Better still . . . stay out of it and let the police do their job."

Jaymie nodded. "I keep telling myself that. It's none of my business." She sighed. "If only I'd listen to me."

She returned upstairs, chose a few books out of her bedroom bookcase to take to the cabin to read, and headed out to pick up Jocie at school. She was a little early so she went in, updated Sybil on what was happening with the plans for a learning through objects course involving the heritage house, and then met her daughter as class let out.

Jocie lingered for a few minutes, the tiniest member of her friend group. Because of her natural self-confidence, fostered by her father, who had done a miraculous job of raising his daughter alone, she had a circle of close friends. But all of them now towered over her. Still, she looked self-assured. Last school year she had been bullied by a boy who supposedly liked her too much to leave her alone; she had taken care of it herself by telling him to back off, and when he didn't, by shoving him. Adults had stepped in, and the problem had been solved.

She never condoned violence, but Jaymie respected Jocie's willingness to take care of herself and was loath to criticize her for it. She'd need that spunk in a world that would look down and patronize her for her size. It was a tough balance, not wanting to see her being bullied, and yet anxious that she feel competent to stand up for herself. Fortunately, so far this school year, despite her getting a late start, there had been no such problems.

In the backseat, belted into her specialized booster seat, Jocie twisted and looked at the pile of books Jaymie had picked up at home. Jaymie glanced at her in the rearview mirror, watching her pretty face with love. Though she had approached stepmotherhood with trepidation, Jakob, who didn't let anything worry him too much, was sure she would be fine, and he was right. She was adapting to the role and loving it far more than she had anticipated. It wasn't always easy, but it was almost always rewarding.

She held her breath for a moment before taking off out of the parking lot, watching Jocie pick through the novels. Some of the scenes in the historical romances were somewhat steamy and she didn't especially want Jocie picking one up and opening to the wrong page. But as she suspected, once her daughter saw the long pages of nothing but prose, she set them aside and picked up *The Poky Little Puppy.* It was too young for her—Jocie was reading at a ten-year-old level or higher—but she laughed at the pictures of the wiggly puppy sneaking under the backyard fence.

"I'm going to read this to Hoppy," she said, waving the book around.

"He'll love that," Jaymie said. Hoppy loved Jocie with an earnest adoration that had previously been reserved for Jaymie alone. And Jocie's kitten, Lilibet, was now his best friend after a few awkward incidents of feline-canine misunderstanding. Hoppy had only ever encountered Denver's grumpy, spiteful hisses and hadn't quite known what to do with the kitten's clambering, insistent devotion. But the two were now inseparable, which Jaymie loved; it meant that her little dog wasn't lonely anymore when everyone was out of the house for a few hours.

"What does it mean?" Jocie asked, having read the whole book within a few minutes of silence.

"What does *what* mean?" Jaymie asked, turning onto a country road after checking for oncoming traffic.

"The story, *The Poky Little Puppy* . . . He's naughty all the time and steals desserts. What does it *mean*?"

"Like a moral, or a point?"

"I guess," Jocie said, frowning at the book and leafing through it again.

So, Jocie was beginning to understand story structure and expect certain things from a book; goodie, another reader in the making!

Though to be fair, she was *already* an avid reader. "You know, I don't think *The Poky Little Puppy* has any point at all."

"But he gets so *many* desserts and the other puppies only get one. That's not fair. They obeyed the rules, finally, and only got one dessert each."

"Well, that's true. Why don't you rewrite it sometime so it makes more sense? But if you do, you have to make it your *own* story. If you use another person's words, or storyline, or thoughts, you're stealing." It was never too early to introduce the notion of plagiarism, and how to avoid it. Jaymie glanced at her in the rearview mirror. "It's the same with your schoolwork. If you have to write an essay, you should never use someone else's words unless you're quoting them directly."

Jocie frowned, her blonde brows drawn down over her round brown eyes. "I could write a whole new story about a puppy, though?"

"You certainly could. As long as it's your story and your ideas, you'll be just fine."

"I'll call it *Slowpoke the Puppy Shares Dessert.*"

"That would be good!" Jaymie said as she pulled up to the cabin.

Inside, Jocie sat at the table and started writing her story while Jaymie rummaged in the freezer, figuring out what to make for dinner. Jakob came home a little early and wrapped her in his arms for a long, lingering kiss, as Jocie blushed and rolled her eyes. He then volunteered to take Hoppy and Jocie for a walk; he had shared his concern for their daughter's activity level with Jaymie, something backed up by their summertime chat with the geneticist. As a little person, it was vitally important to both watch her weight and keep up with physical activity, strength training and flexibility. Her dance classes were wonderful for that, but walking Hoppy was a great excuse for daddy-daughter talk time.

Jaymie watched out the kitchen window as the two headed off across the driveway in the dwindling light to walk the trees. She finished putting together a dinner casserole using leftover chili and macaroni—chili mac was always a hit—pulled out salad greens and contentedly washed and chopped vegetables as she pondered her day, reflecting on how her life had changed for the better since meeting Jakob and Jocie.

And that made her think of people who weren't so fortunate, and that brought her to . . . Heidi! Guilt-stricken, she hurried through making the salad, tucked it back in the fridge, and sat down in the living room with the phone, calling her friend.

"Jaymsie!" she cried, a glad tone in her voice. Heidi was the only one who called her that pet name. "How are you?"

"I'm great. How are *you*? Did you get my message the other day?"

They chatted for a while, catching up, but Jaymie couldn't get past the feeling that there was something that her friend wasn't saying. She tucked her feet up under her on the sofa and pulled a blanket over her lap, tugging at a loose thread. "Heidi, please tell me what's wrong. I feel like there's something going on."

"Oh, it's okay. Nothing . . . nothing to worry about."

That pause spoke volumes, and now Jaymie really started to worry. On an impulse she said, "Can you and Joel come over for dinner? It's just a casserole and salad, but Jakob and I would love to have you. Jocie talks about you all the time. *Please* come." There was silence. Had the last-minute invitation seemed *too* last-minute? "Heidi?"

"Joel and I . . ." She paused. There was just the sigh of her breathing for a moment, and the sense of a sob held back. "Jaymsie, I kicked him out. Joel and I are done."

⌀ Eight ⌀

LUNCH FOR JOCIE MADE and tucked into her book bag, kisses at the door, and Jakob was gone, taking their daughter to school — she had missed the school bus again — before he headed to work for the day, planning to move things around at The Junk Stops Here to make way for another shipment. He had hired a young couple in their twenties to help him at the store, he'd said. New to the area and ex-military, both of them wounded in the line of duty and honorably discharged, they were perfect for many reasons. Their widely varied skills included the wife's ability to handle any vehicle, including the Arctic Cat ATV Jakob and Gus used to move large items around their warehouse-sized store. Raised on a farm and driving by the age of ten, she had apparently crowed with delight at the sight of the Arctic Cat. He had followed up their references and done a criminal background check and was both happy and relieved to have the help.

Jaymie took Hoppy for a walk behind the house, heading off toward the land they were considering buying. It was an uncertain kind of day, with a dark gray ceiling of cloud cover and wind that whipped along the country road, picking up dust and sending it swirling into dust devils. She stood at the top of the hill, among the corn stubble, listening to squawking blue jays and noisy crows squabbling, and thinking about her conversation with Heidi the night before. She had kicked Joel out. He was cheating on her, just as he had cheated on Jaymie. When asked if she was sure, Heidi had said yes. She had received a call from a woman in Ohio who wanted to know who the Heidi Lockland in Joel's cell phone contacts list was. Apparently the woman thought he was moving in with her; he already had a drawer to himself and part of her closet. It was an illuminating discussion, and when Joel got home, Heidi told him to pack his things and leave.

Heidi had cried during the call, but became calmer and agreed to have lunch with Jaymie. Unfortunately the news wasn't that surprising. Joel had cheated on Jaymie with Heidi — though Heidi, new in town and with no friends locally, hadn't known he lived with a girlfriend at the time — so the pattern was entrenched. All the time he was living with Jaymie and then Heidi he had, in fact, still been married to *another* woman. He was a serial cheating rat fink who didn't deserve Heidi or any decent woman. And so Jaymie had vehemently told her friend.

"C'mon, Hoppy . . . home, baby."

The little Yorkie-Poo was so weary from the walk that he only had energy for a few quick dashes around the house with Lilibet, some snackies, and then the two curled up together in his bed in the corner near the fireplace. Jaymie dressed carefully and even put on some makeup and the earrings Heidi had given her for her birthday, a pair of silver feathers with blue crystals *to match her eyes*, her friend had said. She gazed at herself in the mirror: blue eyes, mouse brown hair that was at least shiny and abundant, round face, round body, contented expression. Now, with Jakob, she finally knew she was enough. Joel had never made her feel that. With him she had been fretful and worried and felt inadequate, especially after he started living with the dazzlingly beautiful Heidi. Daniel, her next boyfriend, had loved her the way she was, but they were a mismatch from the start, with different likes and dislikes, goals and expectations. Jakob and she matched so well, it was like they were created for each other. She wished Heidi could find that.

She headed out the front door and paused, glancing up at the sky. Umbrella or no umbrella? It was tough to say in the spring and fall, and the gray overhead worried her. But she decided she was safe enough and headed out to the SUV. Though she and Heidi were to meet at the café in Wolverhampton for lunch, Jaymie had two hours of work with Georgina at the antique store first. Georgina was in an uncertain mood when she arrived, so Jaymie let her be, put her mind to the task and worked steadily on learning about different eras in glassware, and how to spot real Depression, carnival, and art glass. As she finished for the day and closed her notebook, she idly asked Georgina where the set of Buccellati silver came from, the set she was so positive wasn't Miss Perry's. With a sniffy manner the woman said she knew the provenance; it was sold to them by a local woman who inherited it from a great-aunt. Who was the woman? Jaymie asked, despite Georgina getting more and more irritated.

"It happens to be an established family here in town, Beverly Hastings. *Very* embarrassing all 'round," Georgina said frostily, slapping antique magazines together and shoving them under the counter. "The police spoke to her, and I understand she produced her copy of the will in which the set of silver was listed. I have been doing this for some time, you know, Jaymie, and I do *know* what I'm doing."

"I didn't mean to give offense, Georgina. Have a good rest of the day!"

On her way out she ran into Petty Welch, who had started working with Cynthia Turbridge, the owner of the Cottage Shoppe, and Jewel Dandridge, the owner of Jewel's Junk, which was where Petty was headed that day.

A petite gray-haired dynamo, Petty had swiftly become fast friends with her two new employers. She grabbed Jaymie's arm as she enthusiastically extolled the virtues of her new life. "Guess what? I'm selling my cottage and moving to Queensville. I've already found a buyer for my cottage and I'm putting in an offer for the house next door to Cynthia's!" The gray clouds were breaking up and retreating. A ray of fall sunshine shone through. "Brock Nibley has been good to me, very helpful."

"I'm so happy for you, Petty. I think Brock is trying to make up for the past." In which he had lied repeatedly, leading to a decades-long confusion over two girls who had been missing, before their bodies were recovered and it was learned they were murder victims. Petty was the aunt of one of the two, Rhonda Welch, who had been found submerged in her car in the river off Heartbreak Island. Just before her spring wedding, Jaymie had helped solve the murders of Rhonda and Dolores Paget, a teen friend of Becca's. Petty now seemed to be emerging from the dark cloud under which she had once lived, forever wondering where her beloved niece had gone.

"Hey, guess what?" Petty said, her fast-moving mind already changing to a new subject. "I'm dating again! I think you know him, Haskell Lockland?"

"Haskell? Wow!" Jaymie said. Haskell and Petty? She was surprised that his choice was so age-appropriate; he had a habit of flirting with younger women. "He's . . . a good guy." If a bit of a stuffed shirt. "I've known him for years."

"Anyway, enough about me, how are *you* doing, dear?" she asked, still clutching Jaymie's arm.

Jaymie told her the latest but then glanced at her watch. "I have to get going. I'm going to visit a friend in the hospital, and then I have a lunch date!" They hugged, then set off in opposite directions.

Jaymie found a parking spot about midway between Wolverhampton General Hospital and Wellington's Retreat, the tearoom where she was having lunch with Heidi. In the hospital Jaymie went directly to Miss Perry's room. When she entered she was overjoyed to find Mrs. Stubbs, in her mobility wheelchair, sitting by the bed of her cousin.

"I get a two-for-one visiting deal!" she said, seeing that Miss Perry was now conscious. She still looked terrible; she had a black eye and magenta bruises all down her face and neck, as well as along her arm, and her head sported a large bandage on the bruised side, her gray hair matted and sticking up over the top and under it. She looked frail in the sickly blue patterned hospital gown, hooked up to a monitor on a pole with a saline bag almost empty, the monitor with a steady *beep beep beep* measuring her pulse, oxygen saturation level and respiratory rate.

Miss Perry wearily waved her to the visitor's chair. Jaymie gave Mrs. Stubbs a hug, then sat down, setting her purse under her chair.

"I bullied Edith into giving me a ride into town," Mrs. Stubbs said about her son's live-in girlfriend.

"I'm sure she was happy to do it," Jaymie said.

"Darn tootin' . . . it gives her an excuse to go shopping," grumbled Mrs. Stubbs.

"Stop your moaning, Martha," Miss Perry murmured, her whiskey voice fainter than before and lacking vigor. She looked over at Jaymie. "I hear you're the one who found me." She reached out her free hand, the one untethered by an oximeter and saline drip. "I'm old, but I'm not done living, so I'm grateful."

Jaymie took her hand, her eyes misting. "I'm happy I tried the door. What happened? Do you remember?"

She exchanged a look with her cousin. "We were discussing that." She tried to sit up but it was too much of a struggle.

Jaymie released her hand and helped her get the pillow lower under her back, and pressed the button to make the bed head higher so the woman could look into their eyes. She then brought the bedside table closer and moved the sipping cup of ice water within easy reach. Miss Perry took a drink of the water and sighed, giving Jaymie a nod of thanks.

"Lois doesn't remember everything," Mrs. Stubbs said. "She *thinks* Estelle came to the door for their appointment at about nine, but Lois ignored her."

"I *know* that much. That's not where my memory is foggy," the woman said adamantly, contradicting Mrs. Stubbs. "I was *not* going to talk to that woman again. We've said all we need to say and I'm not changing my mind." She clutched her hands together over her little round belly. "I saw her at the door from my bedroom window, which overlooks the circle. She kept knocking."

"So you didn't cancel your appointment with her after your run-in?"

"If she had a grain of common sense she would have known our appointment was canceled, for heaven's sake."

Estelle Arden was persistent, and no assumption would be made if she was trying to get something done.

"Who was your other appointment with?"

"The police asked me the same thing," Miss Perry said, squinting and shifting uneasily. "But I don't remember any other appointment."

"When we spoke on the phone to arrange me coming out to pick up the graters, you told me you had another appointment that morning after Estelle, presumably there, at your place. You said I should come after lunch."

Miss Perry shook her head slowly. "Are you sure I said that?"

"I'm sure," Jaymie said, and glanced over at Mrs. Stubbs, who raised her brows and shook her head. "I suppose a blow to the head could hurt one's memory. One detail that surprised me was that when I found you, you were still in your housedress. You hadn't dressed for your appointment, whatever it was. Do you always dress at the same time of day? It may help the police nail down the time of the . . . the accident, if they knew that."

"Not particularly," she said wearily.

"Have the police already asked you about the housedress?" Miss Perry shook her head. "Do you always dress before lunch, say?" Jaymie pressed.

"Usually, but not always."

"But you certainly would if you were expecting someone else before lunch." The woman nodded. "Is there anywhere you would have written an appointment down?" Jaymie asked.

Miss Perry's eyes were blank for a moment, and she raised one trembling hand to her bandaged forehead. "I . . . I'm not sure. I don't think . . ."

"Lois, you've always been organized," her cousin said. "And you always kept an appointment calendar. *Think!*"

"Stop bullying me, Martha! I don't remember."

She appeared confused. Pain and medications do that to even the most coherent person. "It's okay. Don't worry about it," Jaymie said, putting her hand over the frail lady's. "It's not important."

"Except someone tried to do her in," Mrs. Stubbs said. "Oh, yes, I *heard* about the string across the stairs," she said to Jaymie. "Morgan went on and on about it. How *she* found it. How the idiot police didn't do their job."

"That's unfair! Bernie couldn't exactly charge in and check things out while the paramedics were looking after Miss Perry!"

"I know, dear, you needn't defend your friend. Morgan is like that, very high-handed." She glanced over at Miss Perry. "I wonder where she gets it from."

"Miss Perry, what kind of slippers do you wear?" Jaymie asked, noticing a pair of fluffy blue ones on the shelf of the side table. "Do you have a pair of moccasin-type slippers that are too big for you?"

She shook her head. "I don't think so. I don't like moccasins, and I'd never wear slippers too big for me. Why?"

A nurse came in and charted her signs, then efficiently changed the depleted saline bag. They were silent, but Jaymie's mind was working double-time. Morgan was seeing Fergus Baird on the side, while married. Fergus desperately wanted the shops by the dock, likely not for new shops but to raze them and construct luxury riverside condos. Should she raise the topic of Morgan and Baird?

Just then the young woman herself bustled in and greeted her aunt affectionately. Jaymie was swiftly ashamed of suspecting her of anything. She was clearly devoted to her aunt. Morgan cast a narrow-eyed look at Jaymie, then ignored her.

As the nurse left, Jaymie retrieved her purse from under the chair and stood. "I can't stay; I'm meeting a friend for lunch. You can take my chair, Morgan." She gave Miss Perry an affectionate goodbye, and said she'd visit when she returned home. Mrs. Stubbs followed her out of the room and into the hall, manipulating the joystick of her mobility wheelchair expertly to get through the door and around a laundry cart.

"What do you make of it all, Jaymie?" Mrs. Stubbs said as they slowly headed toward the elevator past a cluster of nurses and residents comparing notes. "Who would want to kill Lois? I'm trying not to alarm her too much, but I'm extremely upset and angry about the whole thing."

"I have some theories, but nothing solid."

"I want you to look into it, Jaymie; you're the only one I trust to figure things out."

"Mrs. Stubbs, the police are more capable than I am. I've just been lucky."

"I'll take lucky over good every time. And I object to that characterization anyway. You've been shrewd, you know all the players, and you have access to gossip and inside information that the police won't pay attention to."

They stopped at the elevator near the nurses' station, a circular desk with banks of computers for nursing staff. Attendants milled about, and a porter stopped with a patient in a wheelchair next to where a man in a suit and carrying a briefcase spoke to a nurse. The gentleman nodded, turned, and headed down the hall and directly into Miss Perry's private room.

"I know who that is," Jaymie said. "That's Parker Bastion, a lawyer. He's the Müllers' contract and will lawyer. I wonder why Miss Perry needs to see him?"

"I don't know, but I'll find out," Mrs. Stubbs said, waving a hurried goodbye and heading back to her cousin's hospital room.

Jaymie descended to the main floor and slipped into the gift shop. Heidi needed something to cheer her up, so a friendship gift was the order of the day. The gift shop was run by hospital volunteers and stocked locally handmade items, from artisanal chocolate to beaded gifts. As usual, there were at least three volunteers, all women of a certain age, as Valetta called herself and other ladies in the forty-to-sixty-year-old range.

"May I help you?" one said.

She was an attractive woman with a smart wedge-shaped bob hairstyle dyed dark brown, wearing a dark suit and a WGH tag with the name Phillipa Zane engraved on it.

"Mrs. Zane. You're Miss Lois Perry's neighbor, Lan Zane's wife!"

"I am. How do you know Miss Perry?"

Jaymie explained as she moved around the gift shop, past the displays of gum, chips, coolers of water and pop, and hospital necessities: tiny shampoo bottles, tubes of toothpaste and travel toothbrushes, flimsy slippers and thin robes. "I was up to visit her. She's conscious now and seems a little better."

"Good to hear. She's a crusty old bird, but I kind of like that. I hope that's me at her age!"

In the front window there was a hanging display that caught the sunlight flooding in; a sign advertised locally made handcrafted stained glass suncatchers, each with a prismatic bead that showered a rainbow of light all around the shop. One was a butterfly with the prismatic crystal as its body and stripes of colored glass for the wings. *That* was Heidi. She took it to the cash register.

"So you're the one who found her, I hear!" Phillipa exclaimed, ringing up the purchase and dipping under the cash desk, taking out a white box and folding it into shape, lining it with silver tissue and nestling the butterfly within.

"I was, fortunately."

"I was here that day, so I missed all the excitement."

"You were here? When did you leave home?"

The woman frowned, wrinkles bunching on her forehead. "I don't know . . . tennish? I left, got into Queensville, then realized I'd forgotten my cell phone, so I came back."

"What time was that?"

She stared at Jaymie but answered. "I don't know . . . maybe ten after ten, a quarter after? It made me late to work, anyway, but who can go a whole day without their phone? Langlow told me all about it later. He has to walk that brutish dog of his—darn thing barks at me like I'm a stranger every time I come in—several times a day or he poops in the house." She wrinkled her nose in disgust.

Several times a day? He had said he was only there in the afternoon. Interesting. "I suppose it was lucky, but I'm sure Morgan would have discovered her soon after. She's such a good niece to take care of her aunt that way!"

The woman sniffed. "Don't be fooled by the prissy butter-wouldn't-melt-in-her-mouth behavior. Morgan Perry Wallace is in it for the inheritance. That's the only reason she takes care of Lois. She *knows* what she's getting and she knows she has to keep her nose clean until she gets it."

"What do you mean?"

"She'd divorce her husband in a second if she didn't think Miss Perry would disapprove. The old lady is from the *marriage is forever and that's why I didn't marry* school of thought."

Maybe that explained the affair with Fergus Baird and the odd look Morgan's husband had when she dissolved on his chest weeping. "How do you know this?"

"I've heard things," Phillipa said, tying a turquoise bow on the box with a flourish.

Gossip: sometimes spot-on, sometimes unreliable. However . . . there was still the cheating. Would that be enough to disinherit Morgan? Jaymie didn't know Miss Perry well enough to understand. Maybe she should ask Mrs. Stubbs, even though she had sworn just minutes before that the police were perfectly capable of finding out who had tried to kill Miss Perry.

"I've spoken to your husband a couple of times," Jaymie said. "You've both agreed to let tourists follow a historic walking trail across your property?" She nodded. "It's Miss Perry who's holding things up. But you must understand her hesitation when someone broke into her house through the back utility room. She's worried about strangers in her backyard."

"We offered to share the expense of a fence across the back all the way along. Haskell said he'd help with the cost, too, but she said no way."

Fences don't stop resolute robbers, Jaymie thought but did not say. "I'd better get going," she said. "I've got a friend who will love this!" She held up the box. "Thank you for making it such a pretty package."

❧ Nine ❧

WELLINGTON'S RETREAT WAS A NARROW TEA SHOP along Wolverhampton's main street. They served tea and desserts, but also did lunches: soups, sandwiches, and salads. Jaymie hustled in the door and Heidi jumped up from her chair, flinging her arms around her and hugging hard.

Jaymie hugged her back, then held her away from her and examined her friend. Heidi Lockland was a slim woman, with long silky blonde hair and impeccable taste in clothing, beautiful in every way, including her heart. They sat down across from each other at the tiny table by the window. Heidi was paler than usual and had lost a few pounds, her cheekbones more prominent, the shadows under her lovely blue eyes not helped by the mustard-colored blouse she was wearing.

Clasping her hands across the table and squeezing, Jaymie said, "Sweetie, I'm so sorry you're going through this. Joel is an idiot. You were the best thing that ever happened to him."

"After you, maybe. But he let go of you, so he's got to be a real jerk, right?" She offered a ghost of a trembling smile.

"Let's agree that he doesn't know when he's got it good. So you know who he's seeing."

"I do," she said, withdrawing her hands and folding them in front of her, no longer wearing the engagement ring Joel gave her. "Like I said, she called me because she found my number and name in his contacts and saw how often he'd called me."

"Why was she going through his phone?"

Heidi shrugged. "She was suspicious. Like I've been, though I've kept it to myself. I started to think something was up a few weeks before you got married."

"This has been going on that long?"

She shrugged. "I didn't know for sure. I was trying to ignore my doubts. We went away in the summer to Italy, and everything seemed fine. But when we got back his business trips were lasting longer than normal by a few days." Joel was a representative for a pharmaceutical supply company and often traveled for work in the Michigan, Pennsylvania, and Ohio area. "And he was spending that time in Ohio."

"The other woman isn't his ex-wife, is it?" Jaymie asked. His ex, from whom he had only recently gotten a legal divorce, lived in Ohio.

"Nope, this is a new one. She met him in a bar and took him home. That was in April. They've been seeing each other ever since. He stays at her place a few nights a week."

"Since *April*?" Jaymie hadn't thought *that* badly of Joel, even though he broke her heart. She had thought that he'd finally found his true love in Heidi. What an idiot. What more could a man want than someone who was kind, good-natured, forgiving, beautiful, and, to top it all off, the cherry on a delicious sundae, was born wealthy? "He doesn't deserve you," she said, using the favorite phrase of supportive female friends since the dawn of time.

"But it hurts."

"I know it does, sweetie, I know. What did he say when you confronted him?"

"Said it wasn't true. That the woman was trying to make trouble for him. That she had come on to him in a bar and was now stalking him."

Well, that *could* happen, Jaymie thought, then shook her head. That was also what a cheating louse would say; blame the other woman.

The waitress came to their table and they ordered one of the soups of the day, vegetable chowder — Heidi had become vegan over the summer — after making sure it was cooked with vegetable broth. They also ordered cheese muffins made with vegan cheese, and hot tea.

As they ate they talked about Jaymie's life. She shared her and Jakob's idea for the Müller Christmas store. Talk finally turned to her reason for being in Wolverhampton, to visit Miss Perry.

"That poor old lady!" Heidi exclaimed, her eyes tearing up. "I saw it on the news, but they didn't say anything about it being a murder attempt."

Experiencing a moment of panic, Jaymie said, "Good grief, I shouldn't have said anything. Maybe they're trying to keep that under wraps." The police did do that sometimes, withhold details from the public in an effort to entrap the culprit. "Don't say anything to anyone."

"I won't. Bernie lets stuff slip sometimes. I know how to keep a secret. Maybe not as good as Joel, but . . ." She sniffed back the tears, dabbing at the wetness gathering under her eyes with a tissue, careful not to smudge her mascara.

"I only know because I was there when Morgan found the wire. Poor Miss Perry doesn't remember anything." Until recently Jaymie would have been able to talk to Chief Ledbetter and hound him for details. He'd used her as a source in the past, and she had even helped him on occasion. But he had retired over the summer; his assistant chief, Deborah Connolly, had been appointed chief of police, the first woman in that position. She was good, but would not tolerate outsiders interfering, she had said in a news conference announcing her appointment.

Jaymie took that personally.

They talked more about Bernie, Heidi's closest friend. The two besties were taking a trip together to New York sometime in the near future to cheer Heidi up. Other than that it was harmless gossip about friends, news about Bernie's brother Beau, who was coming to stay for a while as he convalesced from an on-the-job accident, and Jaymie shared her trials and tribulations with Georgina. Just catching up.

They finished their soup and decided against dessert. Jaymie pulled from her purse the box from the hospital gift shop and pushed it across the table. "A little something to cheer you up," she said. "Open it!"

Heidi gave her that *you shouldn't have* look, but opened it happily and pulled out the butterfly suncatcher. She held it up to the window and the sun streaming in caught the prism crystal, sending rainbow rays around the dim café.

"Because you're a butterfly, sweetie," Jaymie said gently, watching her lovely friend tear up. "Joel was never good enough for you. You deserve someone who will see you for who you are and not try to dull your lovely wings."

Heidi jumped up, raced around the table and hugged Jaymie, who could feel the tears from them both wetting her cheeks.

• • •

JAYMIE STOCKED UP AT KROGER, stopped at a farmers' market for late season veggies, then returned to the cabin to put the food away. Because she enjoyed cooking so much she had taken over much of it, but tonight was Jakob's turn. He was going to pick Jocie up from school and then come home and cook dinner with her. Hoppy was begging for a walk, so Jaymie took him out; when she returned she gave both pets treats. Jocie's cat had outgrown much of her kittenish madness and was turning into a pretty, sweet-natured tiger-striped tabby, who fortunately did not seem to care about going outside. There were coyotes around their home, so it was not safe for a small animal to roam. Jakob was going to build a dog and cat run on the porch so both animals could spend a little time outside unescorted.

What next? She looked around the cabin; it was a homey space with exposed log walls, a big stone fireplace in the living area, a lower ceiling in the kitchen, and a big window over the sink overlooking the covered porch. It had become a second home to her, but someday it would be her only home. Becca and Kevin planned to move to Queensville permanently at some point, and Jaymie couldn't see her and Jakob and Jocie sharing the Queensville home with her sister and brother-in-law for any amount of time.

Today her mind was churning, and she had the familiar feeling of her brain working on a problem in the background, making her fidgety and anxious. She *should* do a couple of loads of laundry. She could clean out the fridge. Or work on her next "Vintage Eats" column, or the cookbook. Or prepare for the radio show with Sid, whom she had emailed back and forth with already. She restlessly roamed the cabin; without Jocie and Jakob it felt kind of lonely.

But in truth she couldn't stop thinking about Miss Perry. What kind of monster would try to kill an elderly woman? And once the lady was released from the hospital and home, how long would it take before the attacker struck again? She couldn't let it be; it was impossible. There were avenues to explore, questions to ask, and problems to solve.

Mind made up, she grabbed her keys, called Hoppy to accompany her, and drove to Queensville, stopping at their house first, where Kevin was helping their neighbor, Pam Driscoll, put up storm windows. Pam was still looking after the Shady Rest Bed and

Breakfast next door until Anna and Clive returned for good next spring with their two kids.

Unlike many Englishmen, Kevin preferred coffee to tea. She waved to him, then went in and made a pot of coffee for them both. Hoppy raced around the home, wobbly as always, sniffing his favorite corners and reclaiming his bed by the stove, empty now that Denver had moved permanently to Valetta's.

When Kevin came in, she greeted him warmly and poured him a cup of coffee.

"I hope Pam's not being too much of a pain," Jaymie said, looking over her shoulder as she fixed the brew the way he liked. Pam had a bit of a needy, clingy personality, but she had done better on her own than Jaymie had expected after their first meeting.

"Not at all," Kevin said, his English accent charming as always. "She was struggling along on her own—her useless son was supposed to help but took off on his bike instead—and I offered. She said no at first; Pam *is* doing her best to learn how to do things. But I prevailed, masculine pride at handiwork surging to the fore, you know. Must step in to aid the damsel in distress." He chuckled, wiping beads of sweat from his high domed forehead.

She set the cup in front of him. "It was kindly done," she said.

"Yes, well, needless to say, it was more work than I anticipated." He was mildly pudgy, an antiques dealer specializing in old radios and Bakelite articles, as well as antique furniture, which was how he met Becca, at an auction. He wore silver-framed glasses and had a salt-and-pepper beard the same color as his thinning hair. Today he wore a professorial outfit: chinos and a suede-elbowed cardigan sweater with a shawl collar over a gray oxford shirt.

"You aren't dressed for it," Jaymie said with a smile. "When I was growing up the bed-and-breakfast was run by an older couple, and he always wore these green work pants and shirt; it was like a uniform for him. But the work pants were like dress slacks, you know, with perfect creases, buttoned pockets and a leather belt."

"Ah, yes, the sartorial elegance of the working man of yesteryear." He took a long drink and set down the cup with a sigh of satisfaction. "I shouldn't say it aloud," he said, leaning forward in conspiratorial fashion, "but you make *much* better coffee than your sister."

"She forgets the eggshell."

"Eggshell?"

"Eggshell is an alkaline and coffee is acidic; it mellows the coffee to put a little crushed eggshell in with the coffee grounds."

"I will gently remind her."

"*Or* you could make the coffee yourself; I'll show you." She paused and frowned down at her cup. "Kevin, I have a question, but I don't want you to take it the wrong way."

"Yes, Georgina has always been prickly and difficult, apparently from the moment she was born, my dear mother once said. She's a hedgehog and can be a pain in the buttocks. She swears she means no harm, and indeed she is rude to everyone, playing no favorites. For some reason Americans love that about her."

Jaymie laughed out loud. Hoppy came over begging for attention, and she lifted him to her lap, cuddling him to her. He licked her chin then settled down. "That's funny, but it's not what I was about to ask. Actually, it's about the antique business." The more she had thought about it the more absurd it seemed to her that Bev Hastings's aunt would have a complete set of valuable sterling flatware in the exact same pattern as Miss Perry. Such an extravagance couldn't be *that* common. "You deal in a lot of valuable stuff, and you buy things that folks bring into the store. What happens if you accidentally buy stolen goods?"

His expression became serious. "We do our best to be sure we know the provenance of articles, but Georgina and I have been burned before. If we do buy something and then find out it is stolen, we make every effort to give restitution, when possible by returning the exact item to the theft victim." He squinted and examined her expression. "Is this about the Buccellati silver set?"

"Georgina mentioned it?"

He nodded, his glasses glinting in the light. "I didn't think anything of it when the police checked it out, but since then I've become worried. That Savoy by Buccellati set is extremely valuable, and if someone stole it from Miss Perry, I'd like to check into it further, but I'm not sure how to go about it without offending Georgina, Mrs. Hastings, or tipping our hand."

"You still have the silver, right? No one has bought it?"

"It was never going to be a quick sale. High-end silver and

antiques require the right buyer. We knew it wasn't going to sell in Queensville, though we do have one place setting and a couple of serving pieces out in the display case. The remaining pieces are locked in the vault." When they renovated the antique store in the spring, Kevin and Becca had installed two vaults, a smaller one under the sales desk for cash, and a larger one in the bookkeeping office for jewelry and valuable pieces. "We expect that it will sell online at some point, for a price somewhat less than we have it listed." He frowned and sighed. "I've been in a quandary as to how to handle it."

"I'll do what I can to help you figure it out."

He nodded. "Until then, I believe I'll have Georgina remove the set from the online catalogue and the showcase. It will ease my apprehension."

"Will she be okay with that?"

He smiled. "She's my employee; she may be older than I, but she has to do what I say this time. It won't be pleasant, but I will do what I think right."

Jaymie departed, after ascertaining their schedule for the next couple of weeks. She was ready to spend another weekend at the house in town, but she didn't want Becca to feel compelled to leave. However, Becca and Kevin would soon be returning to London, Ontario, where their grandmother lived, to take her to some appointments and check in on Becca's assistant in the china replacement business she ran out of her Old South home. As long as their Grandma Leighton was alive, Becca had once said, her time would always be split between Queensville and London.

On her way through town Jaymie checked her watch; Valetta would be taking her afternoon break about now. It was still plenty warm enough for a cup of tea on the Emporium porch, in the Adirondack chairs kept there for that reason. She was just in time. Valetta saw Jaymie and brought out two mugs of tea, handing one to her friend. They sat on the store porch, watched through the glass by Mrs. Klausner, the nonagenarian store co-owner.

"She doesn't approve of me taking breaks," Valetta said, waving over her shoulder at the woman in the store window. Her mug of the day said *Be Nice to Me – I Know How to Kill You!*

"Is it wise to use that mug at work?" Jaymie asked, keeping

Hoppy on her lap as the little dog quivered with excitement, his little nose in the air, catching every scent. "Customers might get the wrong idea."

"Brock had it made for me. You'd be surprised how polite people are once they read it."

"I didn't think your brother had a sense of humor."

"He's trying." She chuckled and followed that with, "Sometimes he's *very* trying."

Mrs. Bellwood, one of the senior Queensville citizens and the lady who played Queen Victoria every May in the heritage society's Tea With the Queen event, briskly walked up the slight rise toward them, huffing and puffing almost as much as Roary, her pug, who was firmly held on his leash, though he strained at it and wuffled a snorty puggish challenge at Hoppy. She was dressed senior-stylish in a violet velour bedazzled tracksuit and had violet streaks in her gray hair. "Good day, girls! Roary and I love this more fallish nip in the air. Makes us think of winter. Jaymie, will we see you at the heritage meeting tonight?"

"I don't think so, Mrs. Bellwood," Jaymie said.

"Hmph. Ever since you married you've shirked your responsibilities."

Jaymie didn't say what she thought, which was that Jakob and Jocie *were* her responsibilities now. To distract her, she asked, "Have you and Imogene Frump found the Sultan's Eye yet?" The Sultan's Eye was a mythic Dumpe family heirloom supposedly hidden somewhere in the heritage house. It was reported to be a brooch in the style of two centuries before, a painting on ivory of a human eye.

Mrs. Bellwood paused and let Roary sniff a clump of bushes by the Emporium porch, then he barked animatedly at Hoppy, who started struggling in Jaymie's arms to get down. "About that, Jaymie, we urgently need Haskell's vote to let us pull up some of the floorboards. Imogene and I are virtually certain there is a spot under the floor where artifacts are hidden, but he won't let us pry up just a *few* boards. Bill Waterman has already said he could repair any damage we did."

"You'll have to fight him on that yourself. I'm already leaning on him to approve funding for a project I have in mind. You know how hard it is to get society money out of him."

Mrs. Bellwood sniffed, said goodbye and hauled her pug away to continue their walk. She paused to watch and speak to Brock, who had parked his Caddy on the street and was hammering a *For Sale* sign into the lawn of the historic house by the green area beyond the Emporium, a yellow brick Queen Anne similar to the Leighton home.

"I hope whoever buys that house wants to live in it," Jaymie said. "I'd hate to see it go to someone who wants to turn it into apartments, or medical offices."

"Brock says he already has someone interested, even before he got the sign up. It's a newcomer, a husband and wife retiring to Queensville from Port Huron."

"If they buy it we'll have to invite them to join the heritage society. I'll get Haskell on it." Jaymie glanced over at the Queensville Fine Antiques store. Georgina was out on the porch washing the big front picture window — probably to avoid having to deal with Becca; the sisters-in-law butted heads often — and it reminded Jaymie about the silver flatware set. "Val, what do you know about Jon and Bev Hastings?"

She glanced at her friend. "That I can talk about?" As a pharmacist she knew intimate details of people's lives and was very careful never to cross a line.

"Well, sure, of course. I mean, I've known them to nod to for years, but I don't even know where they live."

"Well, let's see: Jon was born here, but moved away. He met Bev at some anglers' convention and they married, and moved back here about fifteen years ago, to a house he inherited from an uncle. It's one of those run-down houses near Johnny Stanko's, but he and Bev have fixed it up some, and her nephew lives there with them. He's a skinny goofy kid with nothing on his mind but video games and pot smoking, as far as I've ever seen. About the same time as they moved back, Jon took over the bait shop from the old fellow who used to own it. The previous bait shop owner has since passed away."

Jaymie suppressed a grin at the straightforward recitation. Valetta had an encyclopedic knowledge of Queensville from the last forty years or so. "I meant on a more personal level. Have either of them ever been in trouble with the law, say?"

Val cast her a sharp and quizzical look. "What are you getting at?"

Jaymie shook her head, unsure how to proceed. She didn't want to implicate Bev Hastings in the theft of silver from Lois Perry's home, not without a whole lot more evidence, and not even to Valetta, though she knew her friend wouldn't pass on her suspicions. "I'm not sure what I'm asking. I have a reason, but it's not one I want to share right now."

"You mean you want to hear gossip?"

Jaymie nodded and let Hoppy off her lap to sniff along the porch. "Do they get along? Do they have any friends? Any problems or . . . criminal doings?"

"Good heavens!" Valetta stared at her. "What, like selling drugs out of the bait shop?"

Jaymie chuckled. "Well, you said yourself the nephew was a pot smoker, right?"

Valetta rolled her eyes. "You *will* tell me what this is about, right?"

"Not right now, but soon."

"Okay." Valetta, brows raised high, took in a deep breath. "Well, there is not a thing even faintly shady, that I *know* of. Jon Hastings has always been a stand-up guy. He's the kind of fellow who will espouse two different sides to an argument just to be agreeable and keep the peace."

Jaymie nodded. That's what he had done at the dock. Even though Baird buying the shops would put him out of business, Hastings had still supported the man's plans for the town, all while being kind to Miss Perry. "How do they make a living from a bait shop, though? There are summer tourists of course, and ice fishing in the coldest part of winter, but that's not much."

"I guess they make do. They don't have a lot of bills; they own their house, their rent on the bait shop is minimal . . . they get by." She stood and tugged down her sweater. "That's all I got, kiddo. I'd better get back to work. I've got five scripts coming in from doctors this afternoon that I'll need to start filling!" She took Jaymie's mug.

"And I'd better get doing *something*," Jaymie said, standing and setting Hoppy down gently. "I'm playing hooky from about five things this afternoon."

"Wish I could join you playing hooky, but illegible prescriptions for unpronounceable drugs wait for no woman. At least I have the weekend off. Hey, I heard that Thrifty Dan's in Wolverhampton is closing down after Christmas."

"Really? Aw, I always loved Dan. Next time I'm in town I'll stop in and get the scoop. If he's having a sale we can go together."

Jaymie avoided her sister and brother-in-law's antique store, though she knew Georgina had seen her with Valetta, and headed to the Queensville Inn, straight to Mrs. Stubbs's room. She tapped, heard "Come in" and entered, letting Hoppy off his leash inside the door.

What she saw took a moment to make sense of. Mrs. Stubbs was in her wheelchair in front of her new smart TV, and she wore pink boxing gloves. She was watching a video and following boxing moves, right cross, left cross, *defend*! She briefly greeted Jaymie, then went on with her video until it was over a few moments later. The woman pulled off her gloves, turned off the TV and wheeled toward her sitting area by the window. Her son owned the Queensville Inn and had given her the last room on the main floor, which looked out on a patio terrace. Jaymie followed, but Hoppy was busy sniffing around the perimeter of the room, then disappeared into the en suite bathroom.

"So . . . you're training for the next Olympics?" Jaymie asked.

Mrs. Stubbs chuckled, a dry-as-dust sound. "I've been exercising, as you know. Cynthia is still coming for wheelchair yoga workouts, which I'd prefer without the relentless chirpy monologue from her, but I know she means well. After I came back from Wolverhampton this morning I felt the need to pretend to pummel someone in the face."

"Uh-oh. Who angered you?"

"You'll want to hear this. But first . . . tea."

Jaymie groaned inwardly. *More* tea? After coffee with Kevin and tea with Valetta she was ready to float. However, tea it was. She crossed to the little kitchenette area, a long counter with a bar fridge, hot plate, tiny sink and cupboards, made it, poured, and sat down with her friend at the table in front of the window with sun pouring in, lighting the tops of fresh flowers.

"So, this morning, at the hospital, that lawyer and Morgan Perry

Wallace," Mrs. Stubbs said with a grim expression. "Do you want to know what that was all about?"

"I do."

Her voice trembling with anger, restlessly pushing and pulling her tea mug, sloshing hot tea over the edge, Mrs. Stubbs said, "While Lois was groggy and in pain, bruised and beaten and almost dead, Morgan was trying to bully her into signing a power of attorney so she could do whatever she damned well pleased with Lois's property!"

✑ Ten ✑

STUNNED, JAYMIE BLURTED, "No, *really*? Did Miss Perry sign it?"

"Over my dead body she would have signed it." Mrs. Stubbs took in a long breath and let it out, moving her shoulders. "That smarmy lawyer had the papers out, and I was about to speak up when a lady police detective came in to ask Lois some questions. She was poker-faced, but she strongly advised Morgan not to prod Lois into signing *anything* while she was in pain and drugged up. Said it wouldn't stand up in a court, and that she herself would have to testify that Lois was in no state to sign anything so serious."

"Wow, that's . . . unusual."

"My thoughts exactly. I never imagined the police would take that step, advising someone in that position."

"I'm impressed," Jaymie admitted. "It may be an important step in combating elder abuse. How did Morgan take it?"

Mrs. Stubbs mopped up the tea she had spilt using a tissue. "She was startled, but she seemed fine about it, I'll give her that. Said the power of attorney was so she could take care of things, if need be."

"As long as she doesn't have the lawyer come back later, after the detective is gone," Jaymie said.

"I think the warning was for the lawyer, too, and he seemed to understand."

"Sure. Parker Bastion has a good reputation. But I hope Morgan doesn't go to court to have Miss Perry declared incompetent to handle her affairs. That's another way to get power of attorney, isn't it?"

"Actually it's more likely to be legal guardianship, if Lois was already considered incapacitated. I don't think that's going to happen with Morgan. At least, I hope it won't. I'd fight her on it myself because Lois will bounce back; she's just medicated right now."

Jaymie longed to ask about Morgan and Fergus Baird, but she was uncomfortable sharing what she had seen, even though Mrs. Stubbs wouldn't say a word. "What is Morgan's deal? What about her marriage?"

"Saunders Wallace is a prig, obsessed with his clothes and car and lifestyle. Even at the wedding I thought that man was only marrying her because she was a Perry."

"So no love lost between you two."

"I don't see them much, just at family gatherings once a year or so, but no, I don't like him and he doesn't like me."

"I understand he's not from around here. Morgan said his family is all in Scotland. Isn't it odd that they wouldn't come to his wedding?"

Taking a deep breath, calmer after her outburst, Mrs. Stubbs said, "Not all families are close. Folks have their own lives. For all we know it's his third wedding and they decided to wait a while to see if this one sticks."

Jaymie snorted with laughter, thinking of Joel; he had been married and engaged to three . . . no, *four*, counting this latest, women over the last two years. And Becca! Her own dear sister was on her fourth husband, after a few youthful miscalculations. Not everyone was fortunate enough to find the right one the first time, as she had.

"He's a phony," Mrs. Stubbs added. "You only have to have seen his TV ads for that. *The Wallace Cheese*," she added with a disparaging grunt. "His smile isn't cheesy, it's fake, as phony as processed cheese food and his red hair."

"As long as Morgan loves him, right?" Jaymie said, thinking of his worried look as he semi-comforted his wife.

"Morgan has been good to Lois but . . ." She sighed and shook her head. "Something is wrong, I don't know what, something about Morgan. I can't put my finger on it. Just a feeling, I guess." She grimaced and flexed her knotted fingers. "Or maybe it's the arthritis."

"Did you stay while the detective talked to Lois?"

"No. It was getting crowded and Edith came for me. I felt Lois was safe with Detective Vestry there and the lawyer leaving."

Without access to the police through Chief Ledbetter, Jaymie felt like her arm was cut off. She couldn't ask Bernie for info; it wouldn't be fair to infringe on a friendship that way, and Bernie wouldn't tell her anything anyway. Even finding Lois injured and perhaps saving her life didn't make it her business.

No matter how much she kept saying that to herself, it didn't help.

• • •

AFTER DUMPING HER TEA AND USING THE WASHROOM, with Hoppy staring at her in an unnerving manner, she headed out, carrying her little dog through the foyer and past the café. She looked in as she was passing and stopped dead. Fergus Baird—dressed in his usual eye-catching pastels, mauve and yellow this time, with white leather tasseled loafers—was sitting having lunch with a woman. Well, he wasn't married, so far as she knew, and a man could have lunch with any woman he wanted to without anything sinister going on, unlike what some folks thought.

However, she did want to talk to him. No time like the present. She asked Edith, Mrs. Stubbs's significant-other-in-law, as she called it—her son's live-in girlfriend and co-manager of the inn—to look after Hoppy, and the woman agreed with alacrity. As Jaymie strode away, Edith was coochy-cooing her little dog as if he was a baby.

Baird was still there, and the lunch had taken a more intimate look, with the woman touching his hand, his silvery hair glinting in the soft light as he leaned across the table, speaking to her in hushed tones. Awkward to barge in, but when had that ever stopped her in the past? She was known as nosy and had decided not to fight the reputation.

She approached the table. "Mr. Baird?" she said as the woman snatched her hand away from his. He admitted his identity. Jaymie glanced at his luncheon companion, trying to place her. She looked familiar, an attractive plump woman in her fifties, wearing a wrap top in fall florals and figure-hugging dark gold leggings, with high heels on dainty feet. Or one dainty foot anyway; the other was encapsulated in the kind of boot used when one breaks a leg. Jaymie smiled at her and nodded.

"Can I help you with something?" Baird asked.

"Yes, I . . ." But distracted from her mission, she glanced at the woman again. Something about her was naggingly familiar. She looked again, trying not to stare, but the blonde hair, piled high, with fetching curls dangling, her round cherubic face, right now holding an annoyed expression . . .

"And you are . . . ? I'm sorry, I don't think we know each other," Baird said impatiently, though the chilly look in his eyes warned that he did remember her from Wolverhampton.

"We have a couple of mutual friends," she said, her attention back on Baird. "We met out at the heritage house when you were speaking with Haskell Lockland. And you know Morgan Perry Wallace. You're . . . *friends* with her, correct?"

Baird, his tanned, oddly smooth face devoid of emotion, answered, "Yes, we know each other. We both belong to the Wolverhampton Country Club, as does Haskell."

"*And* Morgan's aunt owns the dockside buildings: the feed shop and . . . oh!" She turned to the woman. "The bait shop! You're Beverly Hastings, right?" Mrs. Hastings was so differently dressed from the last time she had seen her it was no wonder Jaymie hadn't recognized her. "You and your husband run the bait shop."

She nodded.

"May I help you with something?" Baird asked, his tone edging from impatience to irritation. "Mrs. Hastings and I happened to run into each other and are having lunch. If you have something to say I'd appreciate it if you got on with it."

Since Jaymie hadn't asked why they were together—it was odd he felt the need to explain—she didn't reply to that. "I won't keep you. I wondered if you had heard that Miss Perry was in the hospital?"

"The poor dear!" Bev Hastings said, her voice warm. "I was so upset when I heard what happened! I'm sure you were too, Fergie?"

Fergie?

"I was *appalled*," he said, his tone hard with anger. "I heard it was one of those hoodlum kids that have been trespassing all over the place. I had to chase a couple of them away from my house in Wolverhampton."

"We've had to add an alarm system at the bait shop," Bev said. "Imagine that, an alarm system where we sell worms and minnows!"

Jaymie did not think that some supposed hoodlum kids broke into Miss Perry's home and strung a trap for her, but she was not about to expose how much she knew about the incident. "By the way, Mrs. Hastings, are you okay? Have you done something to your leg?" She indicated the boot.

"Oh, yes, well, it was actually at the shop. That old boardwalk by the marina is falling apart. I was walking toward the bait shop and my foot went right through a board. It's not a break, fortunately, but it is a severe strain."

"I'm so sorry!" Jaymie said, shocked. "Someone should do something if the boardwalk is in such bad shape."

She shook her head. "As much as I love her, I've been telling Miss Perry for years that repairs are needed."

"Someone is going to be badly hurt," Baird said. "Now you see why I want to buy those buildings! Ownership of such public property requires someone who understands building mainten-ance."

Jaymie was about to ask what he meant by that, when his real idea was to wipe out the buildings and construct condos, but that was not the most politic thing, with a co-owner of the bait shop sitting right there. Instead she said, "Miss Perry is going to be fine, I believe. My friend Mrs. Stubbs is her cousin. And I'm sure Morgan, her niece, will make sure she has help once she's out of the hospital," Jaymie said, watching Baird's face for any sign of recognition when she said Morgan's name.

"She's fortunate to have family nearby," he said.

"I'll leave you to your lunch," Jaymie said. They said goodbye, and she headed back to get Hoppy before he ended up dressed in a bonnet in a stroller, completely possible with Edith.

"He's such a sweetie," Edith said affectionately as she handed him across the reservations desk to Jaymie.

The little dog reached up and licked Jaymie's mouth, and she laughed. "He is that! Hey, Edith, I spoke with Fergus Baird in the dining room. I guess he ran into Bev Hastings and they ended up sitting together?"

"Well, not exactly," Edith said, sitting back down behind the desk, drawing herself close to her computer. "I take reservations for the restaurant. Bev reserved a table for lunch and said to tell Fergus she'd be a little late if he arrived before her."

That was odd. Why would Baird lie about something like that? Of course, some people lie about anything and everything. The phone rang, releasing Jaymie from lengthy goodbyes. She waved as Edith took the call, and departed, sitting in her SUV for a few minutes with her trusty notebook. A bunch of things were worrying her, and it always helped to write them down physically, which she did as Hoppy propped himself up at the open window, barking at passers-by.

Some of it was what she had been pondering for days, some was new.

One: Who tried to kill Lois Perry?

It had to be someone with access to the house, which limited the number of people, but Jaymie didn't know enough about Lois to know who would be included in that group. And one had to allow for additional folks, like someone pretending to check the smoke alarm for her, or deliver a package, or who knew what else?

Two: Was Morgan in on it? And was that why she was now trying to get her aunt to sign a POA, or did Lois's "accident" make her realize she would need the POA if her aunt was incapacitated or unconscious for long?

Actually, it was surprising a POA wasn't already in place. It was a necessity of life. Becca had power of attorney for their Grandma Leighton so she could take care of things if something happened. Not *everything* had a sinister origin, and she mustn't demonize Morgan or assign murderous motives because she appeared to be cheating on her husband. No one knew the inside of a marriage unless they were one of the partners.

Three: Was the silver set that Bev Hastings sold to Queensville Fine Antiques truly Lois Perry's? And if it was, how did she get it?

How many people in the world owned a full set of Savoy by Buccellati sterling silver flatware worth upward of ten thousand dollars? Maybe it was unfair to speculate that the set was Lois Perry's stolen silver, but still . . . if it *was*, how did Mrs. Hastings get it? Jaymie couldn't see her throwing a rock at Miss Perry's back window and climbing in past the jagged glass. Had someone else done it, and she was merely the fence?

Four: Why were Bev Hastings and Fergus Baird, two people with apparently little in common and contrary goals, having a scheduled lunch together? And why did Fergus Baird feel the need to lie about it, passing it off as a chance meeting?

Hmmm . . . another affair? Bev Hastings and Morgan Perry Wallace, despite a twenty-year age difference, did have a few things in common, including a curvy figure, nice taste in clothes, and blonde hair. *And* both were married. Maybe Baird was having an affair with both, or maybe it was happenstance that he was having lunch with Bev Hastings.

Or . . . perhaps Bev and Jon Hastings were thinking about selling the business to Fergus so he could open his proposed tea shop. She rolled her eyes at her own attempt to be fair and impartial. She already knew that Baird's plans for the land, should he acquire it, had nothing to do with tea shops and boutiques and everything to do with water views and condo HOAs.

• • •

DINNER, COOKED BY JAKOB, was lasagna made with spinach and zucchini—surprisingly delicious, if a little watery. Gently she suggested that next time, should he choose to repeat the recipe, he cut the zucchini and let it drain in a colander over a bowl to get rid of the excess moisture. Jocie's suggestion, given with a wrinkled nose, was that he replace the zucchini with almost anything else.

After dinner, Jakob went out to take care of some business while Jaymie did dishes with Jocie, who stood on a stool to dry, though she was often distracted by Hoppy and Lilibet; Hoppy would entice Jocie with sharp yips of excitement, then lead her to where the kitten was hiding. A mad dash about the living room would ensue, Hoppy's yipping and Jocie's squeals of laughter echoing. But finally the three were worn out. After dishes, Jaymie sat with her laptop at the long trestle table in the kitchen, yellow light spilling on it from the fixture over the window, and worked on her vintage column and cookbook while Jocie wrote, in longhand, her *Poky Little Puppy* fan fiction.

Jakob, who had taken the information Jaymie had obtained about zoning for the farmland they proposed buying over to Helmut, returned. He threw aside his jacket and wearily stretched his back out as he strolled over to see what his two girls were working on. Jocie was at the illustration stage of her book, tongue stuck out a little ways, pencil crayons spilled in a bright array over the wood surface. He sat down and read her work.

"That's very good, Jocie!" he said approvingly. "But it's a school night, kiddo. Time for bed. Put away your pencils."

"Do you want me to come up?" Jaymie said as Jocie packed away her art supplies.

"I got this," he replied, kissing the top of her head and picking up his little girl. He dipped her to kiss Jaymie good night, then disappeared around the corner and carried her up the stairs, his voice trailing behind as he sang a tuneless rendition of James Taylor's "Fire and Rain."

Jaymie tried to refocus on the cookbook, but her mind kept returning to the mystery of who would try to kill Miss Perry. There were so many tangles in which the woman was involved. It could be personal, as most murders were. Did Morgan want her inheritance so badly that she'd kill her aunt to get it?

As silly as it seemed, was anyone from the heritage society angry over Miss Perry's stubbornness . . . angry enough to try to kill her? That seemed unlikely, to say the least. Estelle Arden had had that run-in with Miss Perry, though, and anger *could* boil to the surface. She shook her head. It was too absurd.

There were the Zanes; Lan had a hot temper and hated Miss Perry's cats. Also, Miss Perry had threatened Tiberius. Was the wire across the stairs intended as a warning? She shook her head again. That was no warning, that was a murder attempt.

And then there was the dispute over the dockside shops and property, and her refusal to sell them to Fergus Baird . . . or anyone, for that matter. It had been odd to see Baird and Bev Hastings have a serious discussion over lunch at the Queensville Inn.

Also, Jaymie's suspicion that Bev Hastings was behind the theft of Miss Perry's silver, which she had then hocked to Jaymie's sister and brother-in-law's shop, had increased significantly until she was virtually certain the silver was her friend's. But how dumb was it to sell it to a local dealer, and was Bev Hastings that dumb?

It was the same trail her mind traveled, over and over, and she knew she'd get no rest until she found the answers.

✄ Eleven ✄

"**REALLY, JOCIE?** You couldn't remind me last night when we were sitting at the table that you needed twenty-four cupcakes for *today*?" Jaymie said, staring at the note from Jocie's backpack, feeling a welling of desperation.

Jocie swallowed a mouthful of cereal. "I'm sorry, but—"

"No buts! Next time, make sure I know the night before."

Jakob, knowing his life depended on it, stifled his snicker, swallowed the last of his coffee, and said, "Gotta go; Gus has a court date with Tami and someone has to be at the shop with the new kids until I know them better." His business partner was supporting his sister by appearing in court with her to help her face charges for a crime that occurred decades ago when the siblings were teenagers. He poured another cup of coffee into a huge thermal travel mug.

"Okay, hubby. At this rate Jocie is going to miss the school bus again, but I'll take her and deliver the cupcakes. You pick her up?"

"Will do. Have fun with the cupcakes."

She made a face at him, then turned back to her daughter. "I'm serious, Jocie, got it?"

"I *got* it, already!"

"Jocie, no smart mouth," her father warned as he headed out the door.

Jocie's pudgy cute face held a sullen expression for a few seconds, but Jaymie poked her tummy and she giggled. "I'm sorry, Mama. I'll remember next time."

"That's better. Okay, let's get started. You're going to help me." Jaymie enlisted Jocie to get out the ingredients.

An hour later, cupcakes frosted with icing that threatened to drip off from the treats being too warm—cosmetically they were not the prettiest cupcakes Jaymie had ever made, but they'd have to do—they set out to school. Jaymie carried them inside and handed the plastic containers to the volunteer in charge of cupcake sales that day, kissed Jocie goodbye, and headed out. She finally remembered her cell phone and turned it on to find several text messages awaiting her: Valetta told her that Mrs. Stubbs wanted her to know that Lois Perry was going home in the next day or so with a home helper who would live in for a few days . . . Miss Perry was apparently worried that Jaymie hadn't gotten the spice graters yet for her school display, and would like her to come over the next morning; Becca wanted her to work a few hours in the antique store so they could take Georgina out for lunch before they left to go back to London; Heidi was in crisis . . . she had a date and needed advice on which of her forty-eight cute dresses she should wear.

Easiest one first: she texted Heidi that whatever she wore she'd be a knockout, but sent a photo of her wearing a personal favorite of Jaymie's, a cute plaid bodycon dress her friend had worn to dinner the month before. It didn't matter, because Heidi would ask everyone, then decide on something completely different anyway. But she did also text . . . *So who's the date with???*

She then headed to the antique shop. Georgina gave her a frosty welcome, loudly shuffling antique magazines with a great show of annoyance, only stopping when Becca and Kevin arrived. Jaymie quietly did her best to familiarize herself with prices and other information about the items they had in the store. Kevin had already removed the Savoy sample pieces from the showcase, so that explained Georgina's frigid mood.

Becca gave her a warm hug, whispering, "Don't mind Georgina. We'll get her drunk on gimlets at lunch and she'll be in a fine mood."

Jaymie giggled as they exited.

A busload of seniors stopped in Queensville, headed to the lunch buffet at the inn. But first they were shopping the main street shops, including the Knit Knack Shack, the Cottage Shoppe, and Jewel's Junk, ending at Queensville Fine Antiques. Jaymie sold a few vintage costume jewelry pieces, a tiny piecrust table, and three serving pieces of OCR, otherwise known as Royal Albert's most popular and plentiful Old Country Roses pattern. The pattern was so in demand that there were OCR serving pieces — pie servers and the like — with china handles, OCR figural teapots and even OCR bathroom sets — toothbrush holders and water cups — and figurines.

She was finishing up the last sale and the ladies were clustered near the door ready to leave when Bev Hastings, wearing her bait shop overalls, barged into the antique store, her face red. "I heard you were here. How *dare* you call me a thief!" she yelled, pausing inside the door, her booted foot stuck out at an awkward angle. "How *dare* you?"

Jaymie, taken aback and flustered, felt seven eyes on her from her customers — one lady had a patch over one eye — and babbled, "I don't know what you're talking about." She hastily taped the tissue she had wrapped around the handle of the OCR pie server and slipped the item in the bag with the cash register receipt.

"You *know* what I mean." Bev glared around at the customers. "What are you old bags doing, looking at me. *She's* the crook! She accused me of stealing a set of sterling silver and hocking it to this store." She shifted her gaze back to Jaymie.

"Bev, I'm sorry you're upset. But I never said you stole anything." Not exactly, though she had thought it and perhaps even implied it.

"You had your brother-in-law call the police about it, and they came out *again*, even though I already showed them the proof that the stuff was mine!"

She hadn't anticipated Kevin going to that length. He probably wanted to see the proof of inheritance himself, rather than taking his sister's word for it. But . . . how did Bev figure out it was Jaymie who questioned it?

The ladies had exited the shop in a bunch, chattering and throwing anxious glances over their shoulders. Jaymie could see out the big picture window that one of them trotted down the front steps and bustled over to the bus driver, an older African-American gentleman, who lounged in the open door of his vehicle where it was parked in a spot beyond the Emporium porch. She chattered at him, gesticulating toward the store.

Taking a deep breath, Jaymie calmed herself and focused back on her antagonist. "Bev, where did you get the idea I had been questioning if you stole Miss Perry's silver?"

"Who do you *think* told me?" she asked, flinging her hands up in the air and stumping over to the glass-topped case that acted as a sales desk. "After the cops got done with me I called here and Georgina said it wasn't her, and it certainly wasn't her brother, that it was *you*." She hammered on the glass. It rattled alarmingly. "*You* were the one who had questioned her about it, and then went and squealed to him. She said he felt he had no choice but to pull the silver from the catalogue and call the police in yet *again!*"

The bus driver entered, the door chime jingling, and approached, warily eyeing them both, his dark eyes taking in the scene. "Miss, do you need me to call the police?" he asked Jaymie. "Some of my ladies are alarmed."

Bev glared at him, then at Jaymie, and bitterly shook her head. "Never mind, I'm going. Wouldn't want to be interviewed by the police yet *again!*" She lumbered out, her boot making a *thump thump thump* echoing sound on the wood floor.

The rest of the day was anticlimactic. When her sister's group returned, Jaymie did not tell Kevin and Becca that Georgina had blamed her to Bev Hastings. She didn't want to make things worse, and to discuss it would surely make it into a siblings-against-siblings argument, with the married couple forced to side with each other's sibling or their own. Bev Hastings would surely simmer down. If she was as full of outraged innocence as she seemed, then there was nothing for her to worry about.

• • •

SATURDAYS WERE STILL WORK DAYS for Jaymie and Jakob, so it was a day Jocie often spent with her Oma and Opa and cousins at the farm. That morning Jaymie went with Jakob to an auction, and then home for an intimate lunch at the cabin. They parted ways for the afternoon, he to walk the Christmas trees with Helmut, marking more of them for cutting in another month or so, and she to go to Miss Perry's home to get the spice graters for the exhibition. She had confirmation that Miss Perry had indeed been sent home to recuperate and was out of danger. She called Bill Waterman. He had the cases stained and shellacked; the only thing left was for them to dry completely. Once they had the graters mounted, he would lock the cases and bolt them to the wall in the heritage house kitchen.

The wind was up, and gusts carried drifts of falling leaves raining down over the roads toward town. Jaymie drove carefully, grateful for the gift her parents had given her in making sure she had a better vehicle than the rattletrap van she had nursed along for a decade. Through town, and along River Road up to Winding Woods, she drove as rain started sheeting down, reminding her of the day she found Miss Perry. She couldn't believe the lady was home already, given how frail and battered she had seemed, but if she had twenty-four-seven care, then home was no doubt where she longed to be.

Bill had sent her photos of the cases; she had them on her phone so she could show Miss Perry. She also had a notepad and pen at the ready so she could take down the history of the graters, as she'd be writing a pamphlet to give away at the heritage house. She looked forward to telling Miss Perry her ideas for teaching the kids about the spice trade and Queensville's part in it.

She caught glimpses of the St. Clair River as she followed River Road to her turnoff onto Winding Woods Lane. The stiff wind was gusting the gray water, churning it into whitecaps as rain blew across the surface. Once more it was obscured, now by the stately homes of Winding Woods. She drove past Haskell's house and pulled up to Miss Perry's residence, sullen in the leaden daylight. Morgan's silver sedan was in the drive. Jaymie dashed up to the porch and banged on the door. Morgan answered and nodded when Jaymie told her why she was there.

The young woman stood back to let Jaymie slip through. She took off her windbreaker and hung it on the coat tree to dry, then followed Morgan back to Miss Perry's sitting room. It had been rearranged and a hospital bed brought in. But Miss Perry was not in bed, she was sitting in her favorite chair, her table by her with a cup of tea, a box of tissues, bottles of over-the-counter pain reliever, cough drops, and other inevitable accouterments of old age. The TV was tuned to a colorful game show, kooky costumed contestants laughing and flailing and apparently yelling out answers, though the set was muted.

Jaymie paused at the door; Miss Perry looked so fragile, her thin arms bare, the shawl she had over her shoulders slipping down. Bruised and battered by her fall, who knows what a toll this would take on her, at her age? Jaymie's eyes welled with tears and her stomach roiled. It was infuriating, whoever had done this, and she was shaken by how angry it made her. She *must* find out who was responsible, or how was the woman ever going to be safe?

"Where is her nurse?" Jaymie whispered to Morgan, who stood at her shoulder.

The young woman looked blank. "Nurse?"

"She was released with twenty-four-hour nursing care, right?"

"No, there's just me."

Jaymie took a moment to digest that. The hospital had released Miss Perry to her niece when an attempt had been made on her life? An attempt that, if successful, would benefit Morgan to the tune of at least half a million dollars in property — the house and the riverside land — and maybe more? It was . . . alarming. But what could she do about it? Adjusting her expression to a smile, she entered and approached the woman's chair.

"Hey, I'm surprised you're home!" she said, leaning over and giving her a hug.

"*Hate* hospitals. Suppose I was cranky enough they wanted to get rid of me." She shuffled her feet, which were clad in fluffy slippers.

Jaymie pictured the scene, recalling the moccasin slippers, new-looking, at the bottom of the stairs. Had someone intended to make it look like she had accidentally fallen down the stairs? But how did that fit with the wire across the stairs? Whoever did that must have known it would be found when she was discovered. Maybe they intended to sneak back in and remove the wire once she was dead.

She shivered. It was something to ponder, but right now she knew the lady was staring at her quizzically. "Let's get down to business, shall we?" she said brightly.

This was going to take longer than she had anticipated, she soon decided, because Miss Perry was in no shape to answer the dozens of questions Jaymie had. Slowly, steadily, Jaymie did coax some information about the graters from Miss Perry, but her strength was soon flagging. A cup of tea, she explained, would help her think. Morgan was on the phone and nodded when Jaymie suggested she go ahead and make the tea. She boiled the pot, and went to the back door while she waited for the tea to steep, needing a moment to relax her mind. She looked out the back-door window and noted a flash of red by the bluff . . . a cardinal maybe? She squinted and stared but didn't see it again.

She took a tray in to her new acquaintance. Tea was drunk, the pause refreshed, and they went on with their conversation.

"I've been thinking about it, which graters you should use." Miss Perry twisted in her seat and called, "Morgan! Come here!"

Her niece came to the door, a bottle of prescription eye drops in her hand.

"Can you gather the graters up for me?" She then listed several; Morgan must have been very familiar with the collection to know them by description. She capped the bottle and disappeared.

Jaymie wrote down the names of the graters as she waited for Morgan to reappear. But when the young woman did, it was with a puzzled look. She laid out a bunch of the nutmeg and other spice graters, but then said, "Auntie Lois, I can't find the acorn-shaped one. Did you take it out of the display?"

"I did *not!*" the woman said. "Where could it be?"

Jaymie followed Morgan and they searched the display room, but it was nowhere. Morgan fretfully described it. "It's small . . . the smallest of the collection. Sterling silver, and shaped like an acorn. Where could it be?"

A howl outside startled them both, and Morgan clutched Jaymie's arm. "What was that?"

"Probably just Lan Zane's dog, Tiberius, right? He seems to get away from Lan often."

The howl got closer, the sound moving, heading toward the back; there was more ferocious barking, and the loud, frightened screech of a terrified animal shrilled through the house. Jaymie headed toward the back of the house, ducking in to Miss Perry's sitting room to make sure she stayed put.

"My poor kitties!" Miss Perry cried, alarmed. She got up, leaning heavily on her chair, but then tottered to the sitting room door, hand outstretched. "Save the poor things, will you, Morgan?"

But Morgan, an irresolute look on her face as she stood in the dim hall, shook her head. "Lan will get his damned dog, Auntie Lois. Stop worrying about those stupid strays!"

The screeching got louder and a wail, piercing and heartrending, echoed into the house. Miss Perry, her face drained of color, the bandage still wrapped around her head and seeping, wept, tears racing down and dripping onto her flowered robe. Swiftly, Jaymie made a decision. Morgan was clearly not going to do a thing about it, so *she* would.

"Morgan, help your aunt sit down before she falls down. *I'll* take care of that dog," she said over her shoulder as she raced to the front of the house, retrieved her shoes, and returned, headed toward the back, hopping and skipping as she slipped her shoes on. "I can't bear to hear that poor cat being hurt," she said over her shoulder as she raced past the sitting room.

She ran out the door into the pelting rain, fearing what she'd see. Tiberius was at the farthest reach of the yard, barking furiously at something hidden in the depths of the shrubbery. A yowl told her that the cat was likely badly frightened, but hopefully not hurt. She raced across the grass, slipping and sliding, hearing behind her Lan Zane calling his dog, his voice getting closer. She came up to the animal; the dog was playful, both paws thrust forward, tail wagging, barking at the hidden cat that howled in displeasure.

But she could see something else — was it a pant leg and white leather shoe? A pale blue pant leg and white leather tasseled loafer that she had seen before, worn by . . . she pushed in and parted the branches.

Fergus Baird lay in the brush, his face mottled purple, his mouth agape, a silver nutmeg grater shoved into his mouth. He was dead, and had been for some time.

⌠ Twelve ⌠

"TIBERIUS! DOWN, *TIBERIUS*. What's going on?" Lan Zane, huffing and puffing, raced across the grass.

Jaymie backed out of the brush, turned, and put her hand up. "Take your dog out of the yard." When he stood, staring at her, she grabbed the dog's collar and thrust the pooch at his owner. "Go! *Now!*" Because of her varied experiences over the last two years, she knew what needed to be done, and none of it was for the body that was once Fergus Baird, poor fellow. The only thing anyone could do for him at this point was to find out who killed him.

Jaymie followed, as the neighbor hustled his dog past the house and along the walk between, but diverged from Zane's path to approach the back door of the house. Morgan, her face white, her body trembling, stared out at her through the open door. It was odd that the woman hadn't come out to see if everything was okay. And why, if she was just going to stand there, was she not with her aunt, making sure *she* was all right?

Unless she had known all along what Jaymie would find out there under the shrubbery. Maybe that was why she so absolutely resisted being the one to go out and take care of the problem. Jaymie's suspicions crept down her backbone in a nervous shudder. Nothing about this made sense, especially why Fergus Baird's body had been shoved in the bushes along the back of Miss Perry's property. "Get me my phone, please. It's on the table by Miss Perry." She had been about to show the woman the pictures of the cases Bill had made.

Morgan obeyed without even asking why, retreating and returning, handing Jaymie the phone out the back door.

"Go back to Miss Perry," Jaymie said. "There's been an incident and I have to . . . take care of something, but tell Miss Perry that the cat is fine. Cats are the drama queens of nature. They always sound like they're dying when they're just angry. Tiberius didn't harm it, he scared it." When the young woman disappeared back into the house, Jaymie sheltered under the eaves from the rain, which had plastered her bangs down over her forehead and dripped into her eyes, and made the call to 911.

• • •

IT WAS A CRIME SCENE, of course, with all the attendant confusion and neighborly interest, Winding Woods Lane lined with police vehicles. Jaymie—wet, cold and shivering—sat by Miss Perry. She had been forced to tell the lady that she had found a body, but she hadn't elaborated. She did *not* tell Morgan who it was. Miss Perry assumed it was "one of those foolish walkers" who had fallen down the cliff, and there was no point in clarifying. The police would do that soon enough.

Detective Angela Vestry had arrived on the scene. Chief Ledbetter, Jaymie's friend, had lauded the woman as one of the best detectives he'd worked with in his long law enforcement career, but she certainly lacked his personal charm. However, since when did a detective *require* charm? She was an effective investigator, one the new chief of police, Deborah Connolly, relied on.

Officer Ng summoned Jaymie. She followed him out the back door and he pointed her toward Detective Vestry, who stood inside the taped perimeter that cordoned off the back half of the lawn. At least the rain had stopped, though it still dripped from trees overhead and clung to bushes that had not yet shed their leaves. Jaymie, damp and shivering, approached with trepidation. The detective had once expressed skepticism about Jaymie's habit of finding dead bodies, and this was one more example.

Faced with that skepticism and doubt from the detective and others, Jaymie had pondered the pattern. It seemed to her that it was mostly because she was involved in so many of her community's events, societies and groups. Combined with her innate curiosity—nosiness, Valetta called it—it meant she was more apt than most to discovery. Like today; if she had hauled the dog away without looking to see if the cat was all right, who knew how long Baird would have lain there? Someone else would have found him, but not so soon.

Armed with this argument, she was therefore surprised by Vestry's bland expression when she said, "Tell me what happened, Ms. Leighton."

"Leighton Müller," Jaymie corrected automatically, before launching into a description of her day. She finished by saying, "I went looking for the cat to make sure he was okay. That's when I saw the body stuffed into the hedge. I recognized the pants and shoes right away. Mr. Baird had a habit of dressing in pastels, and I knew the white loafers from seeing them on him the other day. I parted the bushes and saw his face." She paused, but then went ahead, determined to tell all she knew. "I recognized that silver thing in his mouth; it's an antique nutmeg grater. Like . . . like the ones in Miss Perry's collection."

If Vestry was startled by the revelation, she didn't show it. It was plaguing Jaymie, though, because she was trying to remember if it was one Miss Perry had shown her on her first visit. Was it even the missing one Morgan had been complaining about? When she mentioned that, and the detective asked why that mattered, she replied, "It matters because Miss Perry suffered a break-in and theft some time ago. If the grater hadn't been seen since, then it could have been stolen at the same time as the other silver. But if I saw it, it means the grater was stolen between that day and the moment it was shoved into Mr. Baird's mouth."

The wind was coming up and blowing brisk and cold. Standing outside in damp clothes and sodden shoes, without a warm dry sweater or coat, she shivered, frigid to the core of her being. Or maybe it was a belated reaction to finding another body. Her stomach roiled and she swallowed back a rising sick feeling.

Vestry eyed Jaymie. "You have lately been accusing Mrs. Beverly Hastings of playing a part in that theft, isn't that true?"

"No, not exactly." Jaymie told the detective everything about the silver, and how unlikely it seemed that another local would have a complete set of Savoy by Buccellati. "It's my sister and brother-in-law's shop. I was concerned. It seems odd to me, you know? One coincidence too many." She made a swift decision and added, "There's more, Detective. I don't know if they're in it together or not, but I wonder if Bev Hastings, at least—maybe not Jon, I don't know—was trying to help Fergus Baird buy the dockside property from Miss Perry."

The detective gazed steadily at her, pale brows raised in skepticism. "Are you seriously suggesting Miss Perry herself killed Baird and planted him in the shrubbery with one of her silver grater thingies shoved down his throat because he was trying to buy her land?"

"Of *course* not!" Jaymie's cheeks burned with embarrassment, and her back went up, irritation that she was being treated like a flake flooding through her. "I'm telling you what I think."

"Stick to solid information, Ms. Leighton, not conjecture."

Leighton Müller, Jaymie thought, but this time did not say. Her respect for the detective's acuity went down a notch. At least Chief Ledbetter had listened to her, no matter how far-fetched her thoughts had seemed at the time. She was not a trained professional, true, but she did have some insight and it didn't cost anything to listen.

Morgan came to the back door and stared down the lawn at them. So . . . after that warning from the detective, tell about the affair she suspected between Morgan Perry Wallace and Fergus Baird or not? After all, it might not even be an affair, she couldn't know for sure. Jaymie decided only to tell if she was asked directly.

Vestry dismissed her with a casual, "We'll be in touch, Ms. Leighton."

Jaymie returned to the house, slipping through the back door to find Morgan standing in the kitchen waiting, one hand resting on the worn kitchen counter, her index finger following a scar in the work surface, stroking it over and over.

"What did you say to her?" Morgan asked, her eyes clouded and a tense, expectant expression on her round face. She blinked and squinted, looking anxious.

Jaymie paused. If Morgan knew it was Fergus Baird lying dead out there then any feelings of heartbreak or sadness were overlaid with something more worrying. Fear, perhaps, or guilt? Without knowing her better she could not guess.

"How much do you know about what's going on out there?" Jaymie asked.

"I know it's Fergus. I saw the . . . the shoes. Even from a distance I could tell. What happened?"

"He's dead."

"I know that, but I mean . . . how?"

"I don't know."

"Surely you know *something*?" Her nail caught that scratch in the countertop, picking away at the laminated surface, chipping at it until there was a little pile of arborite scraps.

Jaymie shook her head.

"What . . . what did you tell that woman, the detective?"

"You mean about you and Fergus?"

Morgan's breath caught, but she nodded.

"I didn't tell her anything, but if I were you, I'd fill her in completely on your . . . relationship."

The young woman whirled and grabbed the kettle from the stove, filling it with water and slamming it down, turning on the jet. "That's none of your business."

"True," Jaymie said. "I'm going to check on your aunt."

Miss Perry, white with exhaustion and trembling with pain—she was past time for her pain medication, but it made her sleepy and confused, she said, not how she wanted to be when she spoke to the police—was more worried about the safety of her colony of feral cats than her own suffering, or even the dead body in her yard. "Those police won't shoot them, will they?"

"Of course not. I'm sure the cats will be hiding anyway, Miss Perry."

"Call me Lois, dear," the woman said with a confiding look, her eyes watery. "My cousin is right about you, you know. You're . . . solid."

Jaymie smiled briefly.

"Oh, I don't mean physically," she said, waving her blue-veined hand. "Plump girls worry too much about that anyway. I mean solid like . . ." Her voice drifted off, and she winced, some stab of pain giving her trouble. "You're reliable. So few people are anymore. Or maybe that's just me getting old."

The kettle whistled. "I'll make some more tea," Jaymie said, squeezing the woman's hand.

"I don't know what's happened to Morgan," she said fretfully as the teakettle whistle shrilled.

Jaymie retreated to the kitchen, but Morgan had disappeared. She refilled the teapot, got out her phone, texting Jakob that she might be late, then called her mother-in-law to see if Jocie was okay to stay with them for dinner. Mrs. Müller said it was perfectly all right. Jocie could stay over; her cousins were, and they would all be ecstatic if Jocie could, too. When Jaymie fretted about Hoppy and Lilibet, she was assured that Helmut would take Jocie over to the cabin and bring both animals back to the Müller farm, where there was a fenced yard and people who loved them both.

Jaymie gave her a message to relay to Jakob, in case he didn't get her text. She was fine. She would be home the moment she could, but she was not going to leave Miss Perry alone if she could help it. Sighing in relief to have such a brilliant support system, she rinsed out their cups, then made the tea and took it to Miss Perry.

"Miss Perry . . . uh, Lois . . ." She shook her head. It didn't feel right to call her by her first name. "I understood that you were to be released from the hospital with nursing care. Are you sure Morgan's capable of taking care of everything you need?"

"Nursing care?" the woman said with a quizzical frown. "I don't know anything about that. I let Morgan take care of it and she said I could go home, and that she'd stay with me." She picked up the remote and turned the TV up, tuned to another game show, all noise and bright color, then closed her eyes, softly snoring after a few minutes.

Sleep would be a relief from pain; she'd let her slumber. Jaymie picked up the remote and turned down the racket. Worry gnawed and ached in the pit of her stomach. She didn't think she could even handle tea at this point. Who was responsible for trying to kill Miss Perry? Morgan had every motive. On multiple levels her aunt's death would materially benefit her, and she had just tried to get the woman to sign over control of her life and assets with a POA. And now Fergus Baird was dead, his body in Miss Perry's backyard. There were weird happenings afoot. Jaymie could not, in good conscience, leave Miss Perry alone with just Morgan.

Decision made, and knowing Morgan—if she was the murderous niece Jaymie hoped she wasn't—wouldn't try anything with the current police presence, Jaymie slipped out to her SUV. No one stopped her, no one questioned her, so she drove away to the Queensville Inn. Afternoon was waning. Weak sunlight was trying to burn off the clouds, but unsuccessfully so far. Dull shadows were lengthening over the still-green grass as she went directly to the sliding glass doors on the terrace by Mrs. Stubbs's room.

Her friend had been dozing in her mobility chair, an open large-print book on her lap, the sun streaming in on her, warming her arthritic hands, but waved Jaymie in when she tapped on the sliding glass doors. After Jaymie's long relation of what had happened that afternoon, Mrs. Stubbs was lost in thought.

"Well, what do you think?" Jaymie said, fidgeting anxiously. She paced to the glass door, worrying over the dwindling light and her sureness that the police would be wrapping up the investigation for the night very soon. "Am I being paranoid?" she asked, turning to her friend. "Tell me I'm nuts."

"I wish I could. Get me my phone and my address book on the shelf above the counter."

Jaymie did as she was told, and Mrs. Stubbs took the phone. She kept the coil-bound book open on her lap and followed a number with one crooked finger as she punched it in. She gave her name; it was clear by the ensuing conversation that they knew her. They put her through to someone, as she covered the mouthpiece.

"There are few benefits to being my age," she said to Jaymie, "but one is, I know exactly how to get proper care." Her gaze shifted, and she answered yes to someone on the other end of the line. It swiftly became clear what she had decided as she ordered twenty-four-hour-a-day nursing for her cousin, who had come home from the hospital and was doing poorly. The nurse would arrive within the hour at the address on Winding Woods Lane and would work a twelve-hour shift, before being replaced by another. He — Mrs. Stubbs asked for a certain nurse named Skip Buchanon — was registered and adept with geriatric patients, and would provide his identification when he arrived. Mrs. Stubbs made it very clear that she was worried about her cousin's safety, as there had been a murder near the house and the perpetrator might be lurking anywhere.

"Now, go back there. I'll call Morgan and tell her what I've done. I'll say it was my idea because Lois is so fragile. You did the right thing."

Relief flooded through Jaymie and she even teared up. "Thank you, Mrs. Stubbs. I wouldn't have been able to leave Miss Perry alone but for your excellent idea."

"Now, go pick up soup or something and take it back, and tell Morgan you had errands to do. Remember . . . it's not necessarily a bad thing if she thinks you had anything to do with what I've done. If she's guilty, then she'll know multiple eyes are on her. And if she's not, then she has nothing to fear, right?"

℘ Thirteen ℘

BECAUSE SHE STOPPED AT THE EMPORIUM to get some things for Miss Perry — soup, pudding, Jell-O and ice cream — she arrived at the Winding Woods Lane residence about the same time as the nurse, a young African-American fellow, Skip Buchanan, who was driving a smartcar with the name of the nursing service on the side. She pulled up to the curb, waited while he got out his bag, and noticed him looking at the police cars. Round-faced, with a fringe of close-cropped beard rimming his chin, about the same length as his close-cropped hair, he was dressed in green scrubs and around his neck had a lanyard with his identification tag and affiliation.

She strode over to him, her grocery bag dangling from one hand, and introduced herself, shaking his hand and telling him she was acquainted with both his patient and her cousin, who had called the service to arrange his help.

"I know Mrs. Stubbs; *love* her!" he said with a broad, toothy smile. His voice was light, pleasant, with a soothing quality. "Whenever I've looked after her we play euchre and she beats me every time. So what's going on here?" he asked, following her up the steps to the porch, hoisting his duffel bag on his muscular shoulder.

"They didn't tell you?"

"No."

She stayed him with one hand on his arm as he grabbed the doorknob, and quickly filled him in. He held her gaze, his dark brown eyes thoughtful as he nodded and interjected occasional sharp questions. When she was done, he paused, then said, "There's something you're not telling me. Is Miss Perry in danger?"

"I don't know," she said, relieved at not having to raise the idea herself. "But obviously I don't want her life at risk."

"And so, twenty-four-hour care. You're not even sure of the people closest to her, am I right?"

"I didn't say that," Jaymie said, shying from the notion of accusing Morgan, or anyone else. "I . . . I don't know *anything* for certain," she said, feeling tears well up. "But I didn't want to take any chances. She's a cranky, difficult, *dear* old lady, and she's important to Mrs. Stubbs."

"Don't worry," Skip said, turning the knob. "I got this."

Morgan was furious, Jaymie could see that right away as Skip Buchanon introduced himself, told her he was sent by Miss Perry's cousin, Mrs. Stubbs, who was concerned for the well-being of her relative. He took her hand, shook it briefly, and said he'd see his patient now, so they could get acquainted.

"I don't want you here," Morgan said, facing the nurse, her whole body stiff with outrage. Her fierce whisper echoed in the dim hallway.

This was a delicate and difficult spot, and as much as Jaymie wanted to tell the woman this was how it was going to be, she hesitated. If Morgan talked Miss Perry into telling Skip to go home, there wasn't much he could do but comply. No one could force nursing on her if she didn't want it. Jaymie slipped away from the confrontation in the hall and headed to Miss Perry's temporary bedroom.

The woman was awake and fretful. "What's going on out there? I heard a man's voice. Who is it?"

"Miss Perry, how are you doing?"

"Not so good. Have I . . . did I take my pills? Where is Morgan . . . that *girl*! *Morgan*! Did I take . . ." She shook her head, and her gaze drifted back to the TV.

Jaymie, alarmed, took her hand. "Miss Perry, *Miss Perry*!"

"Mhm?"

"Mrs. Stubbs was worried about you, so she sent a registered nurse to look after you. Is that all right?"

She nodded, closing her eyes. "Good."

"Miss Perry, the nurse is a man. Is that okay too?" She nodded again. "He'll stay all night to make sure you're safe, and have the right meds, and that your vitals are okay. That way Morgan can go home and get some sleep."

"Okay, dear."

Skip Buchanan came in that moment and stood by the door, assessing the situation. He eyed the hospital bed, the recliner, his patient. Morgan was throwing things around in the kitchen; it appeared she had lost the battle. Jaymie met Skip's gaze. He nodded, smiled, then indicated for Jaymie to let him replace her. He sat down on a low stool next to Miss Perry and took her hand, gently placing fingers on her pulse and looking at his watch.

She opened her eyes. "Who are you?"

He softly explained, and Jaymie chimed in, reminding her what they had discussed. She smiled, nodded, and let him go about his task, which was to review her medication schedule, as given on her hospital release papers. There was comfort, it seemed, in having a professional in charge.

"Your pulse is a little quick, Miss Perry, but some of the meds you're on can have that effect. I'm going to call the hospital in a moment to make sure your current prescriptions are the right dose. One of these concerns me."

"The local pharmacist is a good friend of mine," Jaymie said. "She's available at all times, and will open her pharmacy if something is needed. I'll give you her number."

"Is that Valetta Nibley you're talking about?"

Jaymie nodded.

"I've spoken to her many times, and have her number. Miss Perry, when was the last time you ate?"

Jaymie slipped out to the hallway, where Morgan stood, appearing undecided. "I had nothing to do with this. Mrs. Stubbs called the nursing service when she heard her cousin was home." Walking past her, then, through the kitchen, Jaymie gazed out the back door. The light was dwindling into twilight, and Jaymie longed for her home and her husband and her little girl with a fierceness that surprised her. She hadn't processed finding that poor man's body yet; the thought of it haunted her, the sense of life's fragility, the razor's-edge dance we all perform.

One moment; life rested on one single moment in time, a pinpoint, one bad decision, one mistake. It was terrifying.

The police were still on scene, but it appeared that while she was in town the coroner had taken away Fergus Baird. That, at least, was good. She didn't know him well, but no human should have so undignified a fate.

Morgan followed her to the back door. "I wasn't having an affair with him, you know," she said, her voice tight, fraught with indecipherable emotion.

Jaymie turned. Morgan's round face was ghostly white in the darkness of the back hall, by the stairs where Miss Perry had fallen, the normal pinkness of her cheeks paled to faintest peach, her eyes rimmed with red. "I never assumed that," Jaymie replied. "I was surprised, that's all, when I saw you two kissing in the drugstore in Wolverhampton."

"That . . . the kiss took me completely by surprise. I didn't know he thought of me that way. I would have told him . . . I would have said . . ." She shook her head and choked back a dry sob.

"I'm sorry, though, if he was a friend. I know Miss Perry didn't like him. I saw them having a ferocious argument about the fate of the marina buildings that she owns." Baird had said right then and there that Miss Perry was better off dead so Morgan could inherit and sell the land to him. They must have already spoken of it for him to be so certain. And yet *he* was the one who lay dead.

Morgan made a face. "She's such a crank about those decrepit old buildings."

"Your family has owned them for a long, long time. They represent something to her; they're a symbol of another time, I suppose."

"Fergus wanted what was best for the town, to see some *real* progress there instead of stinky old bait shops."

Progress: condos for the wealthy rather than shops for the regular folks. There was no point in telling Morgan that right now. "Did you know he was friends with Bev Hastings, too? That's the woman who co-owns the bait shop with her husband. Did Mr. Baird ever tell you they had some sort of relationship?"

She looked blank and shook her head. A noise behind them made them both turn; it was Morgan's husband, Saunders Wallace. How long had he been standing there? Jaymie wondered.

"What's going on out there?" he asked. "Why are there police everywhere? And a car from some nursing service?"

"There was . . . an incident," Morgan said.

"Is Aunt Lois okay?"

"She's all right," Jaymie said, watching his face. He was visibly relieved and nodded. "The nurse is looking after Miss Perry so Morgan can go home and get some rest."

"So what's the incident? Are *you* okay, Morgan?"

"It's Fergus Baird, that developer who was trying to get Auntie Lois to sell her land down by the river," Morgan replied. "He's . . . he's dead. Someone killed him."

"What was he doing *here*?"

"Nobody knows."

Jaymie wondered the same thing. Had he been killed on the spot or moved there? When the couple moved off toward the front of the house to talk in private, she turned on the overhead light in the back hall. She had been curious about the wire, and its placement. She hunkered down to see if she could tell where it had been and there, about four steps from the bottom, she could see a screw eye, shiny against the dark stain of the stair stringer. No attempt had been made to make it blend in. Maybe whoever did it knew Miss Perry's eyesight was not great, and perhaps they intended to come back and remove the assembly before the woman was found, dead.

When she rose and headed back to the kitchen, she heard her own voice floating through the home, telling Miss Perry she'd be there in two minutes. It was her message from the other day. Morgan was at the old-fashioned answering machine patiently erasing each message.

Jaymie stopped, stock-still, remembering coming up Winding Woods Lane and the dark pickup truck tearing downhill at her, forcing her to swerve. Was that why the wire assembly hadn't been removed? Had someone been in the house about to do it, but her call told them how soon they'd have company? And yet, Miss Perry had been lying there for some time, evidenced by the crusted blood in her hair and the housedress.

It was something to ponder.

Weary and heartsick, she finally headed out the door, reassured by Skip Buchanon's solid presence, calm manner, and skilful handling of Miss Perry's crankiness. Morgan seemed to have accepted the nurse; she'd stated her intention of heading home with her husband. The police would be there overnight, since there was still a search on for the perpetrator of the murder on the bluff. They would be canvassing neighbors and searching the whole area.

Jaymie paused out on the walk, in the twilight, shivering and pulling her windbreaker around her, hugging herself as she gathered her thoughts. She eyed the house, and the police cars, and pondered poor Fergus Baird, not just *why* he had been killed but why *here*, and why with the nutmeg grater in his mouth? It was a message, but to whom? Or was it deflection? He appeared to be a successful home builder and as such would have assets; who inherited them? There was so very much she didn't know.

Lan Zane, his red Columbia windbreaker zipped up to his chin against the cold evening breeze and the perpetual dog leash wound around one hand, strode toward her. "So . . . I heard that someone fell and broke their neck or something? Is that true? But the body was in the bushes, not at the bottom of the bluff, so . . . did they fall, then crawl up the hill?" His voice was jittery and tense, and he bounced from foot to foot.

"I don't think I can talk about it, Lan. The police are involved now."

"Oh, come on! You can tell *me*. Is there some mad killer out there we should know about?" His jocular tone fell flat, and so did his smile. "My wife is worried, that's all. She was upset when Miss Perry's home was broken into."

"Did you see or hear anything that time?"

He shook his head. "Not a thing, and as far as I know, no one else's place was broken into, just hers. Of course, *we* all have up-to-date security systems. I have a gun safe full of rifles and a valuable coin collection, and Phillipa's jewelry alone would make a junkie say hallelujah."

"What about the day I found Miss Perry hurt? Were you or your wife home? Did you see anything?"

"No to both!"

Lan eyed a police car that pulled up to the curb, and retreated abruptly. Jaymie watched him go, wondering about his jitteriness.

Bernie got out and approached Jaymie, smiling. "How did I know you'd still be here? When I got the word that you'd found another body, I just shook my head."

"It has not escaped me that I'm a trouble magnet."

"Jaymie, don't say that. Especially in this case. Don't you think his family would rather he was found? My understanding is, if you hadn't discovered his body he may have lain there for a while."

She nodded, but Bernie's words had made her thoughts hare off in another direction. Did the killer want Baird to be found or not? The facts indicated both. Where he was, hidden in the bushes, was concealed enough she hadn't seen him until she was right there. But the nutmeg grater in his mouth? That was done to send a message. Or perhaps to mislead.

"What are you thinking?"

She was thinking about Lan and Phillipa Zane. Jaymie explained to Bernie that they had a contentious relationship with Miss Perry. If they murdered her, it wouldn't be the first time a fight between neighbors resulted in death. So the attempt to kill *her* could have been planned by the Zanes, but why Fergus Baird? That didn't make *any* sense if they were the culprits. But surely an attempted murder and an actual murder at the same residence were likely connected.

And . . . the nutmeg grater was a pointed tie-in with Miss Perry, her collection, and perhaps even her position in the community. Was it planned simply to point the finger of blame *away* from the Zanes, so it would look like someone was after *both* Miss Perry and Fergus Baird? Lan clearly knew that Miss Perry had no security system for her house. And the timing of the body find was suspicious; Lan knew that when his dog was loose it invariably headed for Miss Perry's backyard on the hunt for the feral cats she valued and cared for. A devious mind would plant the body, and if it wasn't found in a timely manner send the dog into the yard. The pooch would surely find the dead body and bark like crazy, alerting her, as it did, or anyone else who was in the house. It was a circuitous plot, but possible. "Lan knows my car," Jaymie said after explaining her thoughts. "He'd *know* I was here and that I would follow the dog to collar it because I've done it before."

"That's not the *most* far-fetched possibility," Bernie said, pursing her lips in thought.

"But pretty close, right? I don't dare say all this to Detective Vestry. She basically told me to take a hike."

"I know you and the detective don't get along, but she likes me, so I'll mention it to her. The rest of the department might not appreciate me, but *she* does."

"What do you mean, the rest of the department doesn't appreciate you?"

Bernie shrugged. "It started with Chief Ledbetter. Some of the guys insinuated that he favored me because I'm a woman. Now, no matter what I've done since, there's always muttering that I don't deserve the promotion, or I'm being favored for assignments, and lately, with Chief Connolly and Detective Vestry in charge, it's gotten worse. Some of the fellows are getting downright rude about it. I can't even say out loud the names they're giving the department now, with women in charge."

Jaymie felt a burning anger well up in her. Bernie worked harder than any one of the other cops, and everyone knew it. She took extra training; she worked out; she was taking online courses in criminology toward a master's: in other words, she dedicated herself one hundred percent. But still, some would say that her advancements were because she was a woman, and more particularly a woman of color, that she was favored because of some diversity targets in the department. It was crap. Jaymie glanced around, then stepped forward and hugged her friend. "Bernie, you're the most driven person I've ever met," she murmured in her ear. "And I know you don't need me to say it, but you'll blow those other guys out of the water and make detective before any of them."

She smiled and nodded, stepping back. "Thanks, Jaymie. I'd better get going; I'm relieving Ng. At least he's been cool about everything. He's not one of the dicks who are giving me trouble." She had dated him briefly, but a relationship between police officers was difficult to maintain. Waving, she turned and headed off around the side of the house toward the backyard and the cluster of police still investigating.

Rattled and feeling overwhelmed, Jaymie drove home. Jakob was there and waiting. When she came in and dropped her purse, he wrapped her in his arms. They stood for several minutes, in a tight embrace, her head on his shoulder.

"You okay?" he finally asked, his voice gruff.

"I am now."

ẞ Fourteen ẞ

JAYMIE WAS STILL DEEPLY DISTRESSED by the day's events. She kept thinking of Baird's family, and what a shock it was going to be to learn the news. She offered to go pick up Jocie at her in-laws' place. Jakob suggested that instead they spend some alone time: no animals, no child, just the two of them. Jocie and the animals were completely happy at the Müllers' home, he assured her.

Their marriage was still so new. She hadn't even known Jakob a year. His willingness to invest his time, his passion, his love into her was what made it work. Sharing it all, their love was growing day by day. Of all the things she had ever done in her life, this was the most impulsive, but sometimes when it's right, it's right.

And this was right on every level. She happily acquiesced.

An autumnal wind came up, shuddering outside the cabin, making the windows rattle. It was only October, but it was Michigan. The temperature dropped, and the wind howled on, but inside it was toasty warm. Jakob had built a fire in the big stone fireplace he had constructed himself from stones picked over the years from the Müller farmland; he had used it to heat the whole cabin before he married, had a child, and installed a furnace. By the warmth of it they talked, ate pizza, drank — cheap wine for her, beer for him — made love, then talked some more, long into the night. In his arms all of the violence and fear, all the heartache she witnessed, melted away.

Sunday morning they went to the Müllers to pick up Jocie and the animals but stayed for brunch. Jaymie made a frittata for them all while Sonya, Helmut's significant other, cooked bacon and ham. Jakob and Helmut spent more time discussing the launch of their tree nursery business, set to go within the next year; the new Christmas store business was next on the roster for full-scale planning. Jaymie had married someone like her in so many ways: they shared a deep love of home and family, the aptitude to keep a lot of businesses and jobs going at once, and the knack of going with the flow.

The senior Müllers' home was family headquarters and was always full of people, chatter, children, animals, and chaos, with Dieter Senior and Renate, usually known as Opa and Oma, the blissful, calm center. Becca, who had only spent a couple of afternoons with the whole Müller clan, had come away dazed, and wondering, she said, how Jaymie managed. In that sense Jaymie fit in better with the Müllers than with her own calm, quiet, laid-back, small Leighton family. The chaos whirled around her and she smiled through it all.

The rest of Sunday they spent as a family, first with Jocie's cousins, then taking Hoppy and Jocie for a long walk over the new property, through the corn stubble and to the top of what would someday be a toboggan hill. Jaymie described it all, and how much fun it would be, a real family business right next to the log cabin. She also pointed out a clump of bushes around an old oak tree in the middle of the property, and how, in the distance, they could see a long line of pine trees. "That's probably the wind break for the house on the next road, the one the former landowners were keeping." The sale had gone through and they now owned the land, her savings invested too, giving her a stake in their future. It was a gamble, but even if they couldn't change the zoning to include a commercial aspect, they could still use the land.

Then it was home for dinner, a board game or two, and a movie. It was a school night, so bedtime was early. While Jakob was reading a story with Jocie and talking about their day, Jaymie cuddled Hoppy on the sofa and called around, once to check in on Miss Perry, who was improving under professional nursing care—Skip was back on duty for another twelve-hour shift after his replacement left—and a few more calls to set up a girls' night for Valetta, Heidi, Bernie and herself. It would have been so easy to lose touch with her girlfriends, with the frenetic pace of her new life and all its attendant responsibilities. It did get overwhelming at times, but she made a sustained effort and got together with them all at least once a month, but usually more often.

With Valetta, her best friend, she talked a lot longer. For one thing, Valetta insisted on having the girls' night at her place because she wanted to try a new recipe for appetizers. In honor of Heidi's newish veganism she was making homemade roasted red pepper hummus with veggies, and vegetable skewers grilled on her stovetop.

But also, she had a shocking piece of news. "I just heard this today, Jaymie; you're not going to believe it. Bev Hastings is suing Miss Perry!"

"*What?*"

"I guess she hurt herself on the boardwalk by the bait shop the other day, and she's suing Miss Perry for not keeping the buildings up to code. And get this, she's suing for *two mil.*"

"Two *million* dollars?" Jaymie was jolted. Hoppy, on her lap, reacted with a yip when she squeezed him too hard, so she set him down and he retreated to his basket by the fireplace. "I ran into her having lunch with Fergus Baird at the Queensville Inn and saw the boot she was wearing; she even told me what happened, but not that she was suing."

"I know, right? It's terrible! How can she do that and live with herself? Between you and me and the corner, they're in deep financial hot water."

"Jon and Bev Hastings?"

"Yup."

"Didn't I say that exact thing? It's tough being in business even for go-getters like Jakob." Their financial troubles meant that they were likely having to find ways to make a living, maybe outside of the shop. Did that include breaking and entering? He was in the mix for whomever had broken into Miss Perry's home and stolen the silver. With Bev as his accomplice, maybe?

"They've managed to eke out a living so far, but the last few years have been tough. I wouldn't have said anything, but there's something off about this whole thing, Bev and her injury." She paused and sighed again.

"What do you mean? Val, what's going on? I can tell you're worried."

"I *am* worried, and I don't know what to do. I can't be known to have said anything," she said fretfully. "You know how I feel about my career. Privacy is vitally important among a physician, a patient and a pharmacist. I consider that sacred. People trust me with their secrets."

"I know that, Val. You're one of the most principled people I know, and I mean that sincerely. I know how seriously you take the privacy of your patients." Jaymie waited, certain there was more.

"But I'm also *fiercely* opposed to scams and phonies. I've

reported doctors who misuse or mis-prescribe medications. Sometimes, though, the things I learn don't fall within the limits of my authority as a pharmacist, and yet . . . I can't let it go." She sighed heavily. "This is one of those times."

"Okay, I think I'm getting the connection. Something about Bev Hastings's lawsuit against Miss Perry is hinky."

"Keep talking."

"So, either the accident didn't happen, or maybe she wasn't hurt as bad as she says," Jaymie continued. "But . . . how would you know that if you weren't there? Is it . . . maybe something about the doctor who is providing the information in support of the lawsuit?"

"You're warm."

Jakob came back and plunked down beside her on the sofa, gazing at her quizzically. She raised her eyebrows and shrugged. *I'll tell you after,* she mouthed to him. "I'm guessing you know something about him, like . . . he's got a reputation for being dishonest?"

"*Bingo!* Thank you." She heaved a gusty sigh of relief. "So, now that you've guessed, I'll tell you this much: the doctor who diagnosed her severe leg tendon strain is one I've dealt with before over problems with his prescribing patterns, especially with opioids. He most definitely has a reputation."

"Oh. *Oh!*" Jaymie gasped. "I think I know who you mean. Joel said a local doctor was his best customer when it came to ordering painkillers. He thought it was awesome; said he made more money from him than from the rest of the doctors in Wolverhampton combined." She told Valetta who she was talking about and named the clinic.

"That's the guy. I've had to check a lot of his prescriptions, question the dosages, and even ask why a patient was refilling his prescription after only two weeks, when it should last a month. I've tried to work with him, but it's getting more difficult. I'm on the verge of reporting him for opioid over-prescription. That's a serious step, and I don't take it lightly."

"And you think there's something wrong with Bev's accident."

"I happen to know the doctor has signed off on questionable paperwork before, but there wasn't enough to report him. I'm . . . concerned." Valetta was silent for a long moment, then went on.

"Jaymie, I know I shouldn't say this, but Bev's injured—and I'm using air quotes when I say *injured*—leg is a godsend to her and Jon financially. Money from a lawsuit, or more likely an insurance settlement, could save their home. I know that's on the line if the business fails. I never thought she'd do that—sue, I mean— especially for so much, given how kind Miss Perry has been to them. God forgive me if I'm being judgmental or cynical, but I don't think it happened . . . the fall, I mean. Or if it did, I don't think she's actually hurt." She sighed. "I feel bad even saying that; I like them both. I don't know what to do about it, but I don't want that poor old woman sued unless it's legit. Her insurance will pay, but it's going to be hard on her nevertheless."

Jaymie was silent. Miss Perry had so much else to worry about, between someone trying to kill her and an actual murder on her property. This was the last thing she needed. "Okay, Val, I have a few contacts I'm going to mine about this. I'll talk to you Wednesday night."

"What was that all about?" Jakob asked when she hung up.

She told him, and also told him what she intended to do about it.

• • •

JAYMIE HAD IGNORED A TEXT FROM NAN ON SATURDAY, given she had other things on her mind, and she had deliberately stayed off her phone on Sunday. Sunday was family day; unless a meteor was headed for the earth, Jaymie, Jakob and Jocie spent it together.

But Monday morning inevitably dawned. She got Jocie off to school and Jakob off to work, then sat down on the sofa with her tablet and a cup of coffee to catch up on email and read the news. *The Wolverhampton Weekly Howler*—which was in hard copy only weekly; they updated with new stories online daily—had covered the murder of Fergus Baird. It was huge news. The police wouldn't comment except with bare-bones information, but Nan had a new reporter who was resourceful, sneaky, and had some kind of source within the police department who spilled too much, on occasion. The reporter had also been knocking on a lot of doors: neighbors on Winding Woods Lane near the site of the tragedy, as well as Fergus Baird's neighbors, friends and employees in Wolverhampton. She read the previous day's coverage, which had a lot of information she hadn't known.

Fergus Baird, age fifty-three, owner of Baird Construction, died by ligature strangulation with a weapon or tool that was not found at the scene but was assumed to be a belt, rope, or a length of something equally tough and thick. That explained the purpling of the face, Jaymie thought. Baird had been killed somewhere and then, some hours before his discovery, had been put where she had later found him.

To Jaymie that indicated that the killer must be someone strong enough to carry or drag him all the way down the riverbank and up the slope to the bushes. Or there was more than one conspirator. Movies and TV made it look easy, but she had once talked to Bernie about that very topic, and the police officer pointed out how difficult it was to drag a dead weight, especially when it was a human. They had tried a little experiment, with Jaymie attempting to drag Bernie, her hands under her arms and Bernie offering no help. She could do it, barely, but then she was strong for a woman, and Bernie was smaller than her, though heavy for her size because of her toned musculature. Dragging a body up a hill and into bushes? *That* was difficult.

The news report went on to state that the police thought the body had been moved down the riverbank using an ATV; tire tracks had been found. That explained moving the body, but didn't explain why. Why did the body have to be discovered on Miss Perry's property?

Nan would be furious with her, Jaymie thought, given that she found the body and yet had been out of touch all weekend, but the reporter had done very well in ferreting out information. Picking up her phone, she scanned it. There were several angry texts from Nan, becoming more and more frantic, until one screamed in all caps WHERE ARE YOU, JAYMIE? A year ago it would have worried her, but maybe Mrs. Bellwood was right: her priorities had shifted. She had a husband and a child, and they came first.

She would deal with Nan in a while, after she read the rest of the story on the crime.

Baird had been scheduled to meet with someone, his secretary said, when he left for the day on Friday. He didn't have the meeting in his day-timer, nor on his computer, which was now in the hands of the police, but the article said nothing about his phone. That was where busy people kept their whole lives, on their phones. They could be closing in on someone even now.

An autopsy had been done and findings would be released soon. Though the cause of death had already been leaked, there would be more information coming, at some point. Next of kin — two daughters, a son, a daughter- and son-in-law, three very young grandchildren, and an ex-wife — had been notified. They all resided away from Wolverhampton in Maryland, where Baird had lived for many years after leaving Queensville in the early eighties. Reached by telephone, family members had nothing to say except to ask for privacy. His children were on their way to Queensville. So his family didn't even live in the same state, and were unlikely suspects.

No mention was made of the nutmeg grater in the mouth; the reporter probably didn't know about it. She would not be the one to tell Nan about that, nor was she ready to be interviewed by the reporter. She pictured the scene again. She had assumed that the grater in his mouth was the one missing from Miss Perry's collection, but something wasn't right. Morgan had said an acorn-shaped grater was missing. The one in Baird's mouth was shaped like a walnut. Had Morgan misspoken? A nut is a nut, to some. Or . . . was she purposely misleading Jaymie?

Hoppy whined at her feet, and she picked him up, cuddling him on her lap. "I suppose I'd better text Nan, right? Especially since I need to see her today about something else."

She texted Nan, then went about her morning business, including a walk for Hoppy. The days were getting chilly. She put his coat on for him and donned a thick sweater under her windbreaker, but woman and dog were still both shivering when they returned to the cabin. Weather was so completely unpredictable. She remembered one Canadian Thanksgiving years before, in early October, that was so hot her sister had had to have the air-conditioning on while she baked the turkey for their family, who always gathered at Becca's London, Ontario, home for that holiday.

But this year October was setting in chilly and damp. She fed both animals, did dishes and tidied the kitchen. As she worked she thought a lot about Miss Perry. The tangle of troubles kept knotting and fracturing in her mind: who tried to kill her; *why* someone tried to kill her; was it the same person who killed Fergus Baird and put the nutmeg grater in his mouth? Was that a warning, or something else?

And *was* the nutmeg grater Miss Perry's? It *had* to be, Jaymie thought, coming back to that again and again. Sterling silver Georgian nutmeg graters did not turn up every day. It may not be the acorn one but a different one missing from the collection, or perhaps Morgan misspoke. And if that was true, then whoever killed Baird had access to Miss Perry's collection. That access could come in the form of someone close to her, like Morgan, *or* the thief who stole her silver. And Jaymie still didn't know a few things, like . . . who else other than Estelle Arden was Miss Perry scheduled to see the day she fell and hurt herself? Had the nutmeg grater gone missing *before* Jaymie's first visit, or *after*?

• • •

WHEN JAYMIE REACHED WOLVERHAMPTON, she dropped in on Nan and, as expected, her editor grilled her on what she had seen. She kept it brief, and factual. She let Nan record a brief statement, saying, "I was visiting the house and heard a dog barking, so I went to investigate. I chased the dog, who had a cat cornered under the shrubbery along the ridge above the river, and that's when I saw the body of Mr. Fergus Baird, who I recognized. I quickly got hold of the dog and backed away, calling nine one one. And that's it."

Nan was dryly amused and congratulated her on giving the most boring statement ever about a spectacular murder case.

"I do my best," Jaymie said. "Now, what I'm really here for is this . . ." And she gave her a scoop. Like a bloodhound on the trail, Nan was immediately focused on what could be an important breaking news story for the local area, and already doing research and making calls as Jaymie left.

Jaymie returned to Queensville and headed to the dockside buildings, parking in the municipal parking lot used by cottagers who didn't want to take their cars over to Heartbreak Island, those who kept boats in the marina, as well as by those who patronized the two stores. She had been in the feed store a few times, but never the bait store. Fishing wasn't her thing, neither was boating. She and her family were content to take the ferry over to their summer cottage on Heartbreak Island.

She examined the wooden walkway that fronted the four shops: the two boarded up and long abandoned, and the other two, the feed and tack store and the bait shop, open for business. In front of one of the abandoned ones was a raw, broken board cordoned off with yellow nylon rope looped around a piece of wood, with a handmade *Danger* sign nailed to it. Was that where Bev had hurt herself? Why would she be there, so close to one of the abandoned buildings? It made no sense. She bent down closer; there were divots on the wood, like they had been hammered upon to break them.

Jon Hastings, in the door of the bait shop, turned the *Closed* sign over to expose the *Open* side. He saw her kneeling down by the broken board, nodded, then turned away. Though he had seemed a cheery sort the day of the melee, today he appeared troubled. Jaymie entered the small, dim shop, the cash desk by the plate glass window and the rest of the space filled with shelves holding souvenir T-shirts, hats, propane tanks, blue tarps and lengths of nylon rope in packaging, the walls covered in pegboard stocked with plastic packaged lures, bobbers, fishing line and weights. "Mr. Hastings, good morning. Is Bev not here today?"

"Nope," he grunted. "Got a doctor's appointment in Wolver-hampton."

"I understand she hurt her leg. Was it on that broken section of the board walkway by one of the abandoned shops?"

He nodded, his solemn expression not revealing anything. She considered her next move. She had a few suspicions, but no idea how to proceed. "I can't imagine what she was doing right up next to the building."

His eyes narrowed, he said, "What are you inferring?"

Implying. The word was *implying*, Jaymie thought, but did not say. "Nothing. I just . . ." She had been hoping to ask him about his wife's relationship with Fergus Baird, but there was no delicate way to approach such a topic. Also, it could impede the police investigation. She should tell the police about seeing Bev Hastings with Baird, if she truly wanted to get to the bottom of everything. "It's nothing. I'd better get going."

He didn't say another word as she left. She walked along the boardwalk deep in thought.

"What were you talking to my husband about?"

She looked up; Bev Hastings limped toward her from the parking lot. "I was looking for you."

The woman, dressed casually in jeans and a windbreaker over a red bait shop T-shirt, was still using a cane and had the boot on her foot. She stumped toward Jaymie. "Why?"

The wind whirled some leaves along the walkway and into the marina, where they drifted between boats. "You know Fergus Baird is dead," she said.

Bev nodded. "What's it to you?"

"I'm the one who found him. At Miss Perry's place. You were friends with him, right?"

She shrugged.

"You sure looked like close friends while you were having lunch."

She stumped closer to Jaymie, anger reddening her plump face. "What are you saying? Just *say* it. Say what's on your mind."

What was on her mind was complicated and full of twists and turns. She wanted to know more about the silver flatware and the robbery from Miss Perry, but it was unwise to ask those questions. However, one thing did occur to her that she blurted out before she thought it through. "Does this," Jaymie said, waving her hand at the boot, " . . . your injury and your lawsuit against Miss Perry, have anything to do with Fergus Baird? Did he put you up to it to try to influence Miss Perry to sell her marina property?"

Her cheeks reddened, but she stayed silent for a long minute, and her expression blanked. "What a *terrible* thing to say," she finally hissed, her expression venomous, tears welling in her eyes. "You're an awful person, do you know that?" Her voice was choked with tears.

Jaymie steeled herself against the urge to apologize. The woman's hesitation had spoken volumes. "I don't know you, Bev. It happens. People *do* make fake claims." Too late she realized that if the newspaper did an investigation, and the insurance company followed up, Bev Hastings would immediately link it back to her. This was a mistake, one she normally didn't make.

"So you think I'm a thief *and* a cheat? Thanks a bunch, lady." Tears trickled down her cheeks. "Next you'll be accusing me of murder!"

"I'm sorry," Jaymie said. "Finding Fergus Baird like I did . . . it's upset me. Forget I said anything." She walked away, to her SUV. There seemed no way for her to solve any of the current dilemmas on her own: who robbed Miss Perry; who tried to kill Miss Perry; who murdered Fergus Baird. There was no indication the three events were even related, though it seemed a little far-fetched to think that three separate assailants were responsible. She drove up to Miss Perry's home. The police were gone. There was a car in the drive with the nursing company logo on it.

Skip answered the door and looked relieved it was Jaymie. He grabbed her sleeve and pulled her into the hall. "I'm so glad you came. I was about to call Mrs. Stubbs to get your phone number. I'm worried."

"Skip, what's going on? Is Miss Perry okay?"

"She is right now. In fact, she's improved so much I'm not sure I can justify staying here any longer."

"Okay. And you're worried about leaving her alone?"

"You bet I am. I'm *really* worried. Miss Perry and I have talked a lot over the last couple of days. I like to get to know my patients. Jaymie, by my estimation, in the last four months there have been at least *three* attempts on her life."

✍ Fifteen ✍

"**THREE ATTEMPTS ON HER *LIFE*?**" Horrified and stunned, Jaymie was rocked back on her heels. "Skip, what do you mean?"

"Skip?" Miss Perry's voice, sounding hale and hardy, floated down the hall to them at the door. "Where's lunch? I thought you were making eggs."

"I can't tell you now," he muttered, looking over his shoulder and down the hall toward her sitting room. "I'll be right there, Lois!" he called out. Turning back to Jaymie he said, "I'm not sure what to do. Maybe you can help me decide. But right now . . ." He straightened and took a deep breath. "Morgan can't cook to save her life, so I promised my patient soft-boiled eggs. It's one of the many things I learned while I was living with my grandmother when I was a teenager: how to boil the perfect egg. Everything I know I learned from my grandmother and the Marines, and I don't know who the more severe taskmaster was." He flashed a brilliant smile and retreated down the hall.

Mystified and alarmed by what she had learned, Jaymie followed Skip to the sitting room.

"Look who popped in, Lois. It's Jaymie."

"Excellent!" she said, twisting in her chair, staring up at Jaymie. "Did you come to get the graters? I've got a list made up. Skip's been helping me."

Jaymie moved the low stool over and sat on it in front of Miss Perry. "I'd be glad to. I wasn't sure you'd be up to it, but Skip says you're doing *so* much better. You sure look better!" And she did; the bruises weren't fading yet, but the color had sunk down to her neck and the large bandage was gone from her forehead, replaced by a smaller one for the contusion where she had hit the newel post. Her appearance was still alarming, but the brightness was back in her eyes and she had regained her vivacity. Her tightly permed and curled gray hair had been cleaned and brushed so it stood in a poofy halo around her head. "Miss Perry, have you remembered who else you were meeting that morning? You definitely told me you were seeing Estelle Arden and someone else."

She shook her head. "The only place I would mark it would be my

140

appointment calendar, if it was business. I had Skip check it to see if I had any doctors' appointments that needed to be canceled or postponed, and the only person on there for that day was that Arden woman."

"But if there was a friend or relative coming you wouldn't include it?"

She shook her head. "I don't know. Sometimes I do, but not if it's Morgan."

But she had said "appointment." Jaymie decided to leave it alone for the moment. "So did you make that list of graters we can use for the display?"

She brightened and reached over to the small table on the other side of her chair — it was a new table since Jaymie last visited, a hospital-style one that could be swung around for her to use sitting in her chair — picked up a spiral-bound notebook opened to a page, and handed it to Jaymie. In neat block printing that had to be Skip's there was a list of ten graters. She recognized them all from the descriptions as being ones she had seen the first day she visited.

"So, what graters were stolen by the thieves who broke in?"

She scrunched her face into a puzzled look. "There weren't any graters stolen."

Jaymie blinked. No graters stolen. "So . . . what about the missing acorn-shaped one?"

"I'd forgotten that. I don't know where it is."

"But you're sure it wasn't stolen with the other silver?"

"Of course I'm sure," she said, her tone full of her usual asperity. "I had to go through everything I own for insurance. I told you what was stolen: a set of sterling silver flatware, Savoy by Buccellati; a silver epergne; one silver tray and a fruit bowl."

"And that's it?"

"Isn't that enough?" she asked stoutly. "The insurance evaluator gave an estimate of over twenty thousand for the silverware alone. The other items are worth another twenty."

Jaymie quailed at the valuations. What wouldn't someone do to get forty thousand dollars' worth of stuff? Would they try to kill someone? But the theft had happened months ago. And killing Miss Perry wouldn't get anyone anything except . . . Morgan Perry Wallace, who inherited. Was it as simple as that? She shook her head; it didn't add up. Why bring the police's attention to the wire across the stairs? "You went to Queensville Fine Antiques about the flatware set they had there. I don't think I mentioned this, but it's owned by my sister and brother-in-law."

"That starchy Englishwoman they have working for them complained about me to you, I suppose."

"A little," Jaymie said, smiling. "Georgina is my brother-in-law's older sister. She *is* very knowledgeable. I'm taking lessons from her. She was offended because she says she's careful about that kind of thing, provenance and all that."

"I suppose I shouldn't have been so accusatory, but Morgan was doing research for me after the robbery and saw the silver set online. So I went in to ask her. She got huffy . . . very, very huffy. *They* got the police involved, not me. They wouldn't tell me who they bought it from, but the police apparently investigated and it was solved to their satisfaction. Not to mine. I still think it's my set."

Jaymie secretly agreed with her. So . . . Miss Perry didn't know it was Bev Hastings who sold it to the antiques store. Interesting. If the Hastings *did* steal the silver, what had they done with the other things? Wouldn't it be dumb to sell the flatware to a store in the same town as the woman they stole it from? Desperation could make people do dumb things, though.

She went back to the most interesting and troubling revelation, though: if the acorn grater wasn't stolen with the silver, and it was not the one jammed in Fergus Baird's throat, where was it? And what about the grater choking Baird? That was definitely one detail she needed to make sure the police knew about, that the nutmeg grater was not Miss Perry's. They would already know if they referenced the list of stolen silver from the robbery of her home, but perhaps they hadn't gotten that far. It was a small department with limited resources; they'd follow up on every detail but it would take time.

To be absolutely sure, and to cover all possibilities, she asked, "Miss Perry, are you saying there are no graters missing from your collection at *all*?"

She frowned. "Well, now, I couldn't say *that*. There's that acorn one Morgan says is missing. I haven't looked since I showed them to you, but there weren't any missing then. I said none were stolen in that robbery."

Skip brought in a tray with two eggs in egg cups, a rosebud-patterned saucer filled with buttered toast points, silver salt and pepper shakers, and some odd-looking tool alongside the spoon. He unburdened the tray onto the hospital-style table, which he swung around over her lap, and handed her a linen napkin. Her eyes were alight with hunger.

Jaymie smiled; a good appetite was a great sign. "Do you mind if I take the list and have a look through the graters while you eat your lunch?"

"You go ahead, dear," she said, focused on her soft-boiled eggs. She had already used the odd scissors-like silver tool that snipped the tops off the eggs, and was salting the yolk, murmuring at the perfection of the golden runny goodness.

Jaymie took the book and exited the sitting room, motioning for Skip to follow her to the front room, where the cases of graters were mounted. He nodded but headed to the kitchen first with the empty tray. She examined the cases, which were locked and sitting on bespoke tables. Everything was perfectly lined up, and Jaymie remembered that when Miss Perry returned a grater to a case, each had a spot that was equidistant from the others on the dark blue velvet case lining. A gap in the collection would be noticed.

Or would it? A clever thief would simply realign the rest of the graters to disguise the gap. That would take time, though. A robber who broke a window to get in couldn't take that much time and care. Skip joined her and shut the door behind him.

"What did you mean when you said there had been three attempts on Miss Perry's life?"

He paced to a front window and looked out, then returned. His dark eyes were clouded with worry. "Okay, she and I have talked. A *lot*. Especially as she's feeling so much better. I've written this all down and have it stashed in with the file I keep on her meds. So . . . first: Lois takes several medications on a daily basis. She has a plastic dosette that is delivered to her by the pharmacy already stocked. Some of my patients have no idea what they're taking, but she does. One day she noticed a pill she didn't recognize in her night pills section, and in every night compartment for the rest of the week, five days more, she tells me. She didn't take it, and dumped them. She thought the pharmacist had made a mistake and didn't want to get her in trouble, but you know Valetta Nibley even better than I do; she does *not* make mistakes."

"I agree," Jaymie said. "When was this?"

"Just the week before her accident."

"And she didn't tell anyone and just got rid of the pills?"

He nodded and sighed. "Maybe I'm overreacting. Maybe it *wasn't* a murder attempt. Maybe Miss Perry is gaga at times, but if that's the case I've never noticed it. I don't know what else to think. I have had patients who were convinced that the doctor or pharmacist was trying to kill them, but Miss Perry isn't one of them. She thought an error had been made."

"Okay. What else?"

"Second: she was in the backyard in September talking on the phone—she has a cordless handset, not a cell phone—to her yard guy, who was supposed to come out and do some work but hadn't, a mix-up in the days. Someone tried to shoot her. She was winged, but only her jacket was torn. I've seen the jacket but you can't tell much, it looks like a small tear. So I went out to look around and I found a hole in the vinyl siding of the shed. Looks like a small caliber, maybe a twenty-two."

"How do you know it was from a twenty-two?"

"I don't. It's an educated guess. I took my medical training in the Marines, so I understand guns and ammunition."

This was serious. She met his gaze but was silent. She was going to have to tell the police. "And the third attempt? I'm assuming you don't mean the wire across the stairs that caused her fall?"

He shook his head. "I'm not positive about the third one, but it's worth mentioning, given what happened with the wire. She was alone, coming out of the medical building in Wolverhampton from an appointment. She doesn't drive anymore, so she was meeting the car service in the parking lot. Someone tried to run her down. The police were called and a report was filed, but she was so frightened she couldn't describe the car." He sighed. "The police thought it was random, and maybe it was. Someone almost ran me down once on my motorcycle. But Jaymie, I'm worried. This was a bad one, the wire across the stairs. Someone is getting damn close to killing her."

☙ Sixteen ❧

JAYMIE SPENT A LITTLE MORE TIME in the sitting room, examining the cases and thinking. Where had Miss Perry stored the silver flatware and dishes that had been stolen? She headed across the hall to the unused dining room and the answer was right there; by the formal dining table was a hutch and china cabinet. The silver flatware would have been stored in there. The silver bowl and epergne would have been in the upper display case. There were empty spaces among other, larger pieces—maybe too large for the thief to handle: an ornate candelabra and a champagne bucket.

She returned to her hostess's sitting room. Miss Perry was exhausted after the visit and her lunch. She needed a nap, but like most folks of her generation she had made a commitment about the nutmeg graters and was intent on fulfilling it. Jaymie had more pressing concerns, given what she had learned. She made an excuse to come back another day to get the graters, saying she had an emergency. She hugged her new friend. "I'll be back. You get some rest."

Skip followed her to the door. "I don't want to leave her alone, but she's so much better already. I think I can say she needs at least two more days of around-the-clock nursing care, but if she keeps improving at this rate . . ." He shrugged. "I'm worried about her safety more than her health at this point."

"I'm relieved you said two more days. Has Morgan been back so far?"

"She was yesterday. I have to say, she's a nice girl. After she got over her snit about me, she seemed relieved, actually, to not have to stay around the clock. I think she truly loves her aunt. She thanked me for taking such good care of her."

"That's what I would do if I had been unsuccessful at trying to murder someone," Jaymie said. "I'd make sure everyone saw me being super caring and loving toward them."

Skip's eyes widened and he stifled a laugh. "You are sassy, aren't you? I like it."

"I'm becoming cynical, I guess. I think I'll fight that tendency. Most people are good, if not always easy." Smiling, she exited to the porch. "Oh, and Skip?" she said, turning back. "I've learned that

145

Miss Perry is being sued for an incident that happened on her property down by the dock. Bev Hastings, who co-owns the bait shop with her husband, apparently was injured when her leg went through a broken section of the decking. I don't know how long it will be before papers are served on her, but I thought I'd warn you."

"I've nursed people injured in accidents and thinking about suing. They have something like ninety days to serve after a lawsuit is filed, but it's good to be aware."

Jaymie sighed. "It's like the universe has it out for the poor woman, all of this stuff happening."

He shook his head. "Not the universe, Jaymie; it's all about greedy, nasty people."

Jaymie got into the SUV, checked her watch, texted her best friend, and headed into town. Valetta was awaiting her with a steaming cup of tea on the top step of the Queensville Emporium. She was watching with interest as her brother showed the big house that faced the village green, a home that was kind of the centerpiece of the village. It had been used as a vacation home for quite a long time, before being put up for sale.

Valetta handed her a mug of tea but didn't take her eyes off the house. "Brock's got a hot one on the hook," she murmured. "He thinks he's got the right client, an older couple."

"Good!" Jaymie said. "A solid resident in that house will be great. We need access to that land for Dickens Days," she said, speaking of their annual Queensville tradition, a December festival that used the Victorian appearance of the village and often snowy blanket in December to host strolling Victorian Christmas carolers, selling baked goods and cider to benefit the heritage society. Because wind was sometimes a problem, they used anchor lines to keep the little cider house from blowing over, and the only place to run them was onto the land of the house on the green. No one had so far objected.

"The Watsons next door to us are selling, too. I'm going to miss them. Their daughter, Crystal, was a good friend of mine, but she left town years ago."

"I remember her; nice girl."

Jaymie sighed. "Everything is changing." There was no one in the world Jaymie trusted more than Valetta, and no one in

Queensville who knew more about what was going on, and who was who. She told her what she had learned, finishing with Skip's discovery of the three past attempts on Miss Perry's life.

Of course Valetta latched on to the tale of the medications. "Did she say what the pills looked like?"

Jaymie frowned. "I don't know, just . . . pills. Why?"

"If I knew something about the color, shape, and size I could narrow down what kind of pill it was. If it's diamond shape and blue, that's Viagra; she's on nitrates for angina, so the combination could kill her. If the pill was small, round, and pastel in color— green, peach, blue—it could be Coumadin, otherwise known as warfarin. She does take a blood thinner because of her DVT, deep vein thrombosis; additional warfarin could cause fatal internal bleeding, especially in the case of a fall."

"Like the fall down the stairs," Jaymie said, her voice weak.

"She was extremely lucky in that case that the bleeding wasn't worse. She could have died. And she was smart to not take the mystery pill. But I wish she had told me— or *someone!*— about it."

"It would take some knowledge to do that, *and* access to the pills."

"It would take a little planning ahead of time, in the case of warfarin, but it's not hard. In fact, it's simple to look up online, and easy to buy online even without a prescription. That goes for both ED drugs *and* the blood thinners."

Jaymie sighed. "Unfortunately she got rid of the pills, thinking you'd made a mistake."

"Oh, *no!*" Valetta cried, horrified. "You mean all this time she's been thinking I made a mistake and yet she didn't *say* anything?" She set her mug down and took off her glasses with one shaking hand. "That's terrible, Jaymie! This is serious. I *know* I didn't make a mistake."

"Skip knows it wasn't you. I have to tell the police about this, Val. Are you okay with that?"

"Please do!" Swallowing hard, Valetta nodded and put her glasses back on. "And tell them that I want to talk to them, to explain my delivery methods. I need my clients to know they can trust me and ask me *anything*. Our delivery guy, Arlo, takes the dosettes from my hands directly to the client, and takes them inside the house. I *never* entrust them to anyone else. If pills were put in her dosette, it happened after Arlo left it there."

"It's okay, hon," Jaymie said, patting her friend's back, then rubbed in comforting circles. "It wasn't you, we all know that."

"If there is *ever* a problem again I want her to call me and have the dosette brought back in. I'll check it over and call the police, if need be. Please, Jaymie, tell the police soon, or I'll worry about it." She was deeply shaken. There was nothing she took more seriously than her commitment to her clients: their safety, their privacy, and their wellness.

"It's such a weird combination of methods, trying to kill her. It seems to me that it *must* be Morgan, even though I don't want it to be her. Who else could get into the house to put pills in the case? And string a wire across the stairs?"

"But what about the gunshot? Does Morgan shoot?"

"I don't know. Maybe that was random."

"Along the river is not a likely place for a hunter or sport shooter, though, Jaymie."

"You're right about that. But someone could be taking potshots at cans or something."

Valetta took a long, deep breath, settling her nerves. "Let's think this through. Who else would have access to the house on a regular basis?"

Jaymie thought. "I know she doesn't have a housekeeper or cleaner; Morgan told me she does all the housework for her aunt. But there must be others. And Morgan's husband, Saunders Wallace. Other people come in to get paid, maybe, like the yard guy Skip told me about. A handyman? Insurance agent? We had our agent out a few weeks ago."

"What about . . ." Valetta stared into the distance for a long moment. "Her home was broken into months ago; was that a cover-up for anything else? Like . . . stealing a house key?"

Jaymie felt her stomach tighten. "That is *clever,*" she said, gazing at her friend with admiration. "You'd make a great evil genius, Val." That possibility unfortunately left it wide open as to who could be making the murder attempts, and why they would do it. Fergus Baird's words rang in her ears; he had said in his tirade that it was best if Miss Perry die and pass the property on to Morgan, who would sell to him so he could develop the property. Was Baird behind it after all? If so, who killed him and why? A coconspirator? Bev Hastings, maybe?

Jaymie relayed her thoughts to Valetta, then said, "Maybe Nan's reporter has found something out. I suppose I'd better make contact."

Valetta took a deep breath and worked the tension out of her shoulders. "On a lighter note, if you're going into Wolverhampton, check out Dan's thrift store and find out if he'll be doing a closeout sale."

"Good thought." Jaymie got up as Brock came out of the house on the village green with a wiry fellow and presumably his wife; they stood talking by the real estate agent's Caddy. "I'll leave you my mug and get moving."

"Remember . . . tell the police about the murder attempts! I expect a call before the end of the day about the pills in the dosette."

Jaymie looked at her cell phone once she got back in her Explorer. There was a text from Jakob saying he'd be late. Jocie was taking the bus home, so could Jaymie be there to meet her? She texted back an affirmative.

It was still plaguing her who else Miss Perry was supposed to see that day. Had anyone checked with Estelle Arden? she wondered. She'd do it herself. She punched in the number and Estelle answered with a chipper tone. Jaymie made conversation about how the pamphlet for the walking tours was going. The heritage society wasn't only planning the river walk; they were also doing a couple of different ones for the tour of the village itself and its most notable heritage homes, like Stowe House, still for sale since Jaymie's ex, Daniel, had given up on Queensville. There would be walking tours taking in the marina, too, as well as the American half of Heartbreak Island. "Estelle, I was wondering, though I suppose the police have already asked this: the day Miss Perry was hurt you actually had an appointment with her and did show up."

"Ye-es," she answered cautiously, wariness creeping into her tone.

"She was surprised you kept it. After you and she had the run-in on TV she figured you'd assume the appointment was canceled."

"I never assume anything. I thought it would be an opportunity to talk to her one on one, to change her mind. I was still hoping to persuade her. As a woman alone I understand her nervousness, but I hoped she'd see that those of us on the heritage society would ensure her safety." She paused, then said, with laughter in her voice, "So does that mean she was watching me?"

"She was, from an upstairs window."

"I'm relieved. I kept thinking maybe she was lying injured in there the whole time, and I could have done something for her if I'd gone in. I did check the door, but it was locked."

Oh. Oh! "What time was that?"

"Nine in the morning. I'm always prompt."

So the trap was laid after that, but by whom? "Estelle, did you see anyone there that day, any neighbors or strangers?"

"Why?"

"Just wondering." Jaymie held her breath, hoping Estelle wouldn't ask any more questions.

"Not a soul. What's this about, Jaymie?"

But she wasn't ready to tell anyone what she was thinking. "I was curious. You know me." She said goodbye hurriedly and hit the button to hang up.

She kept examining her phone. Another text was from Heidi. Her date went well, and she was happy. Jaymie called her. "Hey, you want to go to a thrift store with me?" she asked.

"Can Bernie come with?" Heidi asked. "We're meeting for lunch."

"That would be perfect. I wasn't sure when her days off were." Maybe she could kill two birds with one stone. "I'll meet you outside Thrifty Dan's at two."

Jaymie returned home and took Hoppy for a long walk while she thought about the attempts on Miss Perry's life, then threw together a casserole, covering it and putting it in the fridge. She checked her email briefly, and was pleased to find one from Sid Farrell confirming her podcast appearance date. Now she could honestly tell Nan that she had set it up. She locked up and headed toward Wolverhampton, knowing she had to fit everything in and be home by four.

She caught her editor in the newspaper parking lot getting into her sports car. Nan's wild and frizzy graying red hair got tossed around in the gusty wind that was sending whirlwinds of dust spiraling around the parking lot.

"Well, I did it," Jaymie said. "I emailed Sid Farrell and we've agreed on a day and time for my appearance on his show. Now I need to calm my nerves."

With the casual manner of every person who doesn't understand the public speaking fears of another, Nan breezily waved one hand and said, "You'll be fine!" She pushed her hair back and held it out of her eyes. "Sid's a nice guy. Joe listens to his radio show all the time."

"Has your reporter found anything out yet, about Fergus Baird's murder?"

"Yes, I have some stuff. I'll get it to you. But right now I have to go. There's a town council meeting, kind of connected to Baird, actually. Now that he's dead some of his projects are up in the air."

"He had a lot going on. Did he have a good reputation as a developer?"

"As good as any, I guess. Not everyone agrees. He bought several buildings in Wolverhampton and was forcing out the tenants. I suppose you could say he was ruthless. The guy who owns Thrifty Dan's probably doesn't have a good word to say about him. His is one of the tenancies that was canceled when Fergus bought the building."

"I'm going there now, actually, with friends. I'll ask him what he thinks of Fergus's death. If I get a colorful quote, I'll let you know."

• • •

JAYMIE PARKED AND WALKED TO MEET HER FRIENDS in front of Thrifty Dan's, a combination liquidation and thrift store. She had always liked it, since Dan made sure his stuff was clean and he didn't overcharge. She had bought, over the years, books, bookcases and other vintage items, especially items for her all-consuming passion, vintage kitchen junk. He had been trying to go a little more upscale of late, with locked cases of statuary—mostly Hummel, Doulton, Wedgwood and Lladró—vintage costume jewelry, and silver.

Heidi and Bernie came toward her, their heads together, chattering nonstop as they bent into the wind. Both looked up and Heidi gave a glad cry when she saw Jaymie.

"Jaymsie, this is so nice and spontaneous!"

All three hugged. "It's so good to see you looking happier!" Jaymie exclaimed, examining her friend's lovely smiling face. "I was worried about you."

"I gave myself a swift kick in the butterooni," she said. "I have a home. I have money. But most of all . . . I have friends."

"Who *love* you!" Bernie said, arm around her shoulders.

They entered Thrifty Dan's, a long, low building that stretched from the main street all the way back to the parallel street, where the back door and loading dock were located. The three friends parted ways, Heidi and Bernie heading to the vintage furniture section. At a thrift store Jaymie always went into a zone, as Valetta called it. The music over the radio, seventies soul and R&B, was a counterpoint, and she hummed to herself as she grabbed a grocery cart and started loading it with books—several old Mary Baloghs and Jo Beverlys that she had probably already read but would read again, as well as two by a romance author friend of hers, Melody Heath, and some kids' books for Jocie. She also found a cute but sturdy wooden step stool that had been painted white and had kitten decals that looked like they were from the fifties. It would help Jocie reach the top shelf of the bookcase in her room.

She glanced up. Bernie and Heidi were now going through the racks of liquidation clothes, exclaiming and holding things up to each other. Jaymie wandered over to one of the glass cases, and Dan himself came to see if he could help her.

Dan was in his mid-forties, bulky, with sparse hair and many chins, all clean-shaven. A Wolverhampton native, he was good-natured and helpful. "Hey, Jaymie. Good to see you. How's that handsome husband of yours?"

She smiled. "Just as handsome as ever. Say . . . I heard you had a Going Out of Business sign up, and then I heard it was because Fergus Baird bought your building. But today the sign is gone. What's up?"

Wide-eyed, he shrugged. "You tell me. I couldn't get a straight answer when I called his office, so I took it down. I guess we won't know until we find out who owns the building now that he's gone whether I need to close up shop or not."

"He had kids, right? But his children live in Maryland, I've heard. Presumably they'll inherit his assets. I can imagine you didn't like him too much, right?"

"Business is business," Dan said, his tone equable. "I wasn't thrilled at being turfed out, but unless you own property that's always a possibility."

"True." Jaymie started examining the items in the glass case. There were some china pieces she recognized from her lessons with Georgina; she identified the maker and pattern from memory. She was getting better at this! "As my grandma says, it's an ill wind that blows no good. His death is a tragedy for some, but I suppose it's a blessing for others. Bev and Jon Hastings, down at the bait shop in Queensville, would have lost their business if Fergus had managed to buy the buildings, but he died before he had the chance."

"Those two would have been fine," Dan said, a disgusted look on his face. "I heard all about it through the grapevine, trust me! By people who know them all. Baird promised the Hastings that if they helped him get the property he'd set them up in business here, downtown Wolverhampton."

Jaymie stopped dead in her perusal of the silver in the case. "How do you know that?"

"Like I said . . . I know people. Bev herself told a friend of mine. She's always hated the bait store. I don't know how Jon felt about this, but apparently Baird was going to set them up in a flower shop in one of his Wolverhampton properties."

Jaymie examined Dan's guileless expression; he was known to be honest, and in this case had no reason to lie. Dan and Jakob were friendly competitors in a way, but her husband always said that Dan's appraisals were spot-on. In Jaymie's experience if someone was honest in business, they were probably trustworthy in other ways. "I'm not sure I understand," she said slowly. "How could the Hastings help him get the property?"

Dan looked around: Bernie and Heidi were now in the farthest reaches of the store rummaging through boxes of cupboard and door hardware. Another customer had come in, but she headed directly for the liquidation appliances at the back on the opposite side. Dan leaned heavily on the glass counter. "Don't tell anyone I said this, but I heard from a source I will not reveal that they were going to find a way to sue Miss Perry, or something along those lines. That would make the poor old gal want to sell the property, they figured, and would net them a pretty penny as well. Bev especially is all about the Benjamins, you know?" He straightened.

"Is that so?" Jaymie's mind spun at the news. So the lawsuit was, as she suspected, a fraud.

"*And* Bev was sweet on Fergus. I saw them in Wellington's Retreat one day and she was cooing over him like a pigeon. Poor old Jon was oblivious, of course."

"How long had the plan to harass Miss Perry been in the works? Do you know?"

"Well, I heard about it first some time ago, but I wrote it off as gossip, you know? It wasn't obvious then what Baird was planning."

So if the plan went back a while maybe Bev had done the robbery, stolen the silver to make it look legit, and took the door key at the same time. Then she would have a way into the house easily to plan the other assaults. Baird may have planned to scare Miss Perry into selling, but it was possible that what he said on the dock that day had confirmed to Bev that Miss Perry had to die. The other murder attempts, if that's what they were, had been half-hearted, but the wire across the stairs . . . that was more pointed and almost successful.

"Earth to Jaymie . . . you're fascinated by the silver sugar tongs?" he said.

She shook her head. "No, I . . . I was daydreaming. What is that?" she asked, pointing at a little silver box.

"Well, I *think* it's a snuff box," Dan said, unlocking the case and bringing it out. "I got a lot of things from an estate sale once, silver items, and I had them displayed in my home for a while, but I'm trying to clear the clutter. This is the last of a bunch of smalls I got," he said, using industry jargon for the small vintage and antique items that made up an antique dealer's bread and butter. "All sterling."

He handed it over. She opened it and gazed down at the perforated insert. "Dan, this isn't a snuff box, it's a nutmeg grater."

✍ Seventeen ✍

"A NUTMEG GRATER? You sure?"

"I'm certain," she said, her voice trembling. "You had a bunch of smalls kind of like this, you said?"

"Sure . . . sterling silver, little boxes and egg-shaped doodads. I knew some of them were graters of some sort, but I didn't even consider that *this* one was, it looked so different. It's not my era; I'm more into mid-century modern, as you know. But they're so pretty, and I got the whole collection kind of cheap."

"How long have you had them to sell?"

"I brought them in and have been selling them since . . . oh, summer, I guess?"

Now she knew where Baird's killer had gotten the silver walnut-shaped nutmeg grater found in his mouth. It hadn't come from Miss Perry's collection at all, but from Dan's. "Do you keep track of who bought these things?"

"Nope."

"Do you remember one shaped like a walnut?"

"I do."

"Do you happen to remember who bought that one?"

"Actually, yes, I do."

"Who?" she asked.

"Do you know Saunders and Morgan Wallace? He's quite well known, a used car salesman here in town. On TV all the time, ginger hair, big cheesy grin. He fancies himself a man-about-town and collects vintage automobiles as well as selling them. Morgan is a cutey . . . one of those cuddly pudgy blondes, cherubic, wears a lot of pink when she's not forced to wear Saunders's gawdawful tartan clothes. Which do *not* suit her, by the way. She's office manager of her husband's company. I think she's related to Miss Perry, right?"

"So . . . Saunders or Morgan?"

"Morgan, natch. Saunders has bought some vintage barware, but he's not into doodads."

Dan talked more, but there was a buzzing in Jaymie's ears and she couldn't hear. She needed to think. She made her purchases and moved toward the door, deep in thought.

"Are you okay, Jaymie?" That was Bernie, who had also checked out.

Jaymie met her eyes. "We need to talk." On impulse, she invited both Bernie and Heidi to come out to the cabin for coffee, since she needed to be home when Jocie got there. "In fact, stay for dinner. I think it's going to take me a while to explain everything."

"What do you have for dinner?" Heidi asked.

"Oh, dear . . . nothing vegan. Cabbage roll casserole," Jaymie admitted. "Made with ground beef. It's a recipe I'm trying for my 'Vintage Eats' column."

Bernie rolled her eyes. "We can do better than that. Can you save it for another day and we'll bring dinner?"

They all agreed to meet at Jaymie's and parted ways. As soon as she got home she called Detective Vestry to leave a message about Miss Perry's dosette and Valetta's concerns. She then put on coffee and went out to sit on the porch. Jocie's bus was right on time; Jaymie sat in one of the Adirondack chairs and watched her stepdaughter trudge up the lane, book bag over her shoulder.

At first she had worried about being responsible for the little girl. Life wasn't always easy for Jocie, whose classmates were swiftly growing so much taller. She had faced her unfair share of teasing. Jakob, with more years of parenting behind him, was more philosophical.

"Lots of kids face teasing, *liebchen*," he told her, calling her the pet name he saved for private moments. "I won't let her be bullied, but I also don't want to make her into someone who always needs outside interference and I will not teach her to see herself as a victim. In life, she's going to face hurdles, and will need to handle things on her own. Our job is to help her deal with each instance. Sometimes that means doing nothing, and sometimes that means getting the school or parent involved. I like her to have a say in how we handle it."

It was reassuring to have someone by her side who was so levelheaded and calm. With his support and reassurance, though she was still finding her way, she had integrated herself into their home and lives. Today, the little girl looked downhearted. "What's up, sweetie?" she said, pulling Jocie into her lap as Hoppy danced around at her feet.

Jocie leaned against her shoulder, her lip pushed out in a pout. "I got picked last for volleyball today."

"Aw, honey, I'm sorry. That's never easy." She thought for a moment, then asked, "Are you always picked last for teams?"

"Not always. Sometimes it's Gemma."

Gemma was one of Jocie's best friends. She was a heavy child with glasses, shy and retiring unless you knew her well, when she became chatty and funny. Gemma was one of Jaymie's favorite people, reminding her of herself when she was that age.

"I used to get picked last too, sometimes," Jaymie said. "Grandma Leighton told me that being good at sports or popular was only one part of a person, and even the most popular kids—you know, the ones always picked first—had secret worries and insecurities. She told me not to worry about it because I was better at reading aloud in class, and writing essays, and I could run a long ways, even if I didn't run fast."

Jocie sat up straighter. "I'm pretty good at dodge ball," she said, brightening.

"And you're smart, you can read above your grade level, and you're on the dance team. You're *really* good at that! You can dance like nobody's business. I'm so proud of you."

She sighed and nodded.

"Honey, someone is always going to be picked last. It doesn't mean kids don't like you." She slid Jocie off her lap and took her hand, grabbing her book bag with her other. "Let's go in. Bernie and Heidi are coming out and bringing dinner. Work on your homework now so you can visit with them before bedtime. Daddy's going to be a little late."

He wouldn't be home in time for dinner at all, he texted her. His truck had broken down in Mansfield, Ohio, where he had been delivering a Duncan Phyfe–style dining table and chair set. He FaceTimed with her briefly from the garage where the mechanic was working on the car. The guy was working overtime to help him out, so Jakob was ordering in pizza for them. Once the truck was repaired he'd head home.

"You be sure the truck is working properly before you head out on the highway, hon," Jaymie said worriedly. "I don't want you getting stuck anywhere else. Drive it around for a few minutes before the mechanic takes off. And recharge your phone while you're waiting!"

He nodded, suppressing a smile at her worry. "If traffic is good it'll be about a three-hour drive. I'll be home by bedtime."

Jocie wanted to talk to her dad, so Jaymie handed her the phone, telling her three minutes was her limit, then it was homework.

• • •

Bernie and Heidi brought vegetarian pizza and salad, with a bottle of wine for them and chocolate milk for Jocie. They ate, Jocie read her rewrite of *The Poky Little Puppy* to them, now called *Slowpoke the Puppy Likes Dessert*, in which the puppies learn to share equally with each other. Then she was off to bathe and bed.

Jaymie came back downstairs and the women retired to the living room, a comfortable place with a little bed by the fireplace that Hoppy and Lilibet shared many evenings.

But Bernie got serious quickly. "Jaymie, you looked white as a sheet at the thrift store. And you said we had to talk. I know you were waiting until Jocie was in bed, so spill."

Jaymie told them everything from the beginning through what she had learned about the other attempts on Miss Perry's life, and right down to the silver nutmeg grater that had been bought at Thrifty Dan's by Morgan Perry Wallace. She had already called and left a message for Detective Vestry about the dosette, she told them, but she hadn't mentioned the other things. "I can't figure out how the attempts on Miss Perry and the murder of Fergus Baird connect, though, beyond the obvious, the silver nutmeg grater. Morgan said she wasn't having an affair with Baird, and I think I believe her."

Bernie reached out and touched Jaymie's hand. "That isn't up to you to figure out. You realize you have to call Detective Vestry and tell her *all* of this, not selected bits and pieces."

"Nooo," wailed Jaymie, fingers to her temples. She had a headache coming on. "I told you so *you* can tell her."

She shook her head. "Uh-uh. You have to tell her this yourself."

"But she doesn't like me."

"Jaymie, no offense, but grow a pair, will you?" Bernie said with asperity. "You're braver than that. She's not going to bite your head off. And this is important, you *know* that."

"She's going to be so annoyed," Jaymie said, dropping her hands to her lap and picking at a chipped nail. "She basically told me to stay out of it."

"This information fell into your lap," Heidi said softly. "You know Bernie's right."

"Yeah. I know."

"I'll call her right now and put you on," Bernie said.

Fortunately, Vestry was willing to take all the information in a phone call, which she asked to record, after thanking Jaymie for the tip about the possible drug attempt on Miss Perry's life. Drained after the conversation, Jaymie drank another glass of wine, and then her friends packed it in and departed, with promises to see her at their girls' night in a couple of days.

Jaymie was in bed but still awake when Jakob got home and wearily dropped into bed with her. They snuggled together under the covers, wrapped in each other's arms, and fell asleep.

• • •

JAKOB HAD ANOTHER BUSY DAY AHEAD at The Junk Stops Here, but over breakfast Jaymie told him what she had learned the previous day, ending with the visit to Thrifty Dan's and the phone call to the detective. She felt much relieved that she had done as Bernie commanded. If she hadn't she wouldn't have slept as deeply, she knew that about herself. Sleep was elusive when she was troubled.

She had a full morning planned, and then was going to meet Becca and Kevin at the Queensville house before they headed back to London, Ontario, so Becca could take care of business and their Grandma Leighton, who had her semi-annual appointment with her heart specialist. She was having some trouble with edema, and it was concerning Becca.

Jaymie walked Jocie out to catch the school bus, then returned. "So we'll spend a few days at the Queensville house?" she asked Jakob as he was pulling on his jean jacket over a lumber jacket coat. One of the first signs of colder weather settling in was when Michiganians started layering coats.

"Sounds good. Are Clive and Anna coming back?" he asked about the owners of Shady Rest, next door to the Queensville house. The two men had become good friends in the few times they had met.

"They're supposed to be. Anna hopes if everything works out they're going to come back to live. He may take a buyout from his company and start his own investment business, working from the bed-and-breakfast."

"I hope he does. I want to pick his brain about some investments. Be good and be careful today," he said, giving her a lingering kiss, then racing out the door to his truck, thermal mug full of coffee in hand.

She watched through the kitchen window, and waved as he backed out and drove off. That's one thing she loved about him; he never asked her to stop looking into things that worried or interested her, and he hadn't from the first moment she ran to his door late at night for protection from a deranged killer.

She worked for the morning at the Queensville Emporium. She had worked there more often in previous years, but a couple of the grandkids and great-grandkids were taking over more and more from the nonagenarian Klausners as the couple finally started talking about retirement. Petty Welch bounced in to buy milk for the Cottage Shoppe, where she was working that morning. As Jaymie rang up her purchase, she asked how Petty was doing with Haskell Lockland, her new beau.

"Taking it slow," she said, tossing her gray curls. She wore a plaid skirt over black tights and a black and gold cardigan. Her lightly lined face was made up delicately. She always seemed, to Jaymie, effortlessly chic, maybe one reason why she and Cynthia Turbridge and Jewel of Jewel's Junk had become such fast friends; all were women of a certain age who nonetheless exuded a youthful vigor. "He's a bit of a stuffed shirt, but I think he's okay taking it slow, too. He's had a bit of trouble recently with a clingy woman."

"Oh? Who was he dating?"

Petty looked around, saw there was no one else in the place, and said softly, leaning across the counter, "Don't say I told you, but he was dating a married woman, Bev Hastings."

Jaymie's eyes widened in shock. "You don't say! And she was clingy?"

"Crazy is more like it! This was last spring into summer, I understand. She kept buying things for him, giving him little gifts. He broke it off because she was talking about leaving her husband, hinting that she'd be coming into money and getting out of the bait business. She wouldn't stop calling him. He finally put his foot down and told her if she didn't leave him alone he'd tell her husband. That worked for a while, but recently she started calling him again. He called her and told her to leave him alone or he'd call the cops and get a restraining order. The next day his car was keyed."

"His house . . . it's up on Winding Woods Lane," Jaymie said.

Petty nodded. "Right above where they found the body of the Wolverhampton businessman!"

So Bev Hastings was familiar with Winding Woods. Interesting. "When was this . . . last week, you said?"

"I think it was almost a week ago. Oh, Tuesday! I had a hair appointment and he told me about it afterward."

Tuesday. Jaymie gave Petty her change, trying not to show the shock she felt. That was the very day Miss Perry supposedly had another appointment. And Beverly Hastings was right there, keying Haskell's car. Or was she? That was just Haskell's assumption. "How did he know she did it?"

"Oh, he *knew*. She had scraped 'Loverboy' on the side. It was a message; that was her pet name for him."

"Did he tell the police?"

"No. He said it was too embarrassing. There were police all over the place—I guess his neighbor was attacked—but he just had his car fixed, that's all. Gotta go! Take care, Jaymie."

• • •

DETECTIVE VESTRY CAME IN AND MET WITH VALETTA that morning about the medication Miss Perry had said was in her dosette. The detective had already been out to Miss Perry's home and interviewed her; she described the pills as best she could, Val said after. It wasn't definitive, but it was most likely a generic warfarin.

"Will you come outside with me for a moment, Ms. Leighton?" Detective Vestry said as she was heading for the door of the Emporium.

There were no customers in the store, so she followed out to the board porch. She plunked down on an Adirondack, but stood back up when the detective declined a seat. Wrapping her cardigan around her against the chill breeze, she said, "Detective Vestry, did Skip Buchanon tell you about the other attempts on Miss Perry's life, the gunshot and almost being run down?"

"He did. I'm not willing to bet that the incident in Wolverhampton was an attempt, and the gunshot could have been an accident."

"What, a duck hunter along the river?" Jaymie asked sarcastically.

"We're keeping our options open and investigating every lead," she said. "Now, I'm curious," she said, glancing around the village as she talked to Jaymie on the board porch. "Why did you tell Bernie about all of this and not me right away?"

Jaymie hesitated, but Bernie's admonition that she had to grow a pair echoed in her brain. She took a deep breath and let it out. "I know I should have come to you in the first place. I was going to call you about it today"

The woman met her eyes. "Tell me why you didn't call me right away."

"I had the distinct impression that you don't like me."

The detective frowned. "Go on."

"And I was worried that you'd think I was 'investigating,'" she said, sketching air quotes around the word. "I wasn't. Sometimes information finds me."

The woman nodded, and for the first time her expression had some warmth and humor. "Chief Ledbetter said that when it came to you, I should make friends with you and let you go about your business. He said you'd be helpful. *And* that you'd never keep anything from us."

Jaymie flushed, embarrassed. "He rates my abilities way too high. I'm Miss Marple, I guess, and Queensville is my St. Mary Mead."

She nodded with a smile. "I read Agatha Christie when I was a kid. Miss Marple was my favorite character. Reminded me of my nosy gossipy maiden aunt. I never like Hercule Poirot much. In future, give me a call. I promise I won't bite your head off.

Sometimes it's been tough, being a woman in a man's world. I have to remember not everyone is out to get me."

She was no doubt referring obliquely to what Bernie had said, about some of the guys in the department griping about the female chief of police and lead detective. "I will, Detective, I promise. I won't go out of my way to investigate, so to speak, I promise that, too. But if information comes my way, like this did, I'll let you know." She took a deep breath. "So did you find out anything about the grater that Morgan had bought at Thrifty Dan's? I'm sure it's the walnut-shaped one in Baird's mouth."

"I'm on my way to Dan's now to have a word with him about the nutmeg grater. I never thought I'd say those words, but there it is."

"Detective, I'm concerned about Miss Perry," Jaymie said, shifting from foot to foot. "What if Morgan *is* the one who tried to kill her? Skip is worried he can't justify being there much longer, because she's getting better so quickly. What if you don't tie things up in time?"

The woman nodded. "I'm troubled, too. The best I can do is solve this murder swiftly. We have solid forensic evidence, but it takes time to process. I have some investigative paths to follow, ones I hope will lead me to the culprit."

Jaymie was so tempted to ask what, but knew she'd get no reply. She could imagine some, like checking ATV tracks on the riverbank, and sightings by neighbors. Footwork by dogged detectives to track down every clue would ultimately lead to the killer. She hoped it didn't take too long. "I don't know how you figure it all out. I'm lucky more than anything," Jaymie admitted. "But in this case I can't figure out how the murder of Fergus Baird could be tied to the attempt on Miss Perry's life. It feels like they don't connect, you know? And yet, it beggars imagination that two such traumatic events in the same place wouldn't be connected."

The detective examined her. "You've thought about this a lot, I see. I do want to say . . . Miss Perry's safety is my deepest concern. I have made it known to the Wallaces that we are investigating every single lead and are watching suspects closely. We don't actually have enough officers to follow them around, but I hope it keeps them on their toes."

Jaymie was relieved to some extent, but not wholly. She'd have been more relieved if the Hastingses had been given the same warning. She bid the detective goodbye and went back to the store to tidy, sell, and visit with locals. When Gracey Klausner came in to relieve her, she said goodbye to Valetta and headed over to the house to see Becca and Kevin.

✄ Eighteen ✄

As always, her Queensville kitchen, with its blend of old and new, vintage and modern, relaxed her. They had lunch and chatted pleasantly. She was going to head up to Miss Perry's, since she did need to gather the graters now that Bill Waterman had the cases ready to install at the heritage house.

"Jaymie, if you could, I'd like you to ask Miss Perry a few questions," Kevin said. "I'm wondering if there are any peculiarities she remembers about her silverware."

"Peculiarities?"

"Yes. There are a few on the flatware that could be identifying features, but I won't tell you what they are. Ask her about any scratches, bent tines, marked serrations, anything like that."

"Good idea," Jaymie said. "She's got a very good memory, and is very observant." She said her goodbyes—the couple were going to be in Canada for a couple of weeks—and drove through town and up to Winding Woods Lane.

Skip Buchanon had texted Jaymie, telling her that he was staying at the home full-time. The service was experiencing a temporary shortage of on-call nurses because of an early-season influenza outbreak. She suspected he had other more serious reasons for making himself available. Morgan's car was parked in the drive, along with the nurse's.

She tapped on the door and Skip answered, ushering her in, rolling his eyes as the sound of weeping and shouting echoed.

"What's going on?"

Skip, whose muscular frame was covered in scrubs and a frilly apron—he had a dishcloth in his hands—sighed. "Not my business. I think you'll know soon enough anyway."

She followed him through the hall, where he parted from her to return to the kitchen. She followed the argument to the sitting room. Miss Perry was clearly much better, because she was back to full-on persnickety mode. She still sat in her chair, and Morgan was on an ottoman at her feet, hands over her face.

"If you do that, I *swear* I'll disown you, Morgan Perry Wallace," she stated, her cheeks spotted by two high circles of color.

"Auntie Lois, you don't understand!" the young woman said, wiping her eyes with the back of one hand.

Both looked toward Jaymie as she stood in the doorway. "Hi, you two," she said as she entered, feeling like she was interfering but not knowing quite what else to do.

Morgan's plump face was twisted in pain and misery. She was shaking as she stood. "I'd better go."

"No, Morgan, I can come back another time if—"

"Never mind," she said, pushing past Jaymie. "I'm in the way here anyway."

"Don't you leave in the middle of this, Morgan!" Miss Perry said, twisting in her chair. "I have a right to my opinion, and I will not be bullied out of it."

Jaymie took a deep breath. "What's going on?"

"It's not just an *opinion*," the young woman said, turning and looking back at her aunt, her voice guttural with unshed tears. "You have no right to tell me what to do with my life."

"I'm *not* telling you what to do with your life," Miss Perry said, looking put out. "You are free to head straight to perdition, if that's what you want. But if you get a divorce, you're out of my will. It's *your* choice, young lady!"

Jaymie felt a tinge of unease. "Miss Perry—"

"Don't even bother," Morgan said, her voice thick. "She's only listening to herself." She stomped off and headed directly to the front door. It slammed behind her.

Jaymie moved the low stool to Miss Perry's chair and sat down, looking up at the woman, whose eyes were clouded with tears. "How did that fight start?"

"She waltzes in here and announces she's getting a divorce. Tired of marriage. Tired of Saunders, who has been nothing but sweet and attentive, far as I can see."

"As far as *you* can see," Jaymie said.

"Maybe that's what he wanted to talk about. He was supposed to come see me, but he never did."

Jaymie was about to ask Miss Perry about that, but Skip came to the door, wiping his hands dry on a towel. "You two like some tea?"

"I know I would," Jaymie said.

"You want to help me?" Skip asked, motioning toward the kitchen.

She followed him. "What was that all about, the argument between Morgan and Miss Perry?"

"Morgan was upset when she came in," he murmured, putting the kettle on the burner. "I didn't catch it all, but the police had been to the car dealership to see them about the Baird murder."

Jaymie didn't offer that she may have been the genesis of that visit, with her revelation about Morgan buying the nutmeg grater. From what Detective Vestry had said, she knew that the police had likely given the couple a heavy-handed warning about Miss Perry, too. "And . . . ?"

"And as I understand it, she and Saunders got into a quarrel and she said she wanted a divorce. He said he wasn't going to give it to her, and told her her aunt would never countenance it. She came here to explain to Miss Perry and ask for her support."

"Which it sounds like she's not getting." Jaymie's mind was speeding over the news. She hadn't heard the conversation with the police, nor had she heard the argument between husband and wife. Maybe Morgan's husband knew she had tried to kill her aunt, and perhaps had killed Baird for some reason, and was holding her to their marriage out of spite, or . . . a host of other possible reasons. Maybe he was trying to blackmail her into staying. But then, why was she talking about divorce to her aunt?

"I guess not. Poor girl is distraught."

Jaymie picked up the tray, troubled but not sure how to handle it.

"It's not your problem, Jaymie," Skip said. "In my business I hear all kinds of stuff, and can't interfere unless my patient is being abused or bullied. Most of the time it's not my business."

"I'd make a terrible nurse," Jaymie admitted ruefully. "I can't seem to keep my nose out of other folks' business. It's weird, but I feel bad for Morgan, even though . . ." She shook her head, unwilling to say more.

"Me too. She's deeply upset. I guess all we can do is keep Miss Perry safe and hope the police tie up the investigation. Things will sort themselves out. They usually do." He sighed. "You know, I didn't get the sense that the detective took the other attempts on her life — the gunshot and the car — seriously. I'm worried it has nothing to do with Baird's murder, so finding his killer won't protect Miss Perry."

"That's scary," Jaymie said. "But you're right."

She carried the tea tray into the sitting room.

Miss Perry sat in sullen silence. She looked over at Jaymie. "I suppose you're going to side with Morgan."

"Miss Perry, I don't know the answers," she said, setting the tray down. "But if Morgan is unhappy with Saunders, if their marriage is irrevocably broken, what is the point of her staying in it? That isn't good for anyone." She poured tea in a mug. "Why does she want to divorce him?"

"She said he's not who she thought he was when they married."

"What did she mean by that?"

"I don't know. She kept saying it over and over, that he wasn't who he said he was."

"Wait . . . did she say that he wasn't who she thought he was when they got married, or that he wasn't who he said he was?"

"There's a difference?"

Jaymie thought about it for a long few minutes as she fixed their mugs of tea. "Yes, I think there is. The first means that she was mistaken, the second that he lied."

"I don't know, but I don't think she should throw it all away."

"Miss Perry, it might not be a good idea to use inclusion or exclusion in your will as a bargaining point," she said gently. How to tell her that it painted a target on her? That it made it more likely inheritors would think of her simply in terms of her money? "It's damaging to a relationship to try to make someone behave as you want using threats."

Her eyes watered and she set her cup down. "You may be right. I've never done that before."

"Well, that's good to hear." If that was true, then Morgan would have had no reason to hasten Miss Perry's death. "Is she your only heir?"

"No, not at all. In fact, ask Haskell Lockland . . . I'm giving a lot of my collection to the heritage society on the understanding it will be displayed as a part of local history. The Perry family is important to this town and its development. Some of the Perry furniture and most of the spice relics will go to the society."

"But no other family member will inherit."

"She's the only one who doesn't have close family. Poor

Morgan . . . she was an only child and lost her parents when she was twenty-two and still in college. I was so happy when she married Saunders a few years ago. If she divorces him, she might never get married again." She met Jaymie's gaze. "It's a lonely life without someone to live it with."

"It's even lonelier if you live it with the wrong person," Jaymie said gently. "I could easily be in her shoes. I wanted desperately to marry the wrong man, and I'm grateful every day that I didn't. I don't think you want Morgan to suffer the rest of her life through an unhappy marriage."

After a moment, Jaymie changed the topic and asked Miss Perry Kevin's question about the silver flatware, and wrote down everything Miss Perry could remember, which was quite a bit. One of the serving forks had a bent tine; one of the knives had a nick in the serration; a fish fork had a dark stain; there were other faults she listed. Jaymie tucked that paper in her purse, then gathered the spice graters, labeling each one. She left an hour later with a case full of the graters, each wrapped in tissue in a plastic baggie. She stowed it in her car as Haskell Lockland pulled up. They greeted each other.

"Have you convinced Miss Perry to allow walkers across her land?" he asked.

She stared at him, incredulous. "Even though her home was broken into, someone tried to kill her, and a man was murdered on her property? I think that ship has sailed, Haskell."

He sighed. "None of that has anything to do with tourists."

"You can try and convince her of that, but I'm not helping."

"Jaymie, I intend to protect her *and* myself; I'm her next-door neighbor, after all. Do you think I'd expose myself to danger?"

She knew that was true. She debated asking him about Bev Hastings and the damage she had done to his car, but she would wait on that. "Show me what you intend. If I think it's worth it, I'll try to sway her, but I won't bully her, Haskell. Wait a moment and I'll let her nurse know we're going to go to the backyard." Jaymie raced back to the door, let Skip know she and Haskell would be in the backyard, then returned. She led him around the side and through the gate between their two properties.

She was tempted, as she led Haskell through the backyard, to tell him about the shot fired from the approximate area, but now was not the time to reveal that information. He grumbled as they went about Miss Perry's population of stray cats.

"I feel like I'm preparing them a buffet meal every time I fill my bird feeder."

Jaymie was familiar with the argument that stray cats killed legions of birds every year, but the only way to truly solve the problem without killing the strays — not an option in her mind — was to spay or neuter every animal so they wouldn't keep contributing to the stray problem. There was never going to be one hundred percent eradication of stray cats because people weren't responsible enough when they adopted a cat to fix the poor things. A fixed cat was a happier, longer-lived cat, even strays. So she didn't respond.

It was a windy day. She wrapped her jacket around her and slipped through the rose arbor to stand on the hillside above the river, rippled and gray on a blustery, sullen day. Townsfolk watched warily every winter as ice built up, and coast guard boats were dispatched to break up the ice and shepherd ships upriver. An ice buildup could raise the river levels dramatically and swiftly, threatening riverside parks and homes, as well as those on the island.

But thoughts of ice and snow were far off yet, as October cooled with the winds of autumn. Haskell joined her, and both looked south at a rust-colored cargo ship that cruised along in the shipping lane. She did get why the heritage society was supporting creating a walking trail along the St. Clair; this spot in particular was a wonderful vantage point for photographers, and it was evident that despite this being private property, folks had climbed up here even since the police had found the body. There was a gum wrapper and an empty Red Bull can left behind.

"This is one thing Miss Perry is upset about," Jaymie said, indicating the garbage. "How are you going to handle it if people are given the freedom to walk the cliff? Who's going to clean up the mess? Along the boardwalk it's cleaned by municipal employees, but what about along a walking trail?"

"I know, I know. My place gets the same thing. Worse, probably, because that's where the slope is that people use to climb up the bank."

Jaymie paused and looked south to Haskell's property. His yard was fenced, but on the river side of the fence there was indeed a sloped path down to a flat area. She headed that way and followed the sloping path toward the river, stopping halfway when something caught her attention.

Haskell, panting, followed and stopped behind her to rest, his hands on his knees. "Gosh, if we do a walking trail here we'll have to come out and clear all this brush away!"

Jaymie examined a sumac bush that had reached out over the path; sumacs were used on almost vertical cliffsides because they grew quickly and their roots offered good soil retention. The recent winds had torn the brilliant crimson leaves from the bush, and she spotted a torn bit of fabric on a branch. She plucked it off and turned it over in her hands. It was red, with a square of black at the edge and a yellow line running through it. With that coloration it would have blended with the sumac leaves. Where had she seen that fabric before?

"Maybe this whole walking path idea isn't so good," Haskell said. "I'm going back. I don't know what you wanted to see, but this is enough."

He trudged back along the path and Jaymie turned to follow him. That was when she remembered where she had seen the fabric. On TV. Quite often. As she followed Haskell, things that puzzled her fell into place and she knew who killed Baird, suspected why, and how it tied in with the attempts on Miss Perry. She returned to the house and spoke to Skip again, warning him about one certain person. She wanted to be sure of a couple of things before she went to Detective Vestry, so she asked for Morgan's cell phone number and he gave it to her by memory.

• • •

Back in town, she stopped at the antique store, where she knew Kevin and Becca were giving Georgina an afternoon off before they returned to Canada that evening.

"Jaymie . . . I thought we said our goodbyes!" Becca said, looking up from some last-minute china display tidying. She was setting the gorgeous dining table in the window with a more fallish pattern, Johnson Brothers Harvest Time, an inexpensive but attractive pattern in tones of brown and green. She had hand-lettered a sign that told of the availability of a full set with serving pieces.

"I have some information for Kevin." Her brother-in-law came out of the back storeroom at the sound of his name. "I have a list of imperfections Miss Perry remembers," she said, pulling the sheet out of her purse. "I thought you'd like to take a look." She handed it to him.

He perused it, putting on his glasses and squinting at the list. His expression became more sober and he nodded at the end. "I'm afraid the lady is correct," he said, looking up and pulling his glasses off, letting them dangle on their leather string. "I was examining the pieces, and I recognize these imperfections. I'm afraid Beverly Hastings sold us stolen goods. Which means she faked the will she showed as provenance, and is a thief and a con artist. Georgina is *not* going to be happy."

Jaymie sighed. "I'll leave that list with you. Call in the police, I suppose, but give me half an hour. I want to talk to Beverly Hastings about something else first, and she'll never speak to me after the cops are done with her. Heck, she'll probably be in jail after the police speak to her."

She headed directly for the bait shop, wondering as she went if Jon Hastings was involved as well. Hard to tell, and that would be for the police to figure out. A stream of folks were heading up from the ferry, along with a couple of cars. She waited a moment, wondering if Bev was in the bait shop, and if she was, how to get her away so she could talk to her. But the woman left the bait shop, limping with the boot and a cane.

Jaymie headed her off and said, "Hey, Bev, can we talk?"

She looked dreadful, her normally nicely styled hair a rat's nest, deep bags under her eyes. It's like she had stopped caring how she looked in the last few days. "I don't have time," she growled. "I have a doctor's appointment in Wolverhampton."

"I won't take long, Bev." Herring gulls in the parking lot, where they gathered to beg for treats from tourists, were disturbed and took off in a screeching soaring flock, sending some mallards into a similar flight. The cars from the ferry slowly ascended and took off through the parking lot. "I think you should listen to me," Jaymie added with a steely tone. "It's about Fergus Baird's death."

The woman stopped, her eyes wide, her expression solemn. "Okay. But I'm going to sit down. My leg is killing me."

They sat together on a bench on the walkway above the marina, looking out across the river. There was a lot Jaymie wanted to ask but wouldn't, like, how and why did she break into Miss Perry's house? Why did she sell the silver flatware to the Queensville Fine Antiques store, so close to home? The answer probably was she couldn't find anyone to buy it and got desperate for cash, but Jaymie would let the police handle all of that.

Instead, a more important question: "Who do you think killed Fergus Baird?"

"Morgan Wallace," Bev said, spitting the name out like it was poison.

Jaymie nodded. "Why would she do that?"

"Why do you think? She was having a fling with Fergus and he threatened to tell her precious aunt if she didn't help him get the marina property."

"How do you know?"

For a moment, a fleeting wistful expression clouded her face. She pursed her lips and looked down at the boot on her foot. "He told me he was going to blackmail her. That day you saw us in the restaurant. What a dick! He as good as promised . . ." She shook her head.

"That you and he would be together?"

Her eyes welled and one tear trailed down her cheek and splashed on her hand.

"But you thought that about Haskell Lockland too, didn't you?"

The woman turned an angry face to her. "What do you want from me?"

"Just the truth. Do you know something you're not telling any-one?"

"You're an awful snoop, aren't you?" She stood. "A horrible *horrible* girl. I have to go."

Jaymie almost felt bad for the woman, given what she was going to face in the coming days. But giving her the heads-up that they knew she had stolen the silver was out of the question. She'd have to face the music. Bev Hastings stumped away to a rusted silver sedan parked beside the bait store truck, a small dark pickup, in the municipal parking lot. The woman got out her keys, her keychain flashing silver in the sunlight.

A dark pickup . . . Jaymie stared at the bait shop truck. Was that the vehicle that had come at her on the day she found Miss Perry injured? And was that from marking Haskell's truck? If so, who was driving? Jon wouldn't be the first man to take it out on a competitor when their woman strayed. Interesting idea.

And thinking of Haskell . . . she remembered what she had figured out while walking with the heritage society president. She got her phone out of her purse and dialed Morgan's number. No answer. It went to voice mail. "Hey, Morgan, there's something important I need to talk to you about. It's a question I have about Fergus Baird's death. Give me a call, would you?"

She was about to go back to her car when her phone buzzed with a text message from Morgan. *Sorry. In a meeting. Meet me at Roth Park in Wolverhampton; got to tell you something important.*

Roth Park? She knew where it was, but it was an odd place to meet. She called Detective Vestry and left a message on her voice mail, telling her where she was going and why, and about the torn bit of fabric. She then retrieved her car and drove off, noting the police car at Queensville Fine Antiques. She sighed. She was definitely going to be on Georgina's naughty list, but the truth was the truth. The shadows were long this time of day, and it got chilly quickly. The highway wasn't crowded but there was a fair amount of traffic, folks heading home after a long day.

Roth Park was on the near side of Wolverhampton where Roth Creek raced and tumbled over rocks in a gully on its way to the St. Clair River. She followed the winding lane into the park past clumps of trees and bushes. The elevation descended toward the parking area, which gave easy access in nice weather to the open green area used by picnickers and families and, it was rumoured, on warm summer evenings by lovers as a meeting spot. The parking lot was rimmed by hedges, nice and private for secret rendezvous. This time of day with this chill breeze, it was bound to be deserted. She pulled into a parking space next to Morgan's car and got out, looking around for the young woman, who was not in the driver's seat as she had expected.

"You're a freakin' nosy witch, aren't you?"

Jaymie turned slowly, trapped between the two vehicles, to find a gun pointed at her, clutched tightly in the hand of a tartan-clad Saunders Wallace.

๙ Nineteen ๙

TOO LATE SHE REALIZED it had all gone topsy-turvy faster than she had imagined it would. "Morgan figured it out, didn't she?" Jaymie said, trying to calm her racing heart. In that moment, faced with that gun, she fully understood the danger; she could die, right here, right now, in this lonely parking lot. A knife she'd have a chance against. A baseball bat she could hope to fend off. But a handgun? It was made for one thing: killing a human.

"Morgan? Well, yeah, she *did* figure it out, later than I thought she would, sooner than I'd have liked." His face was lined and shadowed, his expression grim. "My wife is not too bright, but she gets there eventually."

His gun riveted her attention. Some people might say that if she had a gun of her own she'd be able to equalize the danger to her life. But unless she had it in her hand, ready, in this moment of crisis, she didn't see how that was possible. Though Jakob had a rifle on the farm, Jaymie was not a gun person. Her brain and persuasive tongue would be her only weapons.

Jaymie worked at slowing her pulse, controlling her breathing. She'd been in tough situations before, and panicking would not help. As much as she longed to wildly look around, searching for escape, for the moment she needed to focus on Saunders. "She's probably been figuring it out bit by bit for a while." If only she had her phone in her hand she could try to figure out how to call 911. Or something . . . *anything.* Her teeth were starting to chatter—nerves or the cold?

"I can't believe I fooled her for as long as I did."

"*You weren't who you said you were,* Morgan said. Miss Perry thought she was disillusioned, but I wondered right away if she was being literal, that you aren't Saunders Wallace." So far, no nervous quaver in her voice. How long could she maintain the façade of courage when her insides were quivering? "*Is* there a Saunders Wallace?"

The guy shrugged. "Yeah, but he died at the age of two years four months in 1986."

"So, who are you *really*?" Jaymie was trying to slide her glance around, to see if there was anyone else in the park. But they were below road level and the park had large clusters of bridal wreath spirea and forsythia, as well as groves of young trees that hid the parking lot from view and the hedge along the parking lot that trapped her from easy escape. He had thought out carefully where to have her meet Morgan, and where he'd park her car. "You must have a name."

He ignored her questions, saying, "I *see* you looking around. Don't even imagine you can jabber at me enough that you can escape. Morgan is dead, and you're going to join her. The police will have your last text exchange to confirm your plan to meet." He smiled, and there was an eerie peace in his expression. "I'll be *heart*broken, of course, to find out what my lovely little wifey was up to. Morgan lured you here, forced you into her car, and then took off, speeding through town and beyond, out to Rock Valley Quarry, where she will accidentally crash the car and it will go up in flames, killing you both instantly."

A chill ran down her back. He had it all planned out, and so quickly.

"And it will become obvious she was on a killing spree . . . I mean, Baird, and you . . . and then her aunt." He shook his head, an exaggerated sad expression on his face. "So sad, but there's proof right on her phone that she's the one Baird was meeting before he died."

"But . . ." She was still confused about some things Saunders was saying, but she remembered hearing that Baird had been planning to meet someone, though his secretary didn't know who; he no doubt thought he was meeting Morgan. There was probably a text on his phone from a phone registered to Morgan, maybe a burner. But poor Fergus was really having an unplanned and lethal meeting with Saunders. Jaymie swallowed hard. Wallace must have filched the silver nutmeg grater Morgan had bought her aunt. He planned all along to use it, knowing it would be traced back to her and tie Baird's death in to the one he planned for Miss Perry. If Morgan had known about the nutmeg grater in Baird's mouth she would have put it all together, but no one was privy to that information but Jaymie and the police. "You seem to be adept at this kind of thing."

"It's not my first rodeo, doll," he said with the trademark grin that locals had come to recognize and call the Wallace Cheese on his TV ads. "Now get in the car."

"Where *is* Morgan?" she asked, stalling, her mind spinning as she tried to think of how to get out of this mess.

"I told you, she's dead." He glanced at the trunk.

"This is never going to work, you know," she said. She had to stay out of that car; once she climbed in, it became her casket. "No one is going to buy that a girl like Morgan could force me into a car and kill us both. I have a bit of a reputation for surviving things like this."

His face reddened, the color flushing up to the roots of his hair; his natural hair color, growing out under the red dye, was brown with a hint of gray. He was older than he pretended, lines and shadows showing his age. The gun wavered as he trembled with anger. "You think you're good, but this will be your last performance, and then you're done. Too bad for the hubs and kid, but you're a goner."

He knew about Jakob and Jocie!

He smirked as he caught her panicked expression, and regained his confidence. "Now, get in the damn car or I'll shoot you where you stand."

"Why, Saunders? What was this all about?" she asked, still desperately stalling, still trying to figure out how to avoid death. "I'm assuming you were trying to kill Lois Perry and . . ." A thought grabbed her and it all made sense. She could see his plan.

"Get in the freakin' car right now!" he screamed.

She put out her hands in a placating gesture. "I will. I *will*! But first . . . I'm one of those people who *have* to know they're right, you know? It'll go quicker if you satisfy my curiosity. S-so, let me get this straight: you tried to kill Miss Perry. You had a key." She paused and eyed the fellow. "Or . . . you had one made from Morgan's. That way you could sneak in and do things like put dangerous pills in Miss Perry's dosette, and string the wire across the stairs. When did you do that? It must have been the very day it happened. The back stairs are closest to her sitting room, so she would have used them to go up to bed the night before."

"That old bat's hearing is awful," he growled. "She didn't even hear me sneak in that morning. I'm a master at planning; I put the screw eyes in place while I was doing home repairs for *dear* old Auntie Lois the day before," he sneered. "That way I just had to let myself back in the next morning, attach the wire, and let myself out." His expression darkened again. "I had told her I'd be by at ten thirty to do a couple more tasks around the house, but I started banging on the back door at ten. *That* part worked out perfectly."

That was why she was still in her housedress, and why she didn't have the appointment marked on her calendar! She didn't write in a notation if it was just Morgan or Saunders coming over. It also explained why the front door was unlocked; Miss Perry, expecting Saunders at ten thirty, must have descended the front stairs after Estelle left and unlocked it, then gone back up to change. But then Saunders showed up early. "You *knew* she wouldn't be ready yet when you banged on the back door. She rushed down the back stairs to let you in."

"She *should* have died, hardheaded old witch!" he grunted, admitting his attempt on her life. "People get caught because the person who dies, their wounds don't look right, so I figured just make her have a real accident, you know?" He smirked, the know-it-all look so familiar from his TV commercials.

"Weren't you worried about the police finding the wire?"

He shrugged. "I'd intended to remove it and the screw eyes after she fell, but I heard someone next door and a dog was barking its fool head off. I didn't want to be seen at Lois's back door, so I headed down to the river and took off."

He heard someone . . . that was likely Phillipa Zane coming back for her cell phone! She said Lan's dog barked every time she entered the house.

"Then I got held up at the office. If everything had gone to plan I would've been the one to find her. *Dead.* I figured the extra time would ensure she was long gone." He sighed and rolled his eyes. "And I had such a great performance planned! I was going to go in, remove the wire and screw eyes, attempt CPR and bawl my eyes out about dear old Auntie Lois while calling 911. I was looking forward to the publicity as I told the newspaper about my heroic rescue attempt. All that planning wasted."

All his planning, she wanted to say, was crappy. On TV mystery shows killers were always cool and collected, but in real life people made mistakes, fortunately for the police. "Everything would have been different if you'd removed the wire and screw eyes."

"Yeah, well, Lady Luck was not on my side, was it?" he snapped.

"No, it was on Miss Perry's!" she retorted.

He grimaced. "She's like those cats she moons over . . . nine lives or more."

"Once Miss Perry died Morgan would inherit the estate, right?"

"Yeah, of course."

"And then what?"

"What do you think?" He glared at her impatiently, waved the gun and growled, "Enough chitchat! Get in the car."

The man seemed completely comfortable with the gun, like it was an extension of his hand. "You had tried to kill her before, hadn't you? Tampering with her medication was one, and the shot from the riverside *was* an attempt on Miss Perry's life." Maybe he was a lousy shot, since he had only winged her, but he was pointing this gun at Jaymie from ten feet or so; if he shot, he wouldn't miss.

A flicker of uncertainty revealed his surprise that she knew about the gunshot.

"*And* the car that almost ran her down in Wolverhampton. One of your car lot cars, no doubt. You're just not very good at murder, are you?"

"Good enough to trick Baird. Dear Auntie Lois was lucky, that's all. What did I say about nine lives? But her luck's about to run out. Look, I'm *not* going to say this again," he growled, his voice taking on a guttural rasp as he took a step toward her. *"Get in the car!"*

Her insides quivered at the increasing anger in his voice, but she hadn't figured a way out of her predicament. Tears welled. She willed them away, taking a deep breath. She had to risk continuing to talk. "You figured that once Miss Perry was dead, you'd kill Morgan and inherit from *her*. Plus insurance money, I'm guessing? You must have had your wife insured. Morgan wanting to divorce you must have precipitated this, right?" A cold breeze flattened the grass in the park and chilled Jaymie, but she was focused on her assailant. She had to maintain that focus if she was going to get out of this alive.

Like other killers she had met, caught up in their travails, he couldn't resist the bait, the chance to relate his clever plan to a willing listener. The hand holding the gun drooped. "So far you've got it. I knew what I had to do; Auntie Lois first, then Morgan. If the old lady had died when she was supposed to, none of this other crap would have been necessary. But that Fergus jerk was sniffing around Morgan and trying to get her to convince her aunt to sell the marina property. That wouldn't have mattered so much, but he was getting in the way, getting too close. I saw his game; he thought he could step on my turf, persuade my wife to leave me. She was stupid enough to tell me he kissed her. She found some . . . well, some stuff I thought I had hidden better and got mad and threw it out that there were other men interested in her."

"I saw that kiss. She looked surprised and didn't properly kiss him back, you know. No matter what he or anyone else thought," Jaymie said, remembering Bev's claim that Fergus intended to blackmail Morgan once he started an affair with her, "she was not interested in him."

"It was just a matter of time. Women like you and her can be flattered into sex, and then you think you're in *lo-ove*," he said, drawing the word out with a sneer.

"Women like me and Morgan? I don't think we have that much in common."

"You have *one* thing." He looked her up and down.

Ah, he was talking about the fact that both of them tended toward chubbiness. It was the old tired trope that overweight or plain women were easily seduced by flattery and a heavy come-on. He wasn't very bright and he didn't know women as well as he thought. "So, was the stuff she found about who you *really* are?"

"That and other things." He smirked. "I *may* have been looking around for my next wife on a dating site. She figured out my password and went snooping."

He was trolling the internet for his next victim—or wife, as he called her—even as he planned a series of homicides. She was careful to keep her disgust hidden. "So you met up with and killed Fergus, and deposited his body in Miss Perry's yard. Oh!" Her eyes widened. "Using one of the ATVs from your car lot!" She thought of Jakob's ATV at The Junk Stops Here, the one that had a front-end bucket that he used to move heavy things. So that was how Saunders got the body up the hill. But he would have needed to

181

climb up and position Baird in the bushes. That was when the scrap of fabric had torn from his jacket on the sumac branch. "Then you set this plan into motion."

"I wouldn't have worried about it if Morgan had shut her trap. This is all *her* fault. For some reason she suspected I was behind the attempts on that poisonous old lady. She was going to go to the police. So . . ." He shrugged. "I did what I had to do. The plan accelerated."

She heard a noise, and the other car moved. Morgan wasn't dead at all, but locked in the trunk! A surge of hope thrummed through Jaymie's blood. "You're still working out your plan, aren't you? Morgan is still alive because you need Miss Perry to die *before* Morgan. If Morgan goes first you get nothing, right?"

"Wrong!" he shouted. "You're *so* wrong. It only has to *look* like the old lady died first. Now, get in the freaking car before I pop you one," he said, waving the gun at her. "No one will be looking for a bullet in a corpse in a burned-out car."

A chill raced through her and her stomach turned. She was close to throwing up, she was so scared. "You don't understand the law, do you?" she said defiantly. "A murderer can't inherit from their victim, so if it looks like Morgan killed Miss Perry, the will is void. You'd get any insurance on Morgan but you would *not* get Miss Perry's estate."

The gun wavered as he pondered her words. Jaymie's Explorer was behind her. Could she circle it and duck before he got a shot off? It was worth trying, if she could summon the guts, but it had to be quick and decisive because she needed to get past him to do it. A distraction would help. Would the old *look behind you* gimmick work on Saunders?

As if sent by heaven, though, a distraction arrived in the shape of a police car with sirens blaring and light bar flashing. Bernie flung herself from the driver's seat, gun drawn and pointed at Saunders Wallace. "Toss the gun down and get on your face *now!*" she yelled.

Her partner, Officer Hien Ng, lunged past Saunders, grabbed Jaymie and pulled her behind her Explorer. Wallace did exactly as he was told. As he lay facedown in a puddle, the sound of pounding and screaming came from the car.

"Bernie, Morgan is in the car trunk!" Jaymie cried, still clinging to Ng's arm. "Saunders—or whoever he is, because he is *not* Saunders Wallace—was going to kill us both."

• • •

AFTER SAUNDERS WAS TAKEN AWAY IN CUFFS and Morgan was rescued from the trunk and taken to the hospital for an examination, the others convened at the police station. Jaymie gave her statement, not only what had happened but everything her chat with Wallace had confirmed. Sitting in a conference room with the detective and police chief, Deborah Connolly, Jaymie wearily explained what she knew of Saunders's plans, finishing with, "He was going to force me into the car, or kill me and *then* put me in the car, send the car off a cliff to make it look like an accident, kill Miss Perry, and claim the inheritance and insurance."

"You did the right thing, calling me," Detective Vestry said. "It saved your life. The *better* thing would have been to stay out of it altogether."

"As far as I knew I was going to talk to Morgan," Jaymie said.

As she told the police all that she knew, she learned that Detective Vestry had gotten her voice-mail message about the same time as a citizen reported that she had seen a man knocking a woman into the trunk of a silver sedan. Wallace, because he was so well known locally, and perpetually wore red tartan, with his dyed-ginger hair, was ID'd as the man doing it. By becoming a minor local celebrity he had broken the number-one rule of a con man, which was to stay out of the limelight. Vestry put Jaymie's voice mail and the abduction report together and came up with mortal danger for Jaymie; she had a squad car race to Roth Park to intervene.

"I *knew* it was Saunders who had killed Baird, at that point," Jaymie said. "Miss Perry mentioning that Saunders was the one who was supposed to come and see her the day she was hurt—something I wish she had remembered earlier—confirmed it. He wanted to be sure she was exactly where he wanted her. He had a key, a copy of Morgan's, so he snuck into the house and laid the wire trap. Then, hidden from neighbors, he banged on the back door to get her to rush down the stairs."

The detective exchanged a look with the police chief, who nodded. "An eyewitness has come forward who saw Wallace in the area. He apparently parked on Laurel and must have walked to the house."

Jaymie frowned. "One thing I hadn't figured out was *that*, why it was so evidently a murder attempt. He made the mistake of overcomplicating it all. He could have snuck in and pushed Miss Perry down the stairs, but he had to go the elaborate route with the wire across the stairs. Thank goodness he did. If he'd *pushed* her down the stairs she probably would have died." She paused, frowning. "But what about the slippers at the bottom of the stairs? They were *not* Miss Perry's."

Vestry sighed. "I'll tell you this much, but don't breathe a word, and I do mean not a word to anyone. Saunders Wallace had a box of shoes, boots and slippers in his storeroom at the car dealership. We think we'll be able to forensically match the slippers with the other shoes jumbled in that box."

"Oh! From the TV ad he did, where he pitches shoes and slippers at the camera!" she said. "I get it. He thought it would look like she was wearing slippers too big for her and fell down the stairs. If he had removed the wire as he intended it may have looked like that."

"Luckily, he was both overambitious and sloppy," Chief Connolly said. She was a woman in her fifties, somber, sturdy and grim-faced. "He made mistakes. Murderers almost always make mistakes."

"True. You know, the only reason I wanted to talk to Morgan was to convince her to turn her husband in, which is why I was willing to meet her."

Vestry nodded. "We do understand that."

"We're grateful that you cooperated, Ms. Müller, and that it turned out well," said the chief. "This could have ended very badly."

"How is Morgan? Have you heard?"

"She's at the hospital, but she'll be fine. She's young," Chief Connolly said with a flicker of a smile. "We're going to take her statement there, since they would like to keep her overnight for observation to be sure her head wound doesn't cause any problems."

"I'm grateful, Chief, and to you, Detective Vestry, truly," she said, watching the woman across the table; she looked tired and worried. What was it like to work every day knowing that lives depended on you? One wrong move could be lethal. It was a weight for someone to carry, especially someone who cared, as the detective so clearly did. "May I call my husband? He's going to be so worried about me."

Vestry smiled ever so briefly, like the first faint warm wind in March, promising spring. She looked over Jaymie's shoulder.

"Mama!"

Jaymie whirled just in time to catch Jocie, who barreled at her full tilt; Jakob, dark eyes full of concern, followed. When he saw she was okay, he bent and took her in his arms, pulling her up and hugging her hard, as Jocie grabbed them both around the legs.

Jaymie turned to Vestry, eyes watering. "Can I go home now?"

• • •

HOME, BUT NOT TO SLEEP. Even wrapped in Jakob's arms, she awoke shaking and afraid every half hour or so, when she finally could get to sleep. The gun had appeared all through her dreams: on the ground; in her purse; pointed at her; and finally, fired. She awoke again with a start at the loud report in her nightmare. Jakob soothed her every time she awoke, getting as little sleep as she did. He held her and caressed her and let her whisper her fears, even as she shivered, no blankets enough to warm a cold that seemed to have invaded her heart. After all she had been through, all the times she had been in danger, she couldn't figure out why this time had affected her so deeply.

But in the morning, watching Jocie eat cereal and work on the pictures for her story, and Jakob drink his coffee while working on the financial plan for the latest Müller venture—glancing up at her from time to time, worry in his eyes after her rough night—she got it. It was worse now because she had so *very* much to lose. It's not that she didn't care before about living or dying, but now the thought of it was more real, more present, more fearsome.

It was time to rethink the way she conducted herself in these instances.

And yet . . . it was one of those "instances" that led Jaymie to

Jakob's door. Taunting a sociopath had brought her a husband and instant family that was more important than anything else in the world. Maybe that was the trade-off, she thought. Maybe she had to accept that there would be fear, and there would be danger, sometimes, but there would always be reward, too. This time the reward was that because she had managed to do the right thing and contact the detective at the right moment—and had the good luck that a citizen saw and reported Morgan's abduction—Morgan was alive and Miss Perry was safe, her would-be killer in jail awaiting arraignment on those charges and a murder charge for Fergus Baird's killing. If she had not interfered, things may have turned out very bad indeed. She had no doubt that the police would have gotten Saunders afterward, but it would have been too late for Morgan and Miss Perry.

Jakob took Jocie to school—she never knew and would never know how much trouble Jaymie had been in—then came back, and together they took Hoppy for a long walk, over the new land, making their plans. The store would be about a hundred feet back from the road, leaving room for displays of the pumpkins they would grow, and the Christmas trees they would sell. It was going to be one floor, with room to expand if sales warranted.

But that was a ways off. Right now, they had some immediate plans of their own. Back in the log cabin, as Hoppy and Lilibet retreated to the warmth of their bed by the fire, Jakob led Jaymie upstairs and it was there, in the warmth of their cozy bed, that she let love and security banish fear from her heart.

✄ Twenty ✄

WHEN THEY DESCENDED AROUND LUNCHTIME — as loath as he was to leave her, Jakob did have to get to work, though Gus was covering The Junk Stops Here, fortunately — her phone was full of texts and voice mails. Becca's voice mail was frantic, so Jaymie called her first — they were back in Canada — and reassured her. She then called and texted until she was through all her concerned friends and relatives. Social media, too, was abuzz. The newspaper had run a story, and Nan had demanded her firsthand account. But that was going to wait because first she was going to visit the woman who Saunders had tried to kill.

She called Skip, and he told her that he had taken Miss Perry over to the Queensville Inn to visit Mrs. Stubbs. He had returned to the house on Winding Woods Lane, though, because he was packing his things while the two cousins visited. Once he had fetched Miss Perry back to her home, it was officially his last day on the job.

"She complained every second of the drive. It was like Driving Miss Perry."

"Skip, I've seen your car. You don't even *have* a backseat! Besides, if she's complaining, it means she's feeling better."

He laughed and said he'd see her later.

Her mood lighter from the shared levity, she set out in the Explorer, heading to the Queensville Inn. Mrs. Stubbs was hosting a small tea party, with both Miss Perry and Morgan, who had been released from the hospital that morning.

The young woman leaped up from her chair and raced across the room, grabbing Jaymie in an unexpected hug. "I'm so grateful to you!" she muttered into Jaymie's neck. "So *very* grateful! I thought I was dead."

Jaymie hugged her back. "I hope he didn't hurt you?" She examined her. There was some bruising on her cheek, which she touched delicately.

"He hit me. Knocked me right into the open trunk," she said. She blinked and squinted, then rubbed her eyes. "It all happened so quick, I didn't know what to do." She shivered. "I . . . I don't know when I'll stop shaking, but I'm alive."

They joined the older ladies, Mrs. Stubbs in her mobility chair and Miss Perry in a recliner that had been pulled up close, her silver-headed cane leaning against it. The bruising on her face and neck was still visible but gradually disappearing. She took her great-niece's hand as Morgan sat beside her.

"It's good to see you, Jaymie," she said. "I'm so grateful that you did what you did. We almost lost this girl, and all because of that . . . that *man!*"

They chatted for a while, going over everything, even the attempts on Miss Perry's life.

"I'll never know why you didn't tell anyone about all of that, Lois," Mrs. Stubbs said, her tone reproving. "Someone takes a shot at me, I'm going to the police."

Miss Perry waved it off. "Never once thought someone was trying to kill me!"

Morgan said, "There was something off about Saunders, something I noticed right away."

"Hmph. If you'd noticed right away you wouldn't have married the louse," Miss Perry said, seeming to forget entirely that the day before she was castigating her niece for wanting to divorce "the louse."

"Okay, not right away, but . . . after the glitter wore off. At first I thought he was wonderful, but that was . . . that was *then*." She looked down at her joined hands with Miss Perry's. "He pursued me so hard before we married. But afterward it was like a light switch turned off. He started criticizing everything about me."

"That's what con men do," Mrs. Stubbs said. She had always read mysteries, but now she was binge reading true crime, especially old Ann Rule titles. "Once they have you, they start gaslighting you. Did he make you think you were wrong about everything?"

Morgan's round, pretty face held a startled expression. "You know, he did. He criticized everything I did, from driving to . . . to . . . well, everything! Nothing I did was right, no opinion I had correct, no concern or worry was valid."

"You're better than that," Miss Perry said. "You've always been a clever girl."

"Morgan, one thing I was wondering about," Jaymie said. "I know you bought the nutmeg grater—the one that was, uh . . . found on Fergus Baird's body—but *why* did you buy it, and what happened to it?" She assumed that Saunders had filched it but was interested in hearing Morgan's explanation.

"I was looking around in Dan's shop—thinking how much I'd love to work in a place like that—when I saw the grater and I knew exactly what it was. I bought it to give to Auntie Lois for her birthday, but it disappeared on me. *Now* I know that Saunders took it and hid it."

"He had a plan for it even then," Jaymie affirmed.

"When it disappeared I asked him about it but he made like I was crazy, as usual, saying he'd never seen it." She sighed. She squinted and got out a dropper bottle from her purse and squeezed some drops into her eyes. The liquid overflowed, and she brushed the drops away carefully with one knuckle, trying not to smudge her mascara.

"Do you have eye trouble?" Jaymie asked.

"I've got dry eye. I don't produce enough tears."

Jaymie sighed. Morgan's lack of tears when she was ostensibly upset at the murder attempt on her aunt had made Jaymie suspect her in the first place. That was the danger of jumping to conclusions without all the evidence. "What about the missing acorn nutmeg grater?"

Miss Perry nodded. "I spoke to that policewoman, Bernie . . . is that her name?"

"Yes, she's my friend," Jaymie said.

"They needed me to identify something; they brought me a keychain, and there was that silly acorn nutmeg grater!"

"Keychain?" Jaymie said, startled.

Mrs. Stubbs straightened, looking interested. "Let me guess!" she said, raising one hand. "It belonged to the thief who stole your silver!"

Miss Perry chuckled. "You got it. They found it on Beverly Hastings's keys. How did you know?"

"Trophy," Mrs. Stubbs said, her eyes gleaming. "Con artists, killers and thieves like a trophy of their crime, something to remind them. I'll bet she didn't *just* steal for profit but for the excitement."

"Wow. It's hard to picture Bev Hastings climbing into windows and stealing silver," Jaymie said. "Though she does have a nephew living with them. Maybe she had him sneak in the utility room window, unlock the door and tote the heavy silver. Miss Perry, you need to reconsider an alarm."

"Don't worry about me," she retorted. "This girl is moving in with me and we'll look after each other," Miss Perry said, taking Morgan's hand again and shaking it. Morgan leaned over and kissed her aunt's cheek, eyes still glittering with the liquid ready to spill over.

"Miss Perry, I have one more request of you," Jaymie said, hoping to lighten the mood. "I would absolutely love it if you would give me some help on the spice trade lessons we'll be doing at the heritage house."

"She'll do it!" Morgan said. "No one knows more about Perry family history and the spice trade than Auntie Lois!"

It was a very satisfying end to the almost-tragedy.

• • •

THAT AFTERNOON, JAYMIE AND JAKOB MET AT THE SCHOOL. She dropped in on Sybil, and they talked about the learning through objects curriculum she was developing with the heritage house, *and* about Miss Perry's involvement. Of course it was only one small part of the proposed unit; others included science and nature, and Sybil was bringing in other parents with specialties that connected. Jakob was enthused and offered the Müller farm, with its variety of trees, for a section on nature.

But they were really there to witness Jocie's integration to the dance team. Giving up tumbling had been an emotional blow to her, but that afternoon her dance class was giving a demonstration for parents. Jaymie was happy to see that Jocie was fitting in to the squad and appeared to be enjoying herself. Confident and outgoing, she was a star.

Home, with her husband, daughter and two animals, was a relief. They had an early dinner, laughing over the casserole Jaymie had prepared two days before. It was a rare fail, so PB&J sandwiches was the solution, after the casserole had been trashed. It was Wednesday, the evening of her girls' night with her friends. Jaymie was tempted to cancel, after the events of the previous day.

"What do you *want* to do?" Jakob said. "I'd love to have you home, you know that, but . . . maybe you need to stick to your plans."

So she did, dressing carefully in patterned leggings and a long sweater, her hair up and earrings on, perfume and makeup. It was a night out, after all. As always, she was welcomed warmly by her friends. Valetta's vegan snack menu was a great success, and so were the fruity cocktails she concocted. They laughed and talked and gossiped in Valetta's warm, homey cottage living room, while Denver insinuated himself into the party, winding between people for the maximum fuss. Her surly feline had become a social butterfly, Jaymie noted.

By ten or so, their gathering was winding down, all four women weary from a busy few days. Of course they had talked about Jaymie's dangerous encounter and Bernie's heroics. They had discussed Valetta's ability to tell the police exactly what drug she thought had been slipped into Miss Perry's dosette, a heavy dose of warfarin that would have caused her to bleed to death from a relatively minor scrape. She suspected from the questions she had been asked that they may have found orders for the drug from another country on Saunders Wallace's confiscated computer or phone.

They chatted about the arrest of Jon and Bev Hastings for multiple thefts in Queensville, Wolverhampton, and several more towns. The pair had been supplementing their meager earnings from the bait shop with stolen goods for a couple of years, it appeared, with the aid of her ne'er-do-well nephew. A key clue to their thefts was the silver flatware that Kevin Brevard, Jaymie's brother-in-law, had been able to hand over to the police. Bev Hastings was becoming overconfident and sloppy at hiding her and her husband's crimes. Jaymie suspected that other items would come to light as police investigated.

Bev was no longer wearing the boot for her alleged leg injury, and the morning edition of the *Wolverhampton Howler* had revealed that after a tip and some investigative reporting, a local doctor's clinic had been raided and was now closed after allegations of insurance fraud and over-prescribing. Val kept her mouth shut about it, but there was a knowing gleam in her eyes.

The acorn nutmeg grater that had been missing from Miss

Perry's place and had been fashioned into a keychain was a little bauble Bev had privately enjoyed, a sneaky reminder of her life of crime. But it was the undeniable tie-in to their robbery. The grater theft had not been noticed because the item, the smallest in Miss Perry's collection, had usually been almost hidden in among the others. That it was missing only came to light when Morgan was cataloguing the collection for her aunt before the grater loan to the heritage home.

For Queensville residents, almost the oddest thing about the whole theft was that among them were these serial thieves. People were looking at each other a little more closely. As Valetta said, folks hadn't put it past Bev, but Jon was well liked until he snarled on camera, as he was being arrested, that all the richie rich snobs he'd stolen from over the years deserved it. He hoped the thefts had given them nightmares. Valetta had pinned the clip on social media and replayed it on her tablet for Jaymie, who hadn't seen it yet. It was a surprising and riveting moment on TV news.

"Heather Blake looks like she's loving it!" Jaymie said. The newswoman had clearly relished the moment, smirking on camera as she bantered with the anchor at the end of her report on the arrest.

Valetta's living room, redone in the last year to a new, more modern color scheme, and decluttered from her intense love of froufrou knickknacks, as Becca called it, was warm and cozy, candles flickering and soft music playing. Jaymie pulled a fuzzy throw over her lap and pulled her feet up, tucking them under her. "So, how is the dating going?" she asked Heidi.

Her friend's cheeks pinked, but she laughed. "You would not believe what a weird dating world it is out there. Bernie knows!" She described in excruciating detail her foray into online dating. She told one guy she was a vegan, so he took her to a rib joint to try to "change her mind." Another date told her he was thirty-five and self-employed; his social media profile pic supported his age, though it did look a little dated, like Reagan era. When he showed up at her door it turned out he was sixty-five if he was a day, and retired. "I still went out to dinner with him. He was a nice guy," she said. "I was tempted to ask him if he had a son. Or a grandson."

"Poor Heidi!" Bernie said with a hearty laugh.

"*Not* 'poor Heidi,'" she said, laughing along. "You know what? It's *still* better than being cheated on!" Joel had left town, she was pleased to inform everyone.

Denver sprawled on the hassock in front of the sofa, while everyone took turns petting him. Jaymie glanced over at Bernie, so cute in her baseball-styled T-shirt and jeans, her nails colored bright pink and her nose piercing sporting a pink gem, which she did not or could not wear during work. "Bernie, Jakob wanted me to pass a message along to you from him and Jocie. He wanted to tell you *thank you* for coming to my rescue."

Her dark cheeks burned with color on the apples. "Just doing my job, and it was all down to Detective Vestry. She's the one who put two and two together with the kidnapping report. But I am grateful that I was there and could help."

"And that means group hug, and good night before we all get mushy!" Valetta said, laughing, as she rose. "C'mon, ladies . . . girl power!"

Twenty-one

AFTER LISTENING TO A FEW ARCHIVED PAST SHOWS of Sid Farrell's *Talking Antiques*, Jaymie had talked to the host about her ideas. They decided to do two shows, one on the history of Pyrex and Fire King in the kitchen, and one on vintage cookbooks and how she adapted recipes from them. They were going to be thirty-minute segments, with more to follow if it turned out well. She could become a regular contributor.

She had decided to do the first interview from her kitchen in Queensville, while the second would be from the dining room of the heritage house. Jocie had pleaded to be present at this first one. She had been warned that she must not distract Jaymie, so she sat up on a high stool, her milk chocolate brown eyes wide. Jakob, meanwhile, was doing some yard work at the front of the Queensville house, planting some saplings and cleaning up the mess left by the contractor who was working on the Watson home, which now had a Brock Nibley *For Sale* sign on the front lawn.

Jaymie had the landline phone on the table in front of her. This was where it had all started, in this kitchen, she thought, looking around at the homely touches she loved so much: the Hoosier cabinet she had bought at auction; the vintage tins of Calumet baking soda, Hills Brothers coffee, and Peter Pan peanut butter; the aged but lovely tools, including old egg beaters and spoons and graters.

And now, across from her in her beloved old kitchen, where Jaymie had learned to cook from her Grandma Leighton, sat Jocie, eyes wide, waiting breathlessly, hands pressed between her knees. "Sweetie, you're going to be *very* bored," Jaymie said. "All you'll hear is me droning on about Pyrex and Fire King!"

"I don't care, Mama, I want to stay. I promise I won't be bored. I'm going to do a report on it for the school newsletter."

"My little writer," Jaymie said softly.

She glanced at the clock, her stomach twisting in nervousness. This was silly; it was just talking on the phone! She jumped up, got a glass of water, and sat back down. Sometimes when she had to speak in public she got a very dry mouth. She had all her Pyrex and Fire King in front of her: the Primary Colors bowls, in yellow, green, red and blue; her refrigerator dishes, with their glass lids; a few of the other patterns and colors, along with charts and graphics, in case Sid asked questions. She had some Fire King mugs and bowls with their bright tulip patterns, and the tea/snack set she had received as a wedding shower gift from Petty Welch.

The phone rang, and she jumped. A producer said hello, she identified herself, and he told her to wait; she would hear the show, there would be a commercial break, and then Sid would talk to her. It happened swiftly, and she and Sid spoke about how Pyrex became so collectible, and how there were huge online clubs of collectors, who enthused endlessly about the patterns. Pinterest was full of photos of Pyrex collections. There had been books written about it, and fabric with Pyrex dishes on it, a favorite among collectors, who sewed aprons and even curtains from it. There were fewer fans for Fire King, but they were just as devoted and generally crossed over and collected Pyrex as well.

Then the interview became far more personal. Sid asked her about why *she* was attracted to Pyrex; she talked about her Grandma Leighton, her father's mother, who lived in their home for years and taught Jaymie to cook. Pyrex connected her to those memories. As the half hour wound down to a close, he asked her for any last thoughts.

"My editor at the newspaper—I write a column of revamped vintage recipes—said that nostalgia is big, even on social media. I think she's right, but I don't think it's mindless longing for a simpler time."

"What do you think it is?" Sid asked.

"Well, first, it wasn't a simpler time, was it? Though folks may think it was, or remember it as simpler. But every generation has its challenges. For many of us these old dishes and recipes represent continuity. My grandmother passed her recipes down to me. I have them in a book, in *her* handwriting." She touched the ragged black binder of handwritten recipes and old newspaper clippings. Jaymie glanced over at Jocie and smiled. "And in turn, I'll pass them down to my daughter, Jocie, who is looking across the table at me right now with such love, it fills my heart. And that's what these old dishes and recipes are about, not just filling the belly, but filling the heart."

Jocie jumped in her seat and clapped, then covered her mouth with one chubby hand. Jaymie smiled over at her. Jakob had drifted to the kitchen door, his hands still dirty from planting saplings, and leaned against the doorjamb, watching her with tenderness in his brown-eyed gaze.

"So it's more than the food," Sid said gently.

"It's *much* more than just the food. And it's more than pretty dishes, Sid. We're all looking for home, and security and love. We've learned to associate them with memories, some accurate, some reimagined through rose-hued glasses of our past, or an imaginary past. I'll always remember standing on a stool and mixing cookie dough with my Grandma Leighton, and I know my Jocie will stand on a stool between my husband, Jakob, and me and learn to cook, and she'll carry those memories with her for a lifetime."

"And that's all the time we have today," Sid said, his joy-filled mellow voice in Jaymie's ear, but also out there, for all his fans. "Thank you, gentle listeners. We'll be back with Jaymie in two weeks as she comes to us from the Queensville Historic Manor and talks about recipes, passed down through families or shared among friends. I have a feeling Jocie may be there with her that time, too. Good day, everyone, and may you find your own version of home and security and love—as Jaymie Leighton Müller says—and memories."

From Jaymie's Vintage Kitchen

Jakob's Scrumptious Meat Loaf
by Jaymie Leighton

As followers of my column know, I am recently married. Not to make the ladies jealous, but I hit the jackpot. My new husband was a busy single dad, but he wasn't about to go the frozen pizza and take-out route to feed his daughter. Instead, Jakob worked on his cooking skills, and he has a few go-to recipes. One is his magical meat loaf, which he cooked for me on our first official date, dinner at his house, which we shared with his (and now *my*) wonderful daughter, Jocie.

How is this vintage? Well, the first bite was *so* good, but it strongly reminded me of something from my childhood. So I searched back in my cookbooks and found that this is close to my grandmother's Italian Surprise Meat Loaf. Instead of the marinara sauce she used canned tomatoes she had mashed to a smooth pulp. Jakob's is actually better (I think because he wilted the veggies in olive oil, and didn't put them in raw), but shhh . . . don't tell my Grandma Leighton!

Jakob's Scrumptious Meat Loaf
Serves: 6 (8, if you use the full pound of Italian sausage)

Ingredients:

1½ teaspoon olive oil
1 small onion, finely diced
½ red pepper, finely diced
2 cloves garlic, minced
1 pound extra-lean ground beef
½ to 1 pound Italian sausage, casings removed
1 large egg
¾ cup Italian or plain bread crumbs

1 cup bottled marinara sauce
1 tablespoon dried leaf basil
1 teaspoon dried oregano (or substitute 1 tablespoon of Italian seasoning for the basil and oregano)
1 teaspoon salt
¼ teaspoon ground black pepper
1 cup grated mozzarella cheese

Preheat oven to 375 degrees F.

In olive oil, in frying pan, wilt the onion and red pepper until the onion is translucent, adding the garlic in the last two minutes. LOW heat . . . don't let the onions brown! Then cool the veggies.

Combine ground beef, sausage, beaten egg, bread crumbs, half the marinara sauce, the cooled vegetables, basil and oregano (or Italian seasoning), salt, pepper and mix well, then add half the grated mozzarella cheese. Mix well.

Pack in a 2.5–3-quart (or liter) deep-sided oven-safe casserole, NOT a 13 X 9 pan, but a casserole with at least 4-inch-deep sides. Slather top with the rest of the marinara sauce, then bake 45–50 minutes.

Remove from oven, sprinkle with remaining mozzarella cheese, return to oven and bake another 10–15 minutes.

Remove from oven and let rest 10 minutes, then cut into squares.

This is so good, but filling. Green beans in garlic and butter pair with it well, or a green salad. To make it stretch to 8 people (which it will if you have used 1 pound of the Italian sausage), add mashed potatoes alongside it.

This is a hearty fall dish, good enough for company!

Books by Victoria Hamilton

Vintage Kitchen Mysteries

A Deadly Grind
Bowled Over
Freezer I'll Shoot
No Mallets Intended
White Colander Crime
Leave It to Cleaver
No Grater Danger

Merry Muffin Mysteries

Bran New Death
Muffin But Murder
Death of an English Muffin
Much Ado About Muffin
Muffin to Fear

About the Author

Victoria Hamilton is the pseudonym of nationally bestselling romance author Donna Lea Simpson.

She now happily writes about vintage kitchen collecting, muffin baking, and dead bodies in the Vintage Kitchen Mysteries and Merry Muffin Mystery series. Besides writing about murder and mayhem, and blogging at Killer Characters, Victoria collects vintage kitchen wares and old cookbooks, as well as teapots and teacups.

Visit Victoria at www.victoriahamiltonmysteries.